DEFENDING OUR HOMESTEAD

ROBERT J. WALKER

1

It was a rare evening, for the Atlantic was as calm and flat as a sheet of glass, the black water stretching out from horizon to horizon without so much as a molehill of a wave in sight. The stillness of the sea painted a vast portrait of infinite beauty, the water mirroring the starry sky above.

"It's just…spectacular. I don't think I've ever seen so many stars in my life," Hank Jefferson, the youngest crew member on the merchant vessel, said to Marvin Wagner, the chief security officer of the ship. The two of them were out on the deck, where thirty-nine-year-old Marvin was giving Hank, who was almost half his age, a few pointers about the job.

Marvin chuckled as he turned to face Hank. For a few eerie seconds, he felt almost as if he was pulling back the veil of reality and staring through the mists of time at his younger self. He and Hank looked almost as if they could have been brothers—thanks to a clean lifestyle and a rigorous workout schedule, Marvin looked at least ten years younger than he really was—and indeed, some crew members had asked if they were related when Hank had first come onto the ship.

Both men had the same pale-blond hair, almost platinum in tone, and the same ice-blue eyes. Although Hank's facial structure was clearly different from Marvin's—the younger man had a long, narrow face with a pointy chin, while Marvin had more of a square-jawed visage—they were both similarly built: athletically slim, with narrow waists and strong shoulders, like middleweight boxers.

Neither man had ever seen the other prior to this voyage, though, and their similarities in appearance and build were a mere coincidence. Despite this, though, Hank had taken a shine to Marvin, who he quickly began to regard as a friendly mentor. And Marvin, being naturally kind-natured, helpful, and generous, had been happy to answer the younger man's many questions about life at sea.

"Do you ever get bored of seeing skies like this?" Hank asked as the two men gazed up at the star-sprayed heavens. "Man, I don't think I'd ever get bored of seeing this."

Marvin chuckled and smiled warmly. "You didn't get out of the city much when you were growing up, huh?"

Hank smiled sadly and shook his head. "Not really, sir. My mom, she worked three jobs just to keep my sister and me clothed and fed growing up. We didn't exactly have the money or time to go on camping trips in the mountains or nothing."

"Maybe one day you can come with me to my family ranch," Marvin said. "You see some beautiful skies out there. My girlfriend, Caitlin, she's a total city slicker. She barely left the city in all her twenty-nine years until she met me. Your reaction to the night sky out here reminds me of hers when she first saw the stars at the ranch."

"Yeah, I bet," Hank said, grinning. "I felt like a kid at Disney World or something!"

"It's something every human being should experience," Marvin said solemnly. "A night sky without the taint of light pollution, like humans used to see for most of the history of our species, before cities, electricity, modern civilization, all of that. Really puts things into perspective, you know what I mean? Takes us human beings, who feel almost like we're these invincible gods, down a few notches, really shows us how tiny and insignificant we are in the greater scheme of things."

"Yeah, sure, I get what you mean," Hank said, staring with awe and reverence at the millions of gently twinkling stars overhead. "Out here, it's so quiet, so dark, so beautiful, you could almost forget that civilization even exists…I bet during your days as a Navy SEAL, you saw plenty of skies like these in all the remote places you went to, right?"

Marvin's smile faded a little at the mention of his past as a US Navy SEAL. The fact that he had served his country as one of its most elite servicemen filled him with pride, but he had seen some terrible things during his service, things that had left him with deep scars no eyes could see. When Hank mentioned this, a flood of memories gushed through Marvin's head...and many of these images of his distant past were not pleasant.

"Are you, uh, okay, sir?" Hank asked.

Marvin snapped out of his brief trance and forced a smile onto his face. "Fine, son, just fine...I just got lost in the past there for a second."

Hank's attention was already distracted, though, and he was staring up at the sky again. "Man, I just can't stop looking at it," he murmured. "It's so beautiful, so very, very beautiful."

"Kid, we're not even two days away from the coast. I can still almost see the lights and the haze of the big city just beyond the horizon. Wait until we're deep into the ocean," Marvin said. "Then you'll see—"

A brief but almost blinding flash of light flickered across the sky, causing both men to gasp with surprise. The second after the flash blazed across the sky, the entire ship went dark, and with a weak groan and a few coughs and splutters, the steady, humming roar of the gigantic diesel motors that powered the merchant vessel ground to a halt.

For a few eerie seconds, everything was completely and utterly silent.

"What the hell was that light?" Hank eventually spluttered. "You saw that, right? I didn't just imagine it, did I?"

"I saw it all right," Marvin said grimly, "and although I don't know what it was, I can't say I liked the look of it."

"What's going on with the ship? Why have we lost power?"

Marvin shook his head slowly. "I'm not sure, but it's strange that everything has shut down and the backup generator hasn't come on."

"Here, let me get my phone," Hank said. "Then, at least we can see where we're going."

When he took out his phone, though, he discovered the device was dead. "Uh, sir, my phone's dead," Hank murmured, furrowing his brow deeply with consternation. "That's really weird because it was at around eighty percent battery when I last looked at it a couple minutes ago."

Marvin checked his own phone, and when he saw the device was completely dead, his sense of worry and unease only deepened. He was now quite sure he knew what the bright flash had been and what had happened, and his head was spinning at the implications of it.

"Stupid thing, I bought this because it was supposed to be better than all that cheap Chinese-made crap," Hank muttered, repeatedly pushing his phone's power button as if that would somehow revive the dead device. "And now it does this to me, only two months after I bought the damn thing!"

"Hank, your phone doesn't have a problem," Marvin said softly. "I mean, it does, but so does every other phone on the East Coast of the United States right now…

maybe even every phone in America, depending on how far-reaching the impact is."

Hank looked up at Marvin, his face scrunched into an expression of deep confusion. "Wh-what? What are you talking about? The impact of what? Do you know what that flash of light was?"

"I'm pretty sure I do know now," Marvin said. "And we'd better go find the captain and assemble the crew. This voyage is over, kid. We're dead in the water, stuck out at sea, and this ship will never go anywhere again except where the ocean's currents decide to take it."

2

Caitlin stared out of the window at the ocean in the distance. From up here on the seventy-first floor, she could see far out over the Atlantic, which was dotted with the orangey lights of hundreds of ships, artificial mirrors of the stars in the dark sky above. She wanted to think that one of those dots of light on the dark water was the ship her beloved Marvin was on, but she knew the ship he was on was way farther out at sea by now, farther out than she could see even from up here.

She stretched and yawned and thought about brewing another pot of coffee. She decided against it, though; she had already had too much caffeine. Although she was weary, she felt calm and at peace. She enjoyed working late when the office was quiet and still, and the only sounds she could hear were the gentle hums of the various machines resting in the night before another busy day.

Although she and Marvin had been dating for four years now, she still wasn't used to the fact that he was absent for such long stretches with such frequency. Right from the outset, when she had first started dating him, she had known this would always be the case, given his choice of career as a security officer aboard merchant vessels, but that didn't make the long absences any easier to deal with. Even after he had changed things up, only taking on shorter cross-Atlantic voyages rather than longer Pacific voyages or the lucrative but peril-fraught contracts abroad ships that rounded the Horn of Africa, Caitlin had never gotten used to him being away for such long periods.

What kept her going through these difficult stretches, where all she could do was count down the weeks until she'd see him again, was the knowledge that in a few years, he was planning to retire from his profession, having saved up a lot of money over the last two decades, and take on an easier job on shore. And then they would finally buy a house, settle down, get married, have some kids...

The thought of this rosy future put a smile on Caitlin's face—a pretty face, heart-shaped, with big brown eyes that matched the silky, wavy chestnut locks that tumbled around her slim shoulders. She had always been petite in both height and build, and she looked almost childlike next to Marvin, who was six foot four and well over two hundred pounds. She picked up a picture of the two of them—one of her favorites, one she kept on her desk next to her photos of her parents and her younger sisters—and stared at the image of the man she loved more than anything in the world.

The photograph had been taken three years earlier when they'd gone on vacation to Uganda in Africa to see gorillas in the wild. Caitlin had almost become a primatologist. She'd always had a deep fascination with monkeys and apes, but she had chosen to pursue a lucrative career in law instead—a decision she sometimes regretted, even though she had done well enough in her current firm to have earned a corner office with a spectacular view over the city and the ocean.

There were three figures in the photo of her and Marvin—the third was a giant silverback gorilla, sitting calmly in the background, stuffing his face full of juicy jungle leaves. It was a snapshot of a beautiful and surreal moment from the best vacation in her life. However, Marvin had promised to top that experience with the vacation he had planned out for them in a few months to celebrate Caitlin's thirtieth birthday: a trip to the jungles of Borneo to see orangutans in the wild.

After Caitlin set down the photo, she picked up the scarf on her chair and caressed the soft fabric in her hands. The dazzlingly colorful scarf was a souvenir from the Uganda trip, and Caitlin often wore it for work, its gaudy tones a playful contrast to the muted gray, black, and beige business suits she usually wore.

While holding the garment and reminiscing about the wonderful trip, a sudden blaze of almost blinding light—like a sustained flash of lightning, strangely, though, without an accompanying thunderclap—bathed the entire office in white brilliance.

Caitlin gasped, shocked by this mysterious phenomenon. Her surprise was only amplified when the entire office was plunged into inky darkness a mere second after the strange flash of light. She had experienced a power cut in this office once before, and it didn't take her long to realize that this was no ordinary power failure. In the previous power outage she'd experienced, the emergency lights had come on right away, but now even they were dead.

The office was eerily silent—truly silent, for the first time since it had been first built. Gone was the soft, comforting hum of the various machines that inhabited the space, and in its place was a sinister, almost menacing absence of any sort of sound. A bizarre thought suddenly entered Caitlin's head: this threatening silence was surely what astronauts heard out in the void of space.

The first thing Caitlin did was pick up her phone from her desk. Its handy flashlight app had lit her way through dark spaces many times before. However, she quickly discovered the device was as dead as all of the rest of the machines in this place.

Caitlin had always been a person who had been able to keep a cool head under pressure—she never would have gotten as far in her field as she had without this quality—but even for someone as calm and as level-headed as she was, it was difficult to push down the feelings of panic and fear surging up from deep within her core.

"I've gotta get out of here," she murmured, staring out of the window at the eerie and deeply unsettling sight of the city, which had gone entirely dark as far as the eye could see. Only the outlines of the hundreds of skyscrapers could be seen, silhouetted against the starry sky.

The thought of having to descend seventy-one flights of stairs was daunting, even for someone as fit as Caitlin, but with the building's elevators out of commission, there was no other way down. As she began to hastily gather her things off her desk in preparation to leave, though, there was another flash of light. This one was different from the first. It wasn't nearly as bright, but seeing as everything around her was tar-black, even the light of a single candle would have stood out.

Caitlin turned around to look at the source of this new glow, which, unlike the first one, was sustained rather than a quick flash. It had originated from beyond the horizon, but it was now arcing toward the city at impossible speed, blazing a fiery trail through the night sky like some shooting star…but this was no meteorite. It was a weapon.

It took all of two seconds to cross the sky and slam into the city, and all Caitlin could do was stand and stare in utter horror as the missile struck its target, somewhere just beyond the row of skyscrapers in front of her.

This time she both felt and saw the impact. Although her skyscraper was at least two blocks away from where the missile had struck, the force of the explosion that followed the impact shook her entire building and rattled the windows.

"Oh shit!" Caitlin gasped, horror-struck, stunned, and almost paralyzed with sheer disbelief at what was happening. "Oh my God, what's going on? What is this?"

Before she could even begin to contemplate what was happening, more missiles streaked through the sky, tearing like a squadron of fiery dragons over the horizon, spitting fire and flame as they raced with deadly intent through the darkness and hurtling at terrifying speed toward their targets.

One by one, they smashed into various buildings in the city, each concussive impact so powerful that it shook Caitlin's office with the force of an earthquake. Gigantic fireballs billowed up into the sky, bathing the dark city in a hellish orange-red glow, and even from up here on the seventy-first floor, Caitlin could hear the screams of terrified people down on the streets below. Some sort of Armageddon was unfolding here, and it had come completely out of the blue, with not even so much as a rumor of its approach.

Caitlin had been working in this office long enough that she could navigate it blindfolded—which was essentially what she was going to have to do, seeing as even the emergency lighting had failed—and now, with her heart pounding madly in her chest and her head reeling with confusion and terror, she stuffed what items she could into her bag and stumbled out of the office, making her way toward the elevators and the emergency stairs.

But before she had gotten out of her own offices, one of the hundreds of screaming missiles smashed into her building, just a few floors below her. There was a bright flash of light, a percussive impact somewhere at the back of her skull, and with that, Caitlin sank into the dark, soundless void of unconsciousness.

3

"Sir, what's that?"

Hank was pointing at the same horizon from which the initial blinding flash had originated. Now, though, the distant sky was lit up with a different kind of light. The lights were so far away that they were barely visible, but in the silent expanse of darkness out here on the Atlantic, there could be no mistaking the fact that they were there, zipping through the sky. Streaks of bright orange arced across the sky at dizzying speed, followed by brief but bright flashes. All of this was taking place where the faraway city was located.

As a former Navy SEAL, Marvin knew exactly what these eerie meteor-like lights were. He had seen such things with his own eyes in the deserts of the Middle East and the inhospitable mountains of Afghanistan. They were missiles, and not just plain old rockets fired from the shoulders of men or even tanks, but huge missiles being launched either from hidden submarines or an underground facility on shore. These were missiles capable of bringing down even the sturdiest buildings...and hundreds of them were blasting into his home city.

His first thought was of the woman he loved more than life itself. Just minutes before he had come up here onto the deck of the ship for a breath of fresh air, he and Caitlin had exchanged a few messages. Instead of her usual routine, curled up on the sofa of their home in the suburbs just outside the city, she was working late in her office on the seventy-first floor of one of the biggest skyscrapers in the city.

Marvin's knees felt as if they were about to buckle beneath him, and his stomach churned with sudden nausea. The bitterness of bile and vomit burned at the back of his throat, and he had to grip the railing tightly for a few moments to steady himself.

He fought through the terrible feelings that had him gripped in their cold, scaly talons. Yes, it was true that Caitlin was stuck in the middle of what was turning out to be the most vicious attack on American soil since Pearl Harbor or 9/11, but that didn't mean she wasn't safe...for now. Marvin knew one thing for certain, though, and that was that the longer she was stuck in that city—that warzone—the lower her chances of survival would be. He knew Caitlin had a good head on her shoulders and that she was able to stay calm even in situations of great danger and distress, but she had never come up against anything remotely resembling this type of situation.

"I have to get back there. I have to get her out of that place...I have to," Marvin murmured, his fingers curled around the steel railing with a white-knuckled grip.

"Wh-what are you talking about?" Hank stammered. "Where do you have to go? Who do you—"

"Never mind," Marvin muttered, doing his best to collect his thoughts and calm himself. "Come on, we need to talk to the captain and the rest of the crew."

Thankfully, there were emergency light sources all over the ship completely unaffected by the disaster: flares and chemical lights. Marvin walked over to a cabinet on the side of the ship and took out a few chemical lights, handing one to Hank before cracking open his own one.

"Glow sticks," Hank murmured, his face bathed in the eerie green glow the chemical light emitted.

"Take as many as you can find, and don't lose 'em," Marvin said sternly. "These things are going to be worth more than their weight in gold in the world we're heading into."

"Huh? 'The world we're heading into,' sir? What do you mean?" Hank asked as he followed Marvin, who was striding with speed and a sense of purpose in his step into the ship.

"I'll explain everything when the captain and the crew are all assembled," Marvin answered. "Move your ass, kid." His urgent desire to get off the ship and return to

DEFENDING OUR HOMESTEAD

Caitlin added a curtness rare to hear in his usually soft-spoken tone of voice.

It didn't take long for everyone to assemble in the dining hall, which was the agreed-upon emergency meeting point on the ship. Although the captain of the ship, a white-bearded Floridian in his late sixties named Felix Reid, was the most senior authority figure as head of security, Marvin's opinion carried a fair amount of weight, too.

When every crew member was present, Captain Reid stepped onto a stool to address them. There was a buzz of conversation that hummed in the room, which was bathed in the green light of multiple glow sticks, but the sound quickly died down when Reid got into position to address the crowd.

"All right, everyone, listen up," Reid said. "We've clearly got ourselves a very unusual situation here. I don't know what's going on, and the fact that the ship's emergency power systems haven't kicked in is boggling my mind, but—"

"What about the coms systems?" someone yelled. "We want to know what's going on! All our phones are dead, and even the satellite phones are down! Have you been in communication with anyone, Captain, and if you have, what are they saying?"

"Believe me, I've been trying all the communications systems we have on this ship," Captain Reid said grimly. "I haven't been able to get hold of anyone, not even the coast guard…like I said, I don't know what's going on here. I'm trying, people, believe me, I'm trying, but—"

"I know what's going on."

Marvin stood up on a chair next to Captain Reid. Reid turned and looked at him, and on his weathered face, there was both indignation and surprise. As much as Reid hated being interrupted, particularly by someone below him in rank, though, he was as mystified as anyone else on board about what was happening. He was intrigued to hear what Marvin had to say about the situation, so he allowed him to speak.

"Go ahead, Wagner," he said to Marvin, giving him an approving nod.

"Thank you, Captain," Marvin said. "I don't know if anyone besides myself and Hank saw it, but just before the power outage, there was a blinding flash of light just beyond the horizon, over land. Right after that, everything went off. I'm pretty damn sure I know exactly what that flash of light was."

"What was it?" someone yelled out.

Marvin breathed in deeply, scanned the room while holding the air in his lungs, then addressed the room, speaking in a grave and somber tone. "What Hank and I witnessed up on deck was the deployment of an EMP. It was an act of war as severe as the Japanese attack on Pearl Harbor or Bin Laden's attack on the Twin Towers on 9/11. Actually, in terms of the consequences it'll have, it's far, far worse than either of those two attacks on our country, as bad as they were."

The room exploded into a riot of yells and frantic conversation before Captain Reid, Hank, and a few others yelled over the racket and got everyone to quieten down so Marvin could continue speaking.

"What exactly is an EMP?" Hank asked when quiet returned to the room.

"It's an electromagnetic pulse weapon," Marvin answered. "I'm not going to go into a lot of technical detail or anything, but the gist of it is this: anything electronic, anything controlled by computer chips or circuits is now dead…and I mean dead as in permanently knocked out, irreparable. That's why I said this ship is as dead as a piece of driftwood; the only place it's going is wherever the ocean currents decide to take it."

"That can't be possible," one of the sailors said. "There's gotta be some way to fix the engines! They're diesel motors. They're not freakin' computers!"

"Yeah, but the ignition and everything that makes the motor run *is* controlled by a computer," another sailor countered, "and if he's right about this EMP thing, then those motors are toast. We're dead in the water!"

A roar of frantic conversation began to swell in the room again, but Captain Reid and Hank quickly shut it down so that Marvin could continue speaking.

"There's more," Marvin said. "We also saw missiles raining down on the city in the distance. Whatever is happening here, it's an all-out war. This, right here, could be the start of World War III. And that statement, gentlemen, is no joke. I hope you can fully understand the seriousness of what I'm trying to explain to you here."

This time, there was no cacophony of conversation that followed Marvin's words. Instead, there was only stunned silence, the atmosphere tense and laden with fear, the green glow of the many chemical lights only adding to the surreal collective feeling that this couldn't be real, that this had to be some sort of bizarre, shared nightmare.

"What do we do?" someone finally asked.

"Who's attacking us?" another yelled out.

"The Russians, it's gotta be!" a sailor shouted.

"No, it's the Chinese!" another roared.

Again, a riot of raised voices crashed through the room. This time everyone was yelling louder and more frantically than before, and it took some effort for the captain, Hank, and Marvin to quieten them down.

"Look," Marvin said when some measure of calm had been restored, "I'm not going to speculate about who's behind this attack, what their intentions are, or where things will go from here. All I'm going to say is that the world we're in now is a very, very different one than the one we were in before this happened, and it's extremely unlikely that things are going to go back to how they used to be anytime soon...perhaps ever. In terms of technology, we're probably closer now to 1822 than to 2022. And I'm not joking about that."

"Are you saying that we're literally going to have to live without any kind of technology at all?" Hank asked.

"Most items of technology are now dead, yes, and they can never be repaired," Marvin answered. "There'll be some exceptions, of course—anything shielded from the EMP by a strong Faraday cage, for example. Maybe some very old vehicles—cars and motorcycles made in the seventies or earlier. A few other things, basic items. But if you want to survive the coming days, weeks, months…years, even, you're going to have radically shift your perspective on things and prepare to live in a way you never thought you could or would."

"But right now," Hank asked. "Right here, on this ship…what the hell are we going to do?"

"I don't know about the rest of you," Marvin said, "but I'm going to do my damndest to get back to land. Then, I'm going to get everyone I love out of that city and deep into the countryside…and I'm going to leave *right now*. There's no time to waste."

4

When Caitlin awoke, she was completely disoriented and confused for the first few seconds after opening her eyes. A potent headache throbbed in her skull, the metallic taste of blood lingered on her tongue, and her ears were ringing with a shrill and persistent whine. For a few panic-stricken moments, she thought she was blind, but then she realized it was just the inky darkness in which she found herself.

It all started to come back to her: the strange, blinding flash of light that had turned everything bright white for a split second, the citywide power outage, the terrifying missiles streaking through the air, the skyscraper shaking with the impact of the explosions, then one explosion that seemed much, much closer than the others, and a thunderclap of a boom…

At this point, Caitlin noticed something else: the smell of smoke in the air. It wasn't sharp or thick enough to make breathing difficult, but it was strong enough to be easily noticeable…and she knew whatever fire was burning in this building would spread quickly and that it would rapidly become catastrophic.

"Did that missile hit the building above my floor or below it?" she murmured to herself, trying to struggle to her feet.

She still felt disoriented and confused, and a large part of her was almost in denial about what had happened and what was happening; it was all too much to handle. She did her best to force some clarity into her head, though. It quickly became easier to do this when yet another explosion rocked the building with such violence that a few ceiling panels crashed onto the floor, and a few chairs were toppled over from the force of the impact.

"Get up, Caitlin, get up, dammit!" she muttered to herself through gritted teeth.

Despite the pounding headache and her feeling of dizziness, Caitlin managed to get to her feet, gripping a nearby desk for support. She gingerly reached around to the back of her head and winced when she touched her skull—a stab of pain shot through her head when her fingertips touched her head, and she felt the warm, sticky wetness of blood matting her hair there. She didn't know what had hit her. She could barely see her hand in front of her face in the thick darkness, but she did know it had to have been heavy. It was likely one of the bookshelves that had toppled over onto her when the huge explosion had rocked the building, she thought. Whatever it was, though, didn't really matter. What *did* matter was getting out of this building before the whole thing went up in flames or got utterly demolished by the missiles still streaking through the night sky in a deadly meteor shower.

"Light…I need some light," she murmured.

Although she hadn't smoked cigarettes for years, Caitlin had been a smoker in her late teens and early twenties, and even though she had long since ditched the habit, she still carried a lighter with her everywhere she went. Feeling thankful for this carryover from her smoking days, she rummaged around in her bag lying at her feet until she found a lighter.

She remembered that a coworker kept some ornamental candles on her desk. It would be easier using those as light sources rather than having to keep her finger on the lighter button. Using the little circle of weak light thrown out by her plastic lighter, Caitlin navigated her way over to the desk in question and lit up some of the scented candles. The sweet candy scent they gave off seemed particularly out of place in this current situation, but they were the only viable light source here, so they would have to do.

There was only one thing on Caitlin's mind, and that was getting out of this building as fast as possible. However, seventy-one floors stood between her and escape…seventy-one flights of stairs and possibly a raging fire. Caitlin was fit, seeing as she and Marvin regularly went hiking in the wilderness, but getting down seventy-one flights of stairs in a burning building, with missiles flying around, was an extremely daunting prospect.

Caitlin, however, had never been one to let fear stand in her way. She strode out of her company's offices, her bag slung over her shoulder, her way lit by the gentle light of the candle, and she went straight to the emergency stairs. Her heart was thumping in her chest, and her pulse was racing, while her ears were still ringing and a potent headache was throbbing in her skull, but she didn't allow herself to pause or rest, except by the water cooler—a simple gravity-operated one, thankfully, rather than the fancy digitally operated type like those in her offices, which were now dead, their water inaccessible—near the elevators, where she filled up her water bottle. She didn't know when she would next come across a supply of fresh water, so after she'd filled her bottle to the brim, she drank as much as she could.

After that, she opened the door to the emergency stairs. To her dismay, a cloud of acrid black smoke billowed out of the doorway as soon as she opened the door. Coughing and choking, she staggered back, praying it was just a stray cloud that had drifted up the stairwell. However, the smoke got thicker and thicker, continuing to pour out of the doorway, and Caitlin had to shove the door shut to stop the gushing smoke, which continued to squeeze itself through the little gaps in the door.

With her eyes, nose, throat, and lungs burning from the smoke, Caitlin felt an almost irresistible sense of panic rising within her. The stairwell was a no-go; trying to get through that terrible smoke would only result in death by smoke inhalation. Now she knew the fire was on a floor below her, which was exactly the opposite of what she had been hoping for.

"Shit," she muttered, pacing back and forth. "How the hell am I going to get out of here?"

The panic billowing through her with the intensity of the black cloud of smoke in the stairwell was getting to almost paralyzing levels. Caitlin had to use every ounce of willpower she possessed to stay levelheaded and not give in to it.

Her eyes drifted over to the elevator, and a plan started to form in her head. It was an insane plan, but this was an insane situation, and such situations required extreme measures. She ran over to the elevators and instinctively pressed the button before she had even realized what she was doing.

Of course, nothing happened when she did this. She needed to get into the elevator shaft—it would provide a sheltered passage all the way down to the basement of the building, and there would be no danger of being crushed by an elevator since they were all frozen in place due to the power outage. It was still risky, to be sure, but Caitlin was quite certain the power wasn't about to come back on any time soon, not when there was some sort of actual war going on outside.

She set down her candle and tried to pull open the doors with her fingers, but either they were stuck fast, or she just wasn't strong enough. She suspected it was the latter. She wasn't able to get much of a grip on the doors due to how narrow the gap between them was.

"I need something to pry these open," she murmured to herself, still doing her best to hold back the panic rising inexorably within her, all while trying to ignore the throbbing headache pounding relentlessly in her skull.

She paced back and forth for a few moments, trying to figure out what she could use to pry open the doors. The area in front of the elevators provided no help for this endeavor; there were only large potted plants, a few modern art statues, and some artworks on the walls.

Caitlin stopped and stared for a while at one of the paintings on the wall, barely illuminated by the weak orange glow of the candle, and then she realized what she could use to pry open the elevator doors.

Driven on by a sense of immense urgency, one only made more dire by the muted booms and thunderclaps of multiple explosions taking place outside, she left her bag by the elevator, grabbed the candle, and hurried back into her offices.

She made a beeline for Luke Zellweger's office—he was the head of the law firm, and as such, he had the largest and most opulent of all the offices in the business. Just as Caitlin was about to reach Zellweger's door, though, a tremendous explosion rocked the skyscraper.

27

The thunderclap bang left Caitlin's ears ringing, and the force of it hurled her to the ground and shook the building with such violence that she thought it had to collapse any second now.

Lying on the ground, panting with fear, her eyes wide and her mouth dry, Caitlin felt like a feral creature caught in a snare. As levelheaded a person as she was, it was becoming impossible not to give in to these terrible, utterly debilitating feelings of sheer panic.

The increasingly potent smell of smoke in the office, however, kicked her instinct for self-preservation into overdrive, and a flood of adrenalin through her system allowed her to overcome the paralyzing terror holding her in the grips of its icy claws.

She scrambled to her feet, dusted herself off, grabbed the candle, and headed into Zellweger's office. Luke Zellweger was a travel fanatic, and his high-paid position had allowed him to travel all over the world. He had brought back plenty of souvenirs each time he traveled, and there was one particular souvenir he kept in the office that Caitlin was after.

Mounted on the wall behind Zellweger's desk was a samurai sword from a trip to Japan. This was no cheap display weapon; it was the real deal, sharp as a razor and a blade as sturdy and strong as a crowbar.

And that was exactly what Caitlin was going to use as a crowbar. She removed the sword from its mounts on the wall. The polished blade gleamed attractively in the candlelight, and for a moment, she was struck by the sheer beauty of the sword. It seemed like a terrible shame to be using something this magnificent for such a crude task, but she quickly got past this notion. This was a situation of life and death, and if she couldn't get those elevator doors open, she knew she would end up dying in this office, whether from smoke inhalation, getting burned to death when the fire raging elsewhere in the building eventually reached this floor, or by being crushed when the building collapsed—which, judging from the loud bangs and ominous creaks and groans growing ever louder and happening with increasing frequency, was something that was seeming like far more of an inevitability than a possibility.

With the samurai sword in one hand and the candle in the other, Caitlin rushed back to the elevator. She didn't waste any time jamming the sword blade between the doors and pushing her bodyweight against the weapon. Using it as a lever, she managed to pry open the doors.

Once she'd gotten them open a few inches, she was able to toss the sword aside and open them fully with relative ease. Then she wedged the sword between them to prevent them from closing. With her heart thumping dully with fear, she peered down into the elevator shaft. All she could see, beyond the few feet of space illuminated by her candle, was darkness.

"It's probably better that I can't see too far down," she murmured to herself.

Caitlin had never suffered from a true phobia of

heights, but like most people, she wasn't much of a fan of them. She knew at that moment if she'd been able to see all the way down to the bottom of the elevator shaft, there was no way she would be able to get in and start the long descent. Instead, vertigo would have had her head spinning by now, and it surely would have frozen her limbs and muscles as effectively as any drug.

One thing that gave Caitlin a measure of relief was that, unlike the stairwell, no clouds of acrid black smoke came billowing out of the elevator shaft when she had opened the doors. All along one side of the shaft, heading both higher up and lower down into the darkness above and below, were sets of steel rungs attached to the concrete—this was the maintenance ladder by which technicians could service the elevator.

"All right, all right, it's just a steady climb down," Caitlin whispered to herself, doing her best to try to psyche herself up. "One rung at a time, nice and easy, all the way to the bottom."

She tried not to think about the fact that one slip, one misstep, would result in her dropping hundreds of feet down the shaft to her death below. As long as she didn't think about this, she would be okay.

She slipped her bag over her shoulder and gripped the candle in her left hand, preparing to enter the elevator shaft. It was as she was about to climb in, though, that something made her pause—a strange feeling of foreboding, a tingling of her sixth sense.

At that moment, another missile struck the

skyscraper, but this one penetrated the elevator shaft. Caitlin screamed and dived to the side of the elevator doors as a gigantic fireball came rushing up the shaft. Raging flames came billowing out of the elevator doors, and Caitlin missed being incinerated by mere inches.

A few seconds later, she heard a loud bang from somewhere above her, and then an elevator came hurtling down the shaft, the metal screeching and squealing as it fell until it hit something below with a tremendous crash.

Now, the same searing black smoke pouring out of the stairwell came belching out of the elevator shaft. Caitlin hurriedly removed the sword and closed the elevator doors to prevent more of the terrible smoke from getting onto this floor.

When a wave of debilitating panic crashed against her, she was now powerless to resist it…for her only means of escape from the skyscraper had now been cut off, and she was utterly certain she was going to die within hours, if not minutes…

5

"So, Marvin's off on another voyage to Europe, huh?" Declan Palmer asked before taking a long swig of his whiskey as he stared out at the serenely spectacular sight of the clear, starry sky, broken by the jagged black silhouette of the forested hills surrounding the ranch. The porch of the main house, which was situated near the top of the tallest hill in the area, offered a commanding view of the wild landscape for miles around, as far as the eye could see.

Stanley Wagner took a sip from his own tumbler of whiskey before replying. "He is, yeah...they're taking a bunch of cars across to Europe this time. Marv says it's boring work—you know how much my son craves excitement—nothing at all like when he was working the Horn of Africa and having to defend ships from attacks from Somali pirates—but it pays well, and it keeps his girl happy."

Declan chuckled softly. "Yeah, that Caitlin, huh? I never thought Marvin would fall for someone like her. Not that there's anything wrong with her, she's a lovely woman, she's just such a—"

"City slicker, through and through," Stanley interjected with a laugh.

He and Declan both laughed boisterously—the type of rich, rejuvenating laughter shared only between the oldest of friends. Indeed, Stanley and Declan, who had known each other for almost the entirety of their six and a half decades of existence, were far more like brothers than friends. Nobody, however, would have made such an assumption by looking at the pair of them, though. They couldn't have been more different in appearance.

Declan, a Native American whose tribe had lived in this area for thousands of years, was short and stocky in build, with russet skin and thick black hair streaked liberally with gray that he wore in a long ponytail. His large, dark eyes, set in shallow sockets, burned with an intensity that never dimmed, and this fire in his eyes intimidated those who did not know him well while inspiring those who did.

Stanley was tall, lanky, and slim, but his slenderness was not that of a soft and pasty office worker but rather the tough, wiry build of a man whose entire life had been spent toiling away at hard physical labor. Despite his age, his limbs were still taut with muscles like steel cables. Pale-blue eyes sat beneath bushy white eyebrows in a square-jawed visage. He covered his bald pate with a cowboy hat, which he wore almost everywhere except for bed.

Declan and Stanley were neighbors—Declan's family owned a small property that bordered Stanley's ranch, which had been in Stanley's family since the eighteenth century—but Declan spent a lot more time on the ranch helping out with the horses than he did on his own land. Like his father before him, Declan was a horse whisperer, and like his father, he was employed by the Wagner family to look after their prizewinning horses.

"What are you two laughing about?" asked Eileen, Stanley's wife, as she brought a tray of freshly baked chocolate chip cookies onto the porch. She spoke in a tone of mock seriousness, but there was a grin on her face.

"Oh, nothing, nothing, honey," Stanley answered, still chortling. "Those smell delicious!"

He reached for a cookie as his wife walked past him, but she swatted away his hand playfully. "Hold your horses, mister. These still need to cool for a minute or two!"

Eileen was tall—six feet, very tall for a woman—but her husband stood three inches taller than her. Like him, she was slim and long-limbed in build, and although she was almost sixty, she looked at least ten years younger. Although her shoulder-length hair was dyed, its sandy-blond hue was the same as her natural hue had once been, so it didn't look at all false. While her long, narrow face sported a few deep creases and wrinkles, they did not detract from her natural prettiness, which had barely faded over the course of six decades. Her honey-colored eyes still sparkled with an effervescent joy, and her mere presence was always enough to raise the mood of whatever room she was in.

"All right, all right," Stanley said, chuckling. "You know I find it hard to resist your famous home-baked chocolate chip cookies, though, honey."

"Best in the county," Declan said with a grin, exaggeratedly inhaling the delicious aroma of the cookies. "Nah, scratch that, best in the whole damn state!"

They all laughed, but after a period of warm, cheerful silence, the mood took a more somber turn. "While I was baking, I read a rather alarming article on my phone," Eileen said.

"Oh yeah?" Stanley asked, taking another sip of his whiskey.

"There was another murder just outside town," she said gravely. "They think it was a cartel hit. Drug business."

"I knew it," Declan muttered, shaking his head and scowling. "When I saw those people with Randall, I knew they were Mexican cartel guys."

"And you can bet that this murder is going to stay unsolved, no matter how much evidence there is about who did it," Stanley said. "Randall's had the sheriff and his deputies in his pocket for years now."

"Has he made any more offers on your land?" Declan asked.

"Austin Randall has been trying to get this land from me for forty years," Stanley said with a sigh. "We all know. And yeah, he made another offer—double what the ranch is worth. You can bet that I told that drug-dealing scumbag where to shove his offer."

"Good," Declan growled.

"I've said it before, and I'll say it again—we should have gotten the FBI onto Randall," Eileen said. "The local cops know he grows poppies for heroin. He's been doing it for decades…it's useless trying to get them to do anything about it. Only by going over their heads could we get that evil man arrested and put in prison where he belongs."

"I've heard that he's got a paid-off friend or two in the FBI, too," Stanley said. "Austin Randall may be one of the dirtiest, move evil scumbags around, but he's smart, I'll give him that. Remember, I did contact the FBI a few years back. Nothing ever came of it, as you may recall."

"I wonder when he's going to try offering you three times what this land is worth," Declan mused. "I wouldn't be surprised if he tried."

"I wouldn't either, but that sack of shit could offer me a billion dollars and I'd *still* tell him to shove it where the sun don't shine," Stanley said defiantly. "The thought of my family's land, which we've had for hundreds of years, falling into that disgusting man's hands to be turned into a poppy farm for his heroin factory makes me want to puke. It'll never happen, not while I still draw breath, and not while Marv is alive, either. My boy knows the score, and he'll never, ever sell this land to Randall, not for all the money in the world."

"My worry," Eileen said worriedly, "is that eventually, Randall gets tired of making offers he knows you're going to refuse. Now that he's working with Mexican cartel people, he might try to get them to use some of their famously 'persuasive' methods of convincing you to sell. I don't want it to come down to something like that, Stan. You know what those cartel people are capable of."

"Let the sons of bitches come," Stanley muttered, patting the .45 ACP he always wore on his hip. "I won't let anyone even think of trying to intimidate me. Not—"

Suddenly, the porch and house lights went out, plunging the place into darkness.

"Did you see that?" Declan asked, narrowing his eyes and leaning forward, staring at the distant horizon beyond the jagged outline of the forested hills.

"See what?" Eileen asked. "Looks like we've got a power cut, nothing much to see about that."

"No, I mean out there," Declan said, pointing out at the horizon. "I feel like there was a brief but exceptionally bright flash of light in the distance. Didn't anyone else see that?"

Eileen shook her head. "I wasn't looking that way."

"I wasn't either," Stanley said. "Are you sure you saw something out there?"

"Positive," Declan said. "I don't know what it was, though...Ain't never seen anything like that in my life.

But it must have been crazy bright where it happened if I could see it from here."

"Hmm, that's odd," Eileen remarked. "My phone's dead. I could have sworn the battery was almost full, but now it won't even turn on."

"Mine's the same," Declan said, frowning as he took out his phone and tried unsuccessfully to turn it on.

Stanley turned and locked an intense stare into his best friend's eyes, and even in the darkness, Declan could see just how serious the expression on Stanley's face was. "Are you sure you saw a bright flash of light over there in the distance?" he asked.

"Unless I've spontaneously started suffering from hallucinations, then yeah, I'm sure I did," Declan answered. "Do you know what it was?"

"I think I have a pretty good idea," Stanley said grimly. "Hold on, I'm going to go check out a few other things inside the house. Eileen, honey, get some camping lanterns and light 'em up, please…if this is what I'm thinking it is, the lights aren't going to come back on for a long time…a very, very long time."

"Uh, sure, okay," Eileen said, sounding worried. "What are you thinking this is, Stan?"

"I'll tell you in a few minutes," Stanley answered. "For now, please just get some camping lanterns, honey."

Eileen went inside to find some lanterns while Stanley went around the house, checking various electrical items. When he returned to the porch, Eileen had set up a few gas lanterns, and they were hissing softly as they cast out their pale, yellowish light. Illuminated by this gentle glow, both Declan and Eileen immediately saw the deep consternation on Stanley's face when he returned to the porch.

"What's wrong, Stan?" Eileen asked. "What's going on?"

"I know what that bright flash was," Stanley said grimly, "and what it means for us, and possibly everyone else in this country."

"Well, go on, man, tell us," Declan said, unable to disguise the worry in his voice.

"What you saw was part of an attack on this country, an act of war, possibly the most serious in all of American history," Stanley said. "And I have no doubt in my mind that the primary weapon of this attack was an electromagnetic pulse attack, an attack that seems to have succeeded with devastating effects. The entire power grid is now down, and everything electronic is dead, smashed beyond repair...whoever has pulled off this attack has singlehandedly sent us back into the stone age...nothing is going to be the same for us ever again."

"Damn," Declan murmured. "You told us about this a while back. You said it might happen...I never really believed that it could, but now...now it is really happening, and I can't believe it. It's like...like I know you're right because I trust you, and I know how smart you are, but also...it just, it seems so far-fetched that it feels like it can't possibly be real. I know it's real, don't get me wrong…but my mind is having a little trouble coming to terms with it."

"Don't worry, I know what you mean," Stanley said grimly. "The downfall of civilization in the blink of an eye isn't exactly something that any of our brains can process in even a few weeks or months, let alone a couple minutes. It all feels completely surreal to me, too. It's like…like I somehow went from being awake and alive in the present here to slipping into some sort of bizarre, surreal nightmare."

"My old Dodge will still work, though, right?" Declan said. "I remember talking about this before. Not everything will be completely dead, right?"

Stanley nodded. "Your truck will still work because it's a 70s model. And my old Land Rover will still work, too—this is exactly why I kept it and why I've been so meticulous with maintenance—and that's why we have so many gallons of diesel stored in the barn. Eileen, honey, I'm sorry, but your Range Rover is totally dead. There won't be any resurrecting that vehicle."

Eileen let out a sad sigh, but, true to her optimistic nature, she chose to look at the silver lining behind this dark cloud. "At least we have two working vehicles between us, even if my car is dead and gone," she said. "That's probably a lot more than ninety-nine percent of the population can say right now."

"Indeed, indeed," Stanley said. "But right now, I'm not worried about vehicles or even any of the other essential items that are all dead and wrecked beyond repair."

"You're worried about Marv and Caitlin, as I am," Eileen said, the color draining from her face. "My God, what are they going to do? Marv's out at sea, and Caitlin's stuck in the city…it's got to be absolute pandemonium there, utter chaos if everything has suddenly shut down!"

"Oh, I sure as hell am worried about my boy and Caitlin," Stanley said, "but I'm also worried about *us…real* worried."

Declan turned his head in the direction of Austin Randall's land and nodded slowly. "I think I know what you're worried about, my friend," he said grimly.

"When I said that this is the downfall of civilization, that's exactly what I meant," Stanley said, his eyes focused on some unseen point in the far distance. "It's not just the power grid and our technology that have died tonight. The rule of law is dead and buried, too; I have no doubt about that. And while Austin Randall was ready to stop short of murdering us to get this land prior to this evening, now that the law is as dead as this phone in my pocket, he's going to do whatever it takes to get this land of ours. Especially because of your crops, honey. We've been growing enough food to feed ourselves many times over for years now, thanks to your horticultural skills…plain old food, in these times we find ourselves in, is going to be worth more than its weight in gold. Austin Randall will surely realize this. Right now, with the food we've got growing here, we're sitting on a goldmine. Everyone is going to want a piece of it, especially when hunger starts rumbling in their bellies. And believe me, that hunger is going to start hitting people soon, real soon. Austin Randall will be one of those people because he doesn't grow much besides opium poppies on his land. And now that he's got cartel muscle to back him up, he's going to simply use force to take whatever he wants because he knows nobody can stop him."

"Then that can only mean one thing for us," Declan murmured.

"That's right. We have to prepare for war," Stanley said.

6

"How on Earth do you imagine you're going to get back to shore if the engines in this ship are as dead as you say they are?" Captain Reid asked Marvin.

"We've got life rafts on this ship," Marvin answered. "It'll be a tough trip, I'm under no delusions about that, but right now, we're not far enough out at sea that it's beyond the realm of possibility."

"Are you insane? Those inflatable rafts are for emergencies only!" Reid scoffed.

"As far as I can tell, Captain," Marvin said coolly, "this is about as serious an emergency as I can imagine. Sure, the ship may not actually be sinking, but it sure as hell isn't going to be going anywhere ever again, and the ocean currents are only going to take it farther away from land, not toward it. And believe me when I say this:

nobody is coming out here to rescue us. *Nobody*. Everyone is going to have far bigger problems to worry about than a couple merchant vessels aimlessly adrift on the open sea."

"But regardless of the situation, international maritime law requires that—" Captain Reid began.

Marvin was quick to cut him off. "I'm sorry, Captain, but laws are irrelevant now. We're not only entering what's likely to be World War III, which will probably make even World War II look like a kindergarten playground brawl, but even if there was anyone with a working ship that was able to rescue us, I'm pretty damn sure that they'd be far more concerned with their own survival than for combing the open seas for missing merchant vessels."

"What about the navy?" Hank asked. "Will their ships be disabled, too? You're a former Navy SEAL. What do you think?"

Marvin shrugged. "I can't tell you anything for certain. I'm guessing that at least some of the Navy's more advanced vessels will be EMP-proof, but how much of a shit are they going to give about us when they've got the biggest war of the century, perhaps of the entire modern era on their hands, with civilization as we know it literally collapsing around us? They've got far bigger things to worry about. Look, I know you all have a ton of questions, but I can't answer them all, and quite frankly, I'm wasting precious time here. I've told you all what the situation is, I'm damn sure that no help will be coming soon, if ever, and the longer we sit around with our thumbs up our asses, the farther out to sea the currents are going to take us. I'm going to get on a life raft and do my damndest to get back to shore before we're too far away for that to be a possibility. Anyone who wants to come with me, you're free to do so. I'm leaving right now, though. I'll wait ten minutes for whoever wants to come to grab a few essential things, but that's it. Y'all have about a minute to make up your minds, so you'd better think fast."

"You can't just leave!" Captain Reid protested. "The terms of your contract—"

"With all due respect, Captain, you can take that contract and shove it where the sun don't shine," Marvin said gruffly.

"You walk off this boat and you're gonna have the mother of all lawsuits on your hands, Wagner," Reid growled through clenched teeth, his hands balled into tight fists at his sides. "You can kiss your career goodbye; I'll make sure you never even set foot on a fishing boat ever again!"

Marvin laughed coldly and humorlessly. "You want to sue me; you go right ahead, Captain. I'm leaving now."

With that, Marvin strode out of the room, ignoring the cacophony of frantic conversation and yelling that exploded like a detonated hand grenade in his wake. He made a beeline for his cabin, where he gathered a few essential items: his pistol, ammunition, waterproof clothing, chemical lights, a first aid kit, a multitool, a large knife, and some other items. Then he went to the kitchen and grabbed as much non-perishable food and as many water bottles as he could fit into his gym bag.

When he got to the deck area from which the emergency life rafts were launched, he found Hank and two other crew members—both young men who worked in the kitchen—waiting for him.

"So, you're coming with me, huh?" Marvin asked Hank.

"I sure am," Hank answered, "and Bruce and Jason are coming, too."

"What about the rest of the crew?" Marvin asked.

Hank shrugged. "After you left, Captain Reid spent a lot of time convincing everyone that you were wrong and that you were blowing this whole thing out of proportion. He seems real sure it's not as bad as you say it is, and he thinks that we're gonna get rescued or that the engineers will be able to get the ship's engines up and running again with a little work."

Marvin shook his head and sighed. "Then he's either completely delusional or in total denial about what's happened. I just hope his obstinacy doesn't end up costing the rest of the crew their lives."

"I tried to get some more people to come with us," said Jason, a scrawny young man with a shock of red hair. "But they wouldn't listen. They wanna stay here and wait for rescue."

"Yeah," added Bruce, a portly, middle-aged Filipino crew member. "I think partly it's wishful thinking, but it's also fear. The ocean is calm now, but when the last weather reports—just before this EMP thing hit—were saying a big storm was on the way. And when I say 'big,' I mean humungous. It'll be bad enough to be on a ship when it hits, but way worse to be on a tiny inflatable life raft."

"So, why are you risking your life and coming with us?" Marvin asked.

Bruce grinned. "Drowning is a bad way to go but starving to death—or having to resort to something like murder and cannibalism when the food on this ship finally runs out, and then starving anyway, after you've eaten all your buddies and sucked the marrow from their bones—sounds way worse to me. I believe everything you said about this EMP stuff is true, Marvin, and I'd rather take my chances and do what I can to get back to shore while we still have the chance to do that. If I drown, so be it; at least my suffering will only last a few minutes, not weeks or months."

Marvin nodded. "I'm glad at least a few people believe me. I really, really want to be wrong about this whole thing, guys, but I honestly don't think I am. Like you said, Bruce, staying on this ship may seem wise in the short term, but long-term, it's guaranteed to be a long, slow, and tortuous death sentence."

All of the men murmured their agreement with this.

"All right, have you guys got everything you need?" Marvin asked. "I want to get going right away."

"I've got a few personal items, waterproofs, chem lights, and as much food, water, and supplies I can carry," Hank said.

"Same," Jason said.

"I've got all of that, yeah, but also something else that I think is pretty essential that the rest of you seem to have forgotten," Bruce said, a sly grin on his chubby face and mischief twinkling in his eyes in the green glow of the chemical lights.

"Oh yeah, what's that?" Marvin asked. He was sure he had covered all his bases and that he hadn't forgotten anything important.

Still grinning, Bruce pulled two bottles of whiskey out of his bag. "If it all goes to shit and it looks like we're gonna die, we can at least die happy!" he said.

Everyone chuckled, but their laughter soon faded and somber looks came over their faces. Up ahead, in the direction of land, the starry sky was being devoured by a thick and ominous darkness: storm clouds, in which bright violet flickers of lightning flashed every few seconds.

"Looks like you're right about that storm," Jason murmured. "We're going to be heading right into it."

"Yeah, and this ship is going to get pushed far out into the ocean," Marvin said, wetting his finger and holding it up to check the wind, which was already picking up.

"Yep, the wind is definitely blowing toward us, from the direction of the land. By the time this storm is over, nobody is going to be able to reach land from the ship, not even if there are weeks of perfectly calm weather ahead. As dangerous as it's going to be, this is our one and only shot of getting back to land."

"Let's do it then," Hank said. "Like Bruce said, I'd rather die out there in a storm than have to suffer through what's surely coming on this damn ship. Shit's gonna end up looking like a zombie movie here after a couple months of drifting aimlessly around the Atlantic."

"It's time to get that raft on the water," Marvin said.

Although none of the men except him had ever been on an emergency life raft, as part of their training, they all knew how to get the craft off the ship and onto the water. When they had done this successfully—which was easy in the calm before the storm—they used a rope ladder to get off the deck onto the life raft, an orange inflatable vessel with its own built-in, waterproof tent section for shelter and its own oars. It also had emergency lights and a transponder, which were supposed to automatically activate as soon as the raft was deployed, but the EMP had destroyed these. Nevertheless, the men had their chemical lights, which were bright enough to illuminate the raft and the ocean a few yards around it.

They set up a chem light, hanging it from the top of the shelter dome. Then in grim, nervous silence, they each picked up an oar and started to row. The wind picked up slowly but steadily, and on the horizon, the flickering veins of lightning grew brighter and the rolling peals of thunder became louder and longer. A storm was coming, and it was guaranteed to be a big one, and the four men on the raft were rowing themselves right into it.

7

"I'm going to die in here," Caitlin gasped, struggling to breathe as hyperventilation gripped her respiratory system. "Oh my God, oh God, I'm going to die in this office tonight…I'm going to die in here. I'm going to die."

All escape routes were cut off and all exits blocked. And outside, the rain of missiles continued, their booming, wall-shaking explosions adding further terror to an already horrifying situation.

With her heart pounding so madly in her chest that it felt as if it would burst through her ribcage, her extremities tingling, and her head spinning so badly she was sure she would faint, Caitlin staggered backward until she hit the wall. Then she slowly slid down until she was slumped in a defeated heap on the floor, shaking and gasping, completely overwhelmed by fear and panic.

She had never imagined her life would end like this.

She'd always thought that she and Marvin would eventually get married, have a few children, maybe settle down on his family's beautiful ranch in the hills, and live to a ripe old age with many grandchildren and maybe even great-grandchildren. She'd hoped to have a long and successful career in her field, eventually becoming a partner in her law firm and maybe even going on to start her own firm.

All of these hopes and dreams meant nothing now. None of them would ever come to fruition. All would be ground to dust, would be burned to ashes…just like her body would be when this entire gigantic building went up in flames and came tumbling down.

"Maybe…maybe I should just jump and get it over with," Caitlin gasped to herself. "I don't want to drag this out…I don't want to suffer any longer."

Despite the panic that gripped her so ferociously in its terrible claws, a strange and chilling clarity came over her. This was what she needed to do: to just get it over with. She had tried to escape, and she had failed. All avenues of escape were now closed to her. There was no sense in prolonging the inevitable. She needed to simply accept her fate and be done with it.

"I'm going to jump," she said, forcing herself to struggle to her feet. "I'm going to end things quickly. I'm going to jump…I have to jump…to jump off the seventy-first floor of a skyscraper without a parachute."

As Caitlin said the word "parachute," however, a revelation hit her like a bolt out of the blue. It was so startling, so intense that she almost lost her balance. In the soft orange glow cast by the candle, her eyes grew wide and her jew dropped open.

The flame of fresh hope, formerly dead and black and smoking, sprang to fresh life within her.

"That crazy guy...that conspiracy theorist from the offices on the seventy-fifth floor!" she gasped.

When Caitlin had said the word parachute, it had triggered a memory of a conversation she'd had a few months earlier. It hadn't been a particularly pleasant conversation, either—which was precisely why it had stayed in her mind, unlike so many other casual conversations she'd had.

One day, she had arrived at work and, as usual, had taken the elevator from the parking garages in the basement all the way up to the seventy-first floor with another person. Typically, the other people in the elevator observed the usual etiquette and kept quiet for the duration of the ride, avoiding eye contact and speech and maintaining a respectful distance and personal space.

The man who had been with her on this particular day, however, had not done this. Instead, he had started talking to her the moment she had approached the elevator in the parking garage, where he had already been waiting for it to descend. Unfortunately for her, on this day, only one of the elevators had been working because the others were all having maintenance work done...so the wait for the elevator, as well as the ride itself, had been quite excruciating.

The man—an obese, balding man in his forties with wild, bulging eyes and a bad case of eczema—had turned out to be just as unpleasantly crazy as he looked. From the moment Caitlin had stood next to him to wait for the elevator, he had started talking about various conspiracy theories. Some of them were mild and popularly accepted as being possible—like the fact that he thought that 9/11 had been an inside job—but others, like the fact that he genuinely believed that shapeshifting reptilian beings controlled the government, were far less plausible.

It hadn't really been a conversation—instead, the man hadn't even given Caitlin the opportunity to get even two words in as he had unloaded just about every conspiracy theory known to man on her in the ten very uncomfortable minutes that they had had to share the same small space.

But one thing that the man, who told her he worked for a software engineering firm on the seventy-fifth floor, had said now seemed to be incredibly pertinent. He had told Caitlin he was certain the reptilians were going to pull off a series of further 9/11-style attacks on the American people and that he was sure that this building was going to be hit. For that reason, he kept an emergency parachute hidden in one of his desk drawers... along with some weapons he had smuggled into the building, firearms that he had gotten past security by bringing them in piece by piece over a couple of weeks, which he assembled in the toilet on his bathroom breaks.

Caitlin had been immensely relieved to get away from him, but now she was incredibly grateful he had spoken to her. If he had been telling the truth about keeping an emergency parachute in his desk, it could mean the difference between life and death for her on this fateful night.

There was only one way to find out if he had been telling the truth or lying. Caitlin grabbed the candle and the samurai sword—which she knew would come in handy if she had to break through any doors, which was a likely possibility—and then she wrapped her colorful Ugandan scarf around her face. It wasn't much, but it would protect her from at least some smoke inhalation.

Then she ran over to the stairwell. Getting up to the seventy-fifth floor wouldn't be pleasant in the searing, acrid black smoke, but given the alternative, it had to be done. After psyching herself up for a few seconds, she yanked open the door. Thick smoke came belching out of the stairwell, and all Caitlin could do was charge straight into it.

Holding her breath for as long as she could, with the black smoke stinging her eyes and making the already dark stairwell completely impenetrable, Caitlin stumbled through the gloom, seeking the stairs with her feet. She found them, and then, moving as fast as she could through the choking, blinding smoke, she began her ascent.

Since she could barely see anything, the only way she knew what floor she was on was by keeping count of how many turns she made on the stairs. When she was about halfway up, she couldn't hold her breath any longer, and she had to inhale.

Although her scarf filtered a little of the smoke, a lot of it got through, and it burned her airways and lungs fiercely, causing her to pause and break into a fit of coughing. With a surge of intense determination, though, she fought through the pain and discomfort, held her breath again, and then carried on up the stairs.

She made it to the seventy-fifth floor just as she reached the point of being unable to hold her breath any longer. Gasping, coughing, and panting, she barged through the doors and slammed them shut behind her, staggering away from them so she could pull the scarf off her face and greedily inhale a few large lungfuls of fresh air.

Caitlin hadn't been on this floor before, and she didn't even know what the conspiracy theorist's software company was called. She figured, though, that it couldn't be too hard to find. With hope burning in her heart, she began searching the floor by the weak light of the candle, wincing involuntarily every time she heard the dreadful sound of another missile crashing into a nearby skyscraper or hearing the ground-rumbling boom of one of the many huge explosions that continued to go off.

Although her skyscraper hadn't been hit again, the damage it had taken from the earlier missile strikes had clearly been substantial. The building kept creaking and groaning so loudly that the sound felt as if it were shattering Caitlin's skull, but all she could do was grit her teeth and try to ignore these terrifying noises—and the scary shaking and vibrations that accompanied them, which seemed to clearly indicate that it was only a matter of time before the whole skyscraper came crashing down—and press on.

Striding briskly across the gleaming, polished marble floor, she checked the sign on each of the front doors to the floor's many office complexes. After around five minutes of frantic searching, she finally found a set of offices that belonged to a software engineering company.

"This has to be the place," Caitlin said to herself. "Please God, please tell me that crazy man was telling the truth about having a parachute...please God, please."

She set the candle on the floor and tried the door. She wasn't surprised to discover it was locked.

"Well, that's what I brought this along for," she said, gripping the heavy samurai sword with both hands.

The door, like most of the office doors, consisted of two glass panels in a metal frame. Caitlin took a step back, then swung the sword with all her might at the uppermost glass panel, aiming for the center of it—the weakest part.

The blade smashed through the glass, shattering the entire panel, and Caitlin exhaled a sigh of relief. She had no time to pause, though. The air up here was getting worse by the second. The smoke was finding its way through the gaps in the stairwell doors and slowly but surely filling up the entire floor.

Caitlin used the sword to smash any remaining chunks of glass out of the frame, and then she climbed through the gap. She hurried into the office, keeping the sword tucked under her arm and lighting her way with the candle.

Like most offices, it consisted of a number of cubicles separated by dividers. She searched each of them, checking each cubicle for something that would give her an idea of who it belonged to. She had no idea what the conspiracy theorist's name was—if he had told her, she couldn't remember—but she had a clear image of his face in her mind, and she knew she would recognize him as soon as she saw him.

A sudden, earsplitting groan from the building tore through Caitlin's skull. This one was much louder than the previous ones, and she had to drop everything and clamp her hands over her ears to try to block out the terrible sound. The horrid sound was accompanied by a violent shaking and a terrifying sense of lurching and swaying so bad that it almost paralyzed Caitlin with terror.

All she could do was crouch down and keep her ears covered until it was over and pray the building didn't collapse. After what seemed like an eternity, the shaking stopped, and the sound subsided.

"I have to find this parachute, I have to," Caitlin

gasped. "This building is going to come down any second now."

She grabbed the sword and the candle—which, thankfully, was still burning—and she sped up the pace of her searching. Finally, relief washed over her when she found the conspiracy theorist's desk. There was an autographed photo of him with his arms around a beautiful girl dressed in a very skimpy outfit—clearly a cosplayer at a comic convention.

Caitlin didn't waste any time looking at the photo or trying to work out who the girl who had autographed it was. Instead, she dived straight into rummaging through the desk drawers.

One by one, though, they turned up empty of everything except papers, candy, and stationery, and with each successive failed search Caitlin grew more frantic and desperate. Finally, she got to the bottom drawer, which was locked. She grabbed the sword and shoved the tip of the blade into the top of the drawer, and with a bit of effort and levering, she managed to force it open.

Triumph ripped through her when she saw what was inside the drawer: a parachute backpack, two pistols, some ammunition, some knives, a first aid kit, a gas mask, an oxygen tank, and a number of other useful items.

Caitlin shoved what she could into her bag, then she pulled out the parachute pack and strapped it on. She had never been skydiving, but she did have a vague recollection of how to put on a parachute pack. Back when she and Marvin had first started dating, he had taken her on a skydiving trip—or, rather, what should have been a skydiving trip. After going through the initial instructions on the ground, Caitlin had chickened out, refusing to get onto the plane. Marvin, an experienced skydiver thanks to his Navy SEAL background, had gone ahead and jumped without her.

There could be no chickening out this time. A failure to jump would mean certain death, whereas jumping would only mean…likely death. Caitlin didn't know much about base jumping, in which adrenalin addicts would do things like she was about to do and parachute off skyscrapers in pursuit of a rush, but she did know it was far more dangerous than regular skydiving.

Nevertheless, given the choice between likely death and certain death, there was only one option to choose. Now, the only thing that remained to do was to find a place from which to jump.

She knew many of the executive offices in this building had private balconies. This wasn't ideal, but given how badly the skyscraper had been groaning and shaking in the past minute or two, Caitlin knew she didn't have much time to get out. Also, smoke was pouring into these offices now at an alarming rate; the fire was raging through the building and spreading with exponential speed.

She unclipped the strap of her bag, which was quite heavy now, looped it through her belt a few times until it was sitting over her crotch area, and then reclipped it, leaving her hands free to operate the parachute controls when the time came to jump. With her pulse absolutely racing, she ran through the offices, her candle in one hand and the samurai sword in the other, desperately seeking the executive office of this complex.

Thankfully, it didn't take her long to find it, and she whispered a prayer of gratitude when she tried the door and found it unlocked. The office had a balcony, a discovery that brought great relief to Caitlin, but the door to it was locked. Unlike the glass of the front door to the office, which had shattered with one solid blow from the sword, this glass was, like the floor-to-ceiling windows of the skyscraper, made of reinforced glass, and no amount of hitting it with the sword seemed to have any effect on it.

Desperate and starting to despair and choking on the increasingly thick smoke, Caitlin staggered back. She was just about to start ramming her body into the door with sheer desperation when a little object gleaming in the candlelight caught her eye.

When she took it off its hook on the side of the huge, ornate desk, she felt like a miner who had just discovered a huge gold nugget or a diamond, for the object was a key with the label "balcony" on the keyring.

She tossed the sword aside—it had served its purpose now, and she would have no further use for it—and with trembling hands, she unlocked the door and ran out onto the balcony. As she looked out over the apocalyptic sight below, the city a sea of intense darkness dotted all over with fires, backed by a soundtrack of screaming, yelling, gunfire, explosions, and the shrieks of missiles, her vision swam, and her knees felt as if they were going to buckle beneath her.

Caitlin knew there could be no hesitation. The longer she lingered here, the more difficult it would be to actually go through with this.

With her heart in her throat and feeling as if she were on the verge of a full-blown panic attack, she climbed onto the balcony railing, took a deep breath, then jumped off the seventy-fifth floor of the skyscraper.

8

"I've got a bad feeling about this," Bruce muttered as he dipped his oar into the water, rowing in tandem with the three other men on the life raft.

The formerly smooth ocean was starting to get choppy, and the wind speed was picking up steadily while deep, ominous peals of thunder rolled across the sea, synchronized with the violet flickers of lightning in the increasingly dark sky.

"You wishing you'd stayed on the ship, Bruce?" Jason asked with a grin.

Bruce chuckled and shook his head. "Nope, I don't want to end up getting eaten when the food eventually runs out—and you know those bastards would pick me first, with all this meat I've got on my bones—but I've still got a bad feeling about this."

"We've all got life vests," Hank said, trying to sound

confident, "and if you clip your belt to the side of the raft with a D-ring clip, you'll be about as safe as you can be. We'll get through this storm…it's gonna be crazy, we all know, but we'll get through it."

Marvin, meanwhile, said nothing. His eyes were fixed on the horizon, his jaw set tight with determination, and he put power and effort into every stroke of his oar. One thing and one thing only was driving him on in the face of all this danger: the need to get back to the city, find Caitlin, and get her out of there.

"I think it's time to get our waterproofs on," Hank added after a minute or two of silent rowing. "Things feel like they're getting more intense…quite a lot more intense."

"Agreed," Marvin said. "But let's keep rowing for another five minutes, then take a quick break and do that."

"Boys, how about some liquid courage before this thing hits?" Bruce suggested as a particularly cold and potent gust of wind tore with sudden violence across the ocean, whipping spray into the men's faces. "We're not going to have much chance to take a drink after this, not when things start getting really rough."

"Sure, break it out. I sure as hell could use some whiskey right now," Jason said before Marvin could respond.

Bruce set down his oar, rubbed his hands together with anticipatory glee, and got out one of the whiskey bottles. Jason tossed his oar into the raft and stared at the whiskey, his eager eyes betraying his hunger for the liquor in the eerie green glow of the chem light.

Marvin realized there could be no stopping the two of them, so he reluctantly paused rowing. "All right," he muttered, "but only a few sips each. We can't afford to let drunkenness interrupt our rowing rhythm, and when this storm hits, we're going to need to have keen minds and sharp focus to get through it."

Marvin kept a close eye on Jason as Bruce passed the young man the whiskey. Jason had a reputation for getting blind drunk on a regular basis, and although he was a good man when sober, when he'd had too much to drink, he could be a real idiot.

As Marvin had feared, instead of taking a few swigs of whiskey, as soon as Jason got the bottle in his hands, he started chugging the amber liquid down as if it were water. Marvin scrambled up from his position and snatched the bottle out of Jason's hands.

"Hey, man, watch it! You're spilling!" Jason protested, with spilled whiskey soaking the front of his shirt.

"Get a grip on yourself!" Marvin growled, his eyes blazing with anger. "This isn't a pleasure cruise, you moron! If you get roaring drunk and lose control of your coordination and reflexes, you're going to put all of our lives in danger!"

As if Nature herself wanted to help Marvin emphasize this point, a large wave suddenly came rushing across the water, crashing against the flimsy inflatable raft and rocking it violently in a precursor of what was to come. Just after the wave hit, a cannon-shot of a thunderclap pealed across the ocean, the loudest yet, and a bright vein of lightning streaked across the entirety of the sky, illuminating everything for a split second in bright, violet-tinged light.

"Chill the fuck out, man," Jason muttered sourly. "We're not on the ship anymore, and you're not my fucking boss."

"Shut up and quit being an idiot!" This time it was Hank who snapped at Jason. "Marvin's right, we need to be alert and ready to get through the storm, and that's not gonna happen if you're drunk!"

"Aw, what's the matter, kid? Are you scared of a little booze because you're still below the legal age to drink?" Jason mocked.

Now Bruce joined the chorus of voices objecting to Jason's behavior. "Uh, Jason, I didn't bring that booze along so that we could get drunk before taking on the storm," he said warily. "Come on, man, calm down a little, okay? We've all gotta work together as a team here."

"Fine, whatever," Jason muttered, scowling. "Throw the fucking whiskey overboard then, go on, do it. I don't give a shit."

"From now on, this is going to be rationed," Marvin said sternly, "and I'll be keeping it."

"Go right ahead, *boss*," Jason sneered mockingly. "Yes sir, *boss*…are we in the navy now, *boss*? Yes sir, no sir, left right, left right!" The few glugs of whiskey he'd had were already having an effect on his personality.

"Quit being such a jerk," Hank muttered.

Marvin ignored the bait; he knew now was not the time to be drawn into a petty argument.

"Yeah, come on, man, just zip it and row," Bruce said, somewhat nervously—he was the sort of person who always did whatever they could to avoid confrontation.

Just then, another large wave hit the raft. Now the ride was getting seriously choppy, with the life raft beginning to rise and fall in a lurching motion as it surfed the waves and the troughs between them, the extremes of which were growing steadily greater, while the wind continued to pick up in speed, whipping spray into the men's faces.

Marvin took a quick sip of whiskey and then offered the bottle to Hank, who also took a small swig. After that, Marvin tucked the bottle into his bag, which was strapped around his waist. The men got their waterproofs on, and it was time to resume rowing.

Now that the ocean was getting rough, rowing required a lot more effort than it previously had. Marvin clenched his jaw, gripping the oar tightly, and called out to the others, knowing they needed to work in perfect tandem to keep themselves moving forward against the increasingly unruly waves.

"Move in time with me! Row!" he yelled, dipping his oar in and giving a powerful stroke. He raised it out of the water and prepared to give another stroke. "Row!"

The others obeyed, even Jason. Despite his attitude, he was an experienced seaman and knew how important it was, in terms of sheer survival, for him to work with the others. As they rowed, desperately urging the raft onward as it surfed the crests and dips between the swelling waves in increasingly tough climbs and steep, lurching descents, the first few drops of rain started to come down as thunder and lightning boomed and flashed at evermore frequent intervals.

The squall hit in full force after a few minutes, and the cold rain came at them like a horde of cavalry troops charging across the sea in a sheet of icy water.

"Row!" Marvin yelled hoarsely as the rain bucketed down, hitting them with such force—driven on by the wind, which had become a howling gale—that it felt like thousands of BB pellets being fired into their faces and their waterproofs. "Row!" he yelled over the deafening drumming of the heavy rain on the raft and their waterproofs, the howling roar of the wind, and the deep, bowel-rumbling peals and claps of thunder. "Row! Row! Row!"

The storm grew even fiercer, and as hard as the men were rowing, working in perfect synchronization, it quickly began to feel as if they were getting nowhere as their forward progress was completely halted.

A huge wave came out of nowhere, crashing with such force against the raft that it almost capsized. The wall of icy Atlantic water broke over the raft, drenching everyone in it thoroughly.

"Hold on tight!" Marvin yelled. "There's another big one—"

At that moment, the raft crested a gigantic wave, and they were then sent hurtling down into the trough behind it, their stomachs in their mouths for a few terrifying seconds as they were airborne, dropping like a stone into the trough.

They hit the water with a powerful impact that almost flipped over the raft.

"Holy shit!" Hank yelled hoarsely, his eyes wide with fright in the eerie green glow of the chem light, which, thankfully, was waterproof and clipped firmly in place, providing the only light source for miles in the black ocean—aside from the frequent dazzling split-second blazes of brightness from the tongues of lightning that blasted across the sky.

"Row, dammit, row!" Marvin yelled, driving his oar with desperate ferocity into the water, trying to get the raft up the rising slope of the next wave.

There was no time for debate, protesting, or argument; all the men understood with chilling clarity that their survival now depended on working together in perfect unison as a team. Even the belligerent Jason was doing his utmost to row in time.

"Row!" Marvin yelled, putting every ounce of strength and power he possessed into each and every stroke. "Row! Row!" Every muscle in his upper body ached from the effort of his exertion, and his throat and lungs burned. As much as his body was screaming out for rest, though, this urge was overridden by the adrenalin pumping through his veins and his fierce desire to get back to land, not only for reasons of sheer survival but to rescue his beloved Caitlin from the chaos unfolding there.

Suddenly, from out of nowhere, a far bigger wave than any the men had encountered thus far crashed against them. This one was so massive that it made their craft seem like a mere fly drowning in a raging river.

The wave smashed the raft like a bucket of water dumped on a couple of insects. For a few terrifying seconds, Marvin and the others were completely swamped, pummeled with a wall of water that crashed against them with absolutely irresistible force. All they could do was hold their breath and hang on for dear life as the ferocious wave tossed them around like laundry inside a washing machine.

For a brief moment, Marvin was overwhelmed with a feeling of utter panic. It seemed that the raft was about to be sunk; how could the flimsy inflatable craft prevail against such a vicious and unstoppable force of nature?

After those few horrific seconds had passed, though, the buoyant raft surfaced, filled with water and half-sinking but still managing to stay afloat, defying the wrath of the raging ocean.

"Hank!" Marvin roared hoarsely, his eyes burning from the salty seawater, which meant that he could barely see anything, especially with the driving sheets of rain and sprays of water from the waves.

"I'm here. I'm good!" Hank sputtered, gasping and coughing after having inhaled some seawater.

"Bruce!" Marvin yelled.

"Here!" Bruce yelled back.

"Jason!" Marvin shouted, his voice barely audible over the ceaseless howling of the wind.

This time, there was no response.

"Jason, answer me, dammit!" Marvin yelled, raising his voice as loud as it could go.

Again, there was no response.

"Hold on, let me check!" Bruce yelled.

He was sitting across from Marvin and in front of Jason. He turned around and peered over his shoulder… but even through the lashing rain and the gloom, he could see that the spot where Jason had been sitting moments earlier was now vacant.

"Oh shit!" Bruce yelled. "I think he's been swept overboard! He's gone!"

Before Marvin could respond, another huge wave crashed into the raft with spectacular violence, almost flipping it over, and the men were again thrown around like laundry in a washing machine. It was all they could do to hold on for dear life and hold their breath as the furious waters swirled around them.

Again, though, the raft survived this attempt by the ocean to swallow it, and it surged up through the churning water to the surface. Marvin unclipped himself from his position and crawled across the deck of the raft as the waves tossed it around like a leaf on a flooding river.

"Jason!" he yelled, grabbing the chem light to shine it

into the covered section of the raft. "Jason, where are you?"

The green effulgence of the light quickly revealed that the covered section was empty. Bruce was right; Jason had been swept overboard.

"He's gone!" Marvin yelled. "He probably didn't clip himself in, and now he's gone! Dammit, shit!"

"You have to get back to your place and clip yourself in, sir!" Hank yelled, holding on for dear life to the rope that went around the side of the raft. "He's gone. There's nothing we can do. There's no way to save him. He's already dead!"

It wasn't in Marvin's nature to simply let something like this go—every part of him was screaming out to dive into the churning waves to search for his lost companion—but the rational part of his brain told him that Hank was right. If he dived off the raft, as strong a swimmer as he was, he would be torn away from the raft and pulled under the waves. He would likely drown in mere seconds.

"Hurry up, Marvin, clip yourself back in before you get swept away, too!" Bruce yelled. "You can't do anything for Jason. He's gone, but if you don't—"

At that moment, another gargantuan wave hit the raft, and this time, Marvin wasn't clipped in, and as strong as he was, he couldn't resist the immense power of the water. He was swept overboard into the raging black waves of the Atlantic Ocean.

9

"How soon do you think Randall is going to make his move?" Eileen asked, the worry on her face plain to see in the pale-yellow effulgence of the camping lanterns on the porch.

"I doubt he'll wait long," Stanley said grimly.

"Strike while the iron is hot," Declan said. "That's always been the way Austin Randall has done things. Remember when my father sold that plot of land he used to own next to my place just before he passed on? Randall somehow got word of it before it even went on the marketplace, and he got an agent to make my father an offer fifty percent above his asking price. That snake also paid the agent extra to lie about who was buying the land. My father sold it without even considering any other offers. We only found out after my father's death that it was actually Austin Randall who had bought our land."

"Your father must be turning in his grave," Stanley muttered.

"I'm sure he is," Declan said with a sad sigh and a slow shaking of his head. "He never would have sold it to that scumbag agent if he'd known who was really buying it."

"Oh, I know, believe me," Stanley said. "I'll always consider your father one of the wisest, most honorable men I've ever met, my friend. But anyway, we can't afford to be sitting here, talking about the past right now. The world has changed, and it's changed in a bigger way in the space of the last minutes than it changed over the course of our entire lives. We have to assume that once Randall has figured out what's happened, he's going to move with lightning speed to take what he's been after for decades: our land."

"And my crops, my aquaponics setup, and everything I've worked for to provide this ranch with sustainable, off-the-grid food and drinking water for years," Eileen added.

"You know that's likely going to be the main reason he wants this land now," Stanley said. "Not for his damn heroin poppies anymore, but for food. Anyway, the point is, he's going to want this land more than ever, now, and with nobody to stand in his way, he's going to come to take it with no holds barred."

"How do we prepare for the inevitable attack?" Eileen asked. "You two were both servicemen. How would you plan for what's coming?"

"There's a lot of stuff that needs to be done. First,"

Stanley said, "we need to assess our own resources. Weapons, ammunition, supplies, but, most importantly, people. We're going to have to get everyone on the ranch together right now and tell them what's happened and what's going to happen."

"Then we need an assessment of our enemy's situation," Declan said. "I'll take care of that tonight."

"You're going to scout around Randall's land?" Stanley asked.

Declan gave a subtle smile and a nod. "You bet I am. I'll get my ghillie suit out and get my face paint on. I'll try to get right up to his house, even, see if I can do some eavesdropping."

"I know you were one of the best scouts the US Army has ever had," Stanley said with a smile, "but don't forget that you and me, we ain't spring chickens no more. Don't take any unnecessary risks, Declan. Randall's got his usual goons patrolling his grounds, and I know you can sneak past those boneheads without much effort, but he's also got dogs, and they'll be a lot harder to evade."

"Don't worry, I don't plan on doing anything stupid, and I definitely don't plan on getting caught," Declan said. "Plus, the EMP has given me some pretty favorable conditions in terms of snooping around Randall's land. All his security systems are now permanently disabled, as are all the floodlights he usually has blazing all hours of the night. His entire place is going to be shrouded in darkness…and when I'm scouting, the shadows are my closest allies. The darker, the better."

"All right, my friend, I appreciate your doing that," Stanley said. "See how close you can get without putting yourself in too much danger, and see if you can figure out exactly how and when Randall is planning on making his move."

"Roger that, buddy," Declan said. Without another word, he got up and stalked off into the darkness beyond the light cast by the lanterns on the porch. He didn't take one with him; he had made the two-mile journey between his house and Stanley's so many times he could do it blindfolded—which was almost what he was doing right now.

"Take a gun!" Stanley yelled out as Declan's form melted into the thick shadows beyond the porch. "And don't be shy about using it if you have to! It ain't like you're gonna be arrested if you have to shoot someone!"

"Roger that!" Declan called out.

"All right, honey, we'd better get moving," Stanley said to Eileen. "The workers probably think this is some sort of power cut. We'd better get over to their quarters and tell them what's really going on. Come on, grab a lantern, let's go."

In addition to Declan, a number of other people worked on the ranch, from housekeepers who took care of the guest quarters to guides who took tourists out on horse rides through the forested hills. All in all, there were almost a dozen people who worked on the ranch, with some of them living there part-time, too, owing to the ranch's distance from everything.

As Stanley had expected, the workers were gathered in the courtyard located in the center of their living quarters. There they had built a bonfire, both for light and warmth. Stanley and Eileen approached the workers.

"Stanley, we were just about to go up to your house and see if you guys were okay," said Nathan, a young man who worked as one of the horse guides. "This is the worst power cut I've ever seen! And something weird has happened to all of our phones!"

"We're okay, thank you, Nathan," Stanley said. "Everyone, y'all need to gather around and listen carefully because this isn't a power cut…in fact, this isn't like anything you've ever experienced in your lives; I promise you that."

He climbed onto one of the wooden chairs the workers had positioned around the bonfire, and from this spot, with the roaring flames illuminating his craggy features in tones of deep orange and burned red, he addressed the group of people, who he not only considered friends but also unofficial members of his family.

With everyone listening with rapt attention, Stanley explained everything about the EMP strike, what it meant for the present and the future, both in terms of their lives and the fate of the country and possibly the entire world. When he was finished speaking, nobody said a thing; the silence was so intense that one could have heard a pin drop. The only thing that filled the aural void was the ceaseless sounds of the animals and insects of the night in the nearby woods, who were going on about their lives the same way they had for millions of years.

Stanley said nothing for a while. He knew everyone was going to need a few moments to process what he had just told them. After all, it wasn't every day that someone told you that the world you had known for your entire life, the world you had expected to endure relatively unchanged for the rest of your days, was essentially dead and gone, shattered into irreparable pieces in some sort of insane hit and run.

Finally, someone spoke up. "What…what are we going to do?" Nathan managed to utter, his face a crumpled mess of complete shock and confusion.

"That's entirely up to each and every one of you," Stanley said. "Of course, I'll pay you for the time you've worked this month up to this moment, but it's going to have to be in cash…if you want it, that is. I can't imagine that any bank is going to open up again for years, maybe decades, and I have no idea if cash is going to have any value in the future. It might be useful in the next few days, maybe even the next few weeks, but by the time people start realizing the future is forever changed, I'm not sure how useful it's going to be. Things might just end up like that scene in *Day of the Dead*, that 80s zombie movie, in which the deserted city streets are full of hundred-dollar bills blowing around in the wind like sheets of toilet paper."

"I'm not really worried about pay, Stanley," Nathan said. "Money is pretty much the last thing on my mind now. What I mean is…what are we going to do with our lives? How are we going to live…to just *exist*, even…in this insane new reality?"

"Like I said, that's up to you," Stanley said. "Everyone is free to stay on at the ranch if they want, and those of you who have families elsewhere are welcome to bring them here…within reason, of course. We can't have anyone bringing twenty members of your extended family here; we have to take the carrying capacity of this land into account. Now, before anyone says anything, I need you all to understand that there are some conditions attached to this offer. You're free to live here, and there'll be no rent to pay…at least not in the traditional manner of paying rent. That doesn't mean I'm offering y'all a free ride, though."

"And none of us would expect that from ya, Stan!" one of the workers cried out. "We're proud men and women, and none of us want any handouts!"

Everyone else echoed their agreement with this sentiment.

Stanley smiled warmly. "I appreciate that, and I know y'all are good, honest, hard workers—I wouldn't have kept all y'all on here for so long if y'all weren't. Now, what I was saying is that while you wouldn't be paying rent in the traditional sense of the word, y'all would be expected to contribute to the running of this ranch. In this new era we find ourselves in, that focus is obviously going to change substantially. There aren't going to be any more tourists coming out here for horse rides and hiking; that time is over and gone. We're going to keep all the horses, of course—there's no more reliable form of transport in these new times we're in than a good, healthy horse—but the focus of this ranch is going to be more on what my beautiful Eileen has been doing here for the past couple years: growing food sustainably in the permaculture fashion, making sure we've got enough supplies to get us through every winter. If you want to live here, you're going to have to contribute to that."

"I'm willing to do that," Nathan said, and everyone else voiced their agreement with this.

"Hold your horses, Nathan," Stanley cautioned. "I'm not quite done yet...although this ranch will have plenty of food and fresh water, it may not be the safe haven y'all are thinking it might be in the days to come. You see, even though we're decently far from any town or any other place scavengers, raiders, or worse may come from, we have evil and menace right on our doorstep."

"Austin Randall," Eileen said coolly.

Everyone uttered exclamations of anger and disgust at the mention of his name. Randall's reputation was well-known among all the workers. A number of them had been threatened by Randall's goons when they had ridden too close to his land.

"Randall wants this land, but that's something that y'all already know," Stanley said. "What y'all don't know is how badly he's going to want this land now. This land no longer represents an opportunity for that scumbag to grow his heroin business...now, in this new era in which we find ourselves, this land of ours is going to mean the difference between life and death for Randall and his thugs. All they know how to grow is poppies for their heroin, and we all know you can't eat poppies. They're going to realize very quickly that the only way they're going to be able to eat is by taking our land. Without any form of law enforcement to protect us—not that that useless sheriff and his spineless deputies did much before, seeing as they've all been in Randall's pocket for a very long time—there's nothing to stop Randall and his goons from coming over here and using force to take this ranch from us. If you want to stay on here, you need to understand just how real and how imminent this threat is…and you also need to be prepared to do whatever it takes to defend this property from that threat."

A period of tense silence followed these words. Stanley paused before saying anything else, giving everyone the chance to think carefully about what he had just said, allowing the impact of his words to truly sink in.

Then, when he felt that the pause had been long enough, he broke the silence. "I don't expect an answer from any of you right away," he said, his tone softening a little. "All your lives have just been turned upside down—mine has, too, and I'm still reeling from the impact. I know I will be for a long time to come. One doesn't simply adapt to something like this in a matter of hours or days, weeks or months, even. And now, on top of hearing that the entire world y'all have known for your entire lives has essentially ended, I'm asking you to fight in a war—a war with real guns, real bullets…and a very real chance of dying. It's the cold, hard reality of the situation we find ourselves in."

He paused here, his intense gaze passing from person to person, making and holding eye contact with each and every one of them. He had to be sure they understood the full impact of what he was saying.

Finally, he continued, "You're going to have to kill or be killed; this is down to survival at its most basic and primal level. Austin Randall and his thugs *will* be coming for this land because these crops we have here, this permaculture system my wife has set up, it's the only guarantee of food and, by logical extension, survival in the months and years to come.

"Y'all know what kind of people Randall and his men are…and word is, he's now working with some Mexican drug cartel people as well, who are even worse than the goons that son of a bitch already has working for him.

"I'll tell y'all something. They aren't going to feel a damn thing, not even the slightest hint of remorse, at the prospect of killing every last person on this ranch in order to take it for themselves. We're going to have to expect them to strike soon and to strike hard. And anyone who wants to stay here is going to have to accept that the price to be paid for living on this ranch is being willing to defend it…with your lives if necessary.

"I'm not going to judge any of y'all if y'all don't want to do that; not everybody's cut out to fight, even in situations of sheer survival. But if you can't or won't fight for this land, then I'm going to have to ask you to leave. The battle's coming soon, probably sooner than any of us would expect…but I'll give y'all tonight to think it over. I'm going to be patrolling the borders throughout the night, and I pray that evil snake doesn't strike that fast. If you hear gunfire tonight, though, know you either need to grab a gun and help me or run as fast and as far as you can. This is a life-or-death matter right here; I ain't exaggerating."

"I'll patrol with you, Stanley," Nathan said immediately. "I'm with you until the end. I'll go get my rifle right now."

A few others quickly and enthusiastically voiced their agreement with this sentiment. One by one, they stepped forward, pledging their support and loyalty to Stanley, promising with utter sincerity that they would fight to defend this land, paying with their lives if necessary. Not a single person chose to walk away.

After everyone had spoken, Stanley's eyes were rimmed with tears of pride, and a knot of raw emotion sat in a tight ball in his throat. "Y'all have made me proud tonight," he said hoarsely, his voice cracking. "Prouder than I ever imagined I could be. I'm honored to have y'all as friends, incredibly honored. It's settled then…we prepare for war."

10

Gravity yanked Caitlin earthward with a terrifyingly potent force. She felt as if she'd been shot out of a slingshot as she hurtled down toward the unyielding concrete below at an unbelievable speed, her stomach feeling as if it were trying to escape her body via her throat, her heart pounding with such frantic violence it felt like it was on the verge of exploding.

Even though her mind seemed frozen with an utterly paralyzing sense of panic and terror, her reflexes kicked in with her body acting on what felt like an autopilot mode, and without consciously deciding to do so, her hand yanked the cord that released the parachute.

The parachute exploded out of her backpack, unfurling in a mere second, and the broad sail of lightweight fabric snatched at the air and abruptly slowed

Caitlin's chaotic descent, slamming the brakes on her hurtling, out-of-control acceleration earthward.

Her descent slowed dramatically, and for a glorious second, relief surged through her, but this relief was short-lived. Although the parachute had slowed her fall, she was now sweeping through the skies at a forty-five-degree angle, racing forward and downward at speed... and she realized, with an icy flood of terror that gushed through her veins like an injection of liquid nitrogen, that she had no idea how to control the direction or speed of her flight.

"Oh shit, oh my God, oh shit, oh shit," she murmured, the wind roaring in her ears as she hurtled toward a skyscraper.

If she didn't change course, she would smash into the side of the building at a speed surely high enough to kill or seriously maim her. She knew there were controls for the parachute, but her memory of the instructions she'd been given on how to use them seemed to have spontaneously been wiped from her mind.

In desperation, she grabbed both toggles and yanked hard on them. This had the welcome effect of slowing her descent, but she was still racing toward the side of the building, and the impact of slamming into it, even at this lowered speed, would still be lethal. Caitlin had to change the direction in which she was flying, not just the speed at which she was hurtling through the air.

Pulling one toggle would surely result in a change of direction—that was it, wasn't it? That felt like it was what the instructor had told her all those years ago...but which direction was which? Did a yank on the right toggle turn her right, or would that result in her turning left?

It didn't matter right now—in two or three seconds, she would hit the side of the skyscraper, which seemed to be steaming toward her like a speeding train, so Caitlin did the only thing she could and yanked on the right toggle.

She swung in an arc to the right, whipping through the air as her rapid descent earthward continued. She came so close to slamming into the side of the building that she had to tuck her legs in to avoid having her feet smash into the glass, and even then, her knees brushed a panel. She couldn't help but let out a scream of terror; however, things were happening far too quickly for her to fixate on this near miss, for another obstacle was already coming up as she swept through the smoke-filled skies. She ripped through the air, continuing her forty-five-degree descent at an alarming speed, and now crossing over the broad main street—which was a few hundred feet below her—and racing toward another skyscraper.

Caitlin was faced with the very real possibility of smashing into the side of another huge building, which was looming like a vast cliff before her. Now that she at least had some concept of how to operate the parachute, though, she approached this deadly obstacle with a little more calmness and confidence than the previous one, even though terror and panic were both gushing in equally debilitating measures through her veins.

As she sped toward the wall of glass and steel, she pulled hard on the left toggle, and she banked and swung in an arc to the left, avoiding the deadly obstacle and missing smashing into the side of the building by mere yards.

Although she was more on top of the parachute controls now, her descent was barely controlled. Indeed, all this yanking on the toggles seemed to make it more chaotic. Now she was speeding toward another building, this one an apartment block, and to avoid the inevitable crash, she yanked hard on the right toggle.

This time, though, she yanked too hard, and the parachute dipped sharply and steeply, and Caitlin was flung into an out-of-control spin. She screamed as she spun in a deadly spiral downward, whipping around in careening circles as she felt herself accelerating, rather than decelerating now, tearing toward the unyielding concrete below at a lethal speed.

Now only a hundred feet remained between her and the ground. Now ninety…now eighty…

She couldn't see anything; everything was a terrifying blur of speed—ground, buildings, sky…ground, buildings, sky…all of this playing on repeat in a nauseating and horrifying cycle of doom.

A single, dreadfully sobering thought managed to flash through Caitlin's mind: I can't believe I'm going to die like this. I came so close to making it, to pulling off this crazy stunt ...but now I'm going to die...now I'm going to—

A slamming jolt abruptly ripped through her entire body. It wasn't the bone-shattering impact of smashing into the sidewalk below or the deadly impact of crashing headlong into the side of one of the many tall buildings that lined the streets. Instead, it was a jerking, yanking impact that Caitlin felt through her shoulders and her entire upper body.

Her descent was immediately stopped, and the spinning blur that the world had been throughout these last few terrifying seconds suddenly stabilized. Confusion was the first thing she felt, but this feeling was quickly overtaken by a flood of immense relief.

"I'm alive," Caitlin gasped, her heart hammering wildly in her chest, her system saturated with pure adrenalin. "I'm alive...I'm alive, I'm alive!"

Her relief was short-lived, though. She quickly figured out what had happened, and it only took a second or two to realize that her position was incredibly precarious. She was by no means safe.

In the last thirty or forty feet of her descent, her parachute had hooked on a large sign sticking out of the side of a building. This had immediately stopped her descent, but now she was dangling a good fifteen feet above the ground, completely helpless, trapped in the parachute's strings.

"Oh shit," she muttered when she looked down. "I'm

stuck…I'm stuck here. How the hell am I going to get down?"

The sign stuck out way too far from the building for her to be able to grab onto anything; she was dangling way too far from anything to have a hope of climbing down. And even if she managed to free herself from the parachute, the drop down to the ground would certainly break her legs, or worse.

Once again, as when she'd managed to pry the elevator doors open with the sword only to have an elevator come hurtling down and a fireball come billowing up the shaft, it seemed as if fate had played a cruel trick on her, leading her to the point of safety and escape, but then yanking the rug out from under her feet at the last moment.

She struggled and shifted, but the parachute harness held her fast—and even if she could get loose, how would she get down? The drop to the ground would definitely result in broken bones and possibly even death. All she could do was dangle like an insect caught in a spider's web and pray someone would rescue her.

Now that she was down almost on the ground, Caitlin could see the full extent of the anarchy and chaos into which the city had descended. The streets were packed with cars and buses, but not one of them was running. All were eerily silent, and most were empty, the doors left wide open after the drivers and occupants had fled.

A few people were still sitting in their cars, looking

dazed and stunned, in a state of complete shock. One or two others had popped their hoods and were messing around with their engines, convinced they could somehow bring the dead vehicles back to life.

Aside from the occasional shrieking howl of an incoming missile—the rain of which seemed to have finally slowed—and the deafening booms of explosions and sporadic gunfire, yells, and screams, the streets were unnervingly silent.

They were littered with debris, but Caitlin could only see this in the patches illuminated by the fires that had broken out all over the place from the explosions and the missile strikes. Much of what she could see of the streets was shrouded in patches of deep, ominous shadow. She had never seen the city this black, and although the city had always felt at least a little menacing after dark, even with its bright lights and well-illuminated streets, now it felt as threatening as a jungle filled with hungry, predatory animals.

"Help!" Caitlin yelled, at a complete loss as to what else to do. "Can anybody hear me? Help!"

One of the men working on the futile task of attempting to resurrect his dead car looked up to see who was yelling, but because Caitlin's dangling body was shrouded in shadow, he couldn't see her, so he went back to working on his vehicle.

"Anyone? Please help me, please!" she cried, her voice cracking with emotion as she felt herself slipping into a bout of weeping.

"Hey, who's yelling up there?"

Hope surged through Caitlin as she heard this voice from somewhere down below. "Hello? I'm up here. I'm stuck! I know it sounds crazy, but I'm in a parachute, caught on the sign on the side of this building!"

From out of the shadows just below her, Caitlin saw two young men emerge. One of them was carrying a camping lantern, and he held it aloft as they both peered up into the gloom. The light from the lantern was weak, but it was enough to allow them to see Caitlin and get a view of her predicament.

"How the hell did you get up there, miss?" the young man with the lantern asked.

Both men were large and burly, but they didn't look like thugs or criminals, and although Caitlin was wary about asking strangers for help in this strange and terrifying time, she realized that these two were her only chance of escaping this trap she was caught in.

"I literally jumped out of a burning building," she answered. "I-I thought I was dead for sure, but here I am...please, if you could just help me to get down, please, please."

"You're not an enemy soldier, are you?" the other one asked, his face crumpling into a frown of deep suspicion. "One these motherfuckers who's attacking us...you ain't one of them, are you?"

"Do I look like an enemy soldier?" Caitlin asked. "Seriously, dude, look at me!"

"Come on, man, she looks like a lawyer or an accountant or some shit," the man with the lantern said. "She ain't no soldier. C'mon, let's go inside and get a ladder and get her down."

"Hold on!" the other man yelled to Caitlin. "We're going to get a ladder from the basement of this building. We'll get you down!"

"Thank you. Thank you so much!" Caitlin answered. "Please, hurry…if I fall—"

"Don't worry, we're moving!"

Caitlin dangled helplessly in the air for what felt like an eternity, with the pressure from the parachute backpack straps cutting painfully into her flesh and causing a burning pain to radiate throughout her entire upper body.

Finally, just when it was starting to feel as if she couldn't take any more of this agony, the young men emerged from the building, carrying a long ladder.

"Hold on, miss, we're coming!" the man with the lantern yelled.

They set the ladder up next to her, and the other man climbed it until he was next to Caitlin.

"All right, miss, I'm gonna cut you out of this thing. You ever do the piggyback ride thing when you were a kid? Let me help you into a position like that. Get your legs around my waist and your arms around my neck. I'll get you down the ladder like that."

Caitlin got into position, grabbing the young man's waist and neck, and then he got to work with a hunting knife, cutting her away from the parachute strings until finally, she was free.

"That's the last one," he said after slicing through the final string. "You good to climb down?"

"I'm ready, yes," she said. "Thank you so much. I owe you my life."

She held on tight, and the young man began his descent down the ladder, taking it slow and steady, not flinching or slipping even when the crack of a gunshot went off somewhere down the street or yet another terrifying missile screeched overhead.

The descent felt tortuously long, and Caitlin's entire upper body was in pain from dangling from the parachute, but finally, she and the young man reached the bottom of the ladder. When she got off the young man's back and her feet finally touched solid ground, a greater sense of relief than almost anything she'd ever felt rushed through her. She had often heard the old expression about wanting to kiss the ground, but now she actually felt as if she truly understood it. Indeed, she almost did drop down to her knees and press her lips to the sidewalk, and only the thought of picking up some nasty germs—and looking like an insane person in front of her rescuers—prevented her from doing this.

"I-I don't know how to thank you for saving me," she murmured to the men.

It was only at this point that she noticed how the two men were staring at her—and the gaze in their dark eyes was anything but benevolent.

"Oh, *I've* got an idea of how you can thank us," the man with the camping lantern said, slowly looking Caitlin up and down with a hungry, predatory gaze.

Fresh fear flooded through Caitlin's system. Disbelief and shock paralyzed her from acting, though. She remembered that she had a pistol in her bag, but she just couldn't make herself reach for it. She couldn't believe these men had gone to all the effort of saving her only to now want to…

"You're coming with us, bitch," said the other man— the same man who had spoken to her so kindly and gently when he'd cut her out of the parachute strings.

"No, no, you, you can't do this. What are you trying to do?" Caitlin gasped as the young man lunged forward and grabbed her arm.

"We got you down, and now you're gonna pay us," the young man said, his hand locked around her forearm in an iron-tight grip.

"Look, look, I've got cash in my bag, all right?" Caitlin stammered, fear gushing in icy torrents through her veins as she struggled futilely against the young man's powerful grip. "I'll pay you whatever you want. Just let me—"

The other young man crashed his fist into her jaw. The powerful blow whipped her head to the side and sent her into the cold, dark oblivion of unconsciousness.

11

In desperation, Marvin lunged blindly for anything solid he could grab onto, and somehow, as the vicious and immense strength of the wave tore him off the raft, his fingers curled around one of the oars.

The other end of the oar was in Hank's hands, and the young man held on for dear life as the force of the wave threatened to pull Marvin under. "Help me!" Hank screamed. "I'm losing my grip on it!"

"Shit, hang on!" Bruce yelled. The only way he could get across the raft to help was to unclip himself—and thus put himself at risk of being swept away, too—but if this was what was needed, then he was prepared to do it.

Bruce unclipped his D-ring from the side of the raft and half-lurched, half-fell across the flooded deck of the inflatable craft, which was now full of icy, waist-deep seawater, and floundering in the violent waves, pitching and rolling with a terrifying intensity.

"Hurry, man, I can't hold on much longer!" Hank howled, gripping the oar with all his might.

Bruce dove across the remaining distance and grabbed the oar just as it slipped out of Hank's hands. "I've got him. I've got him!" he yelled, bracing his legs against the side of the raft. "Hold on, Marvin, we've got you!" he roared, unable to see Marvin in the raging waves but feeling the weight of his body on the other end of the oar. "Help me pull him in, dammit!" he yelled at Hank.

Hank slipped on the water in the boat and fell, but he hastily scrambled to his feet, then grabbed the oar and braced his feet against the side of the raft. Another huge wave washed over the craft, and this one almost swept all of them—even Hank, who was still clipped in—off the raft. Hank and Bruce pulled with all their might, and finally, after what seemed like an impossible length of time for anyone to survive being submerged, they saw Marvin's head emerge from the waves.

"Hurry, get him in, get him in!" Bruce yelled.

With Marvin coughing and spluttering, soaked to the bone, the two of them managed to help pull him back onto the raft—where there was no relief from the frigid waters of the Atlantic. The waves had completely swamped the little vessel, which was now in serious danger of sinking.

"Are you okay, sir?" Hank cried, having to yell to make his voice heard over the howling, gale-force winds and the roar of the stormy ocean.

Marvin was on his hands and knees in the water on deck, coughing up lungfuls of seawater and shivering from the cold. Despite what he was going through, he managed to utter a few words to the other men. "I'm…fine…I'm…alive…bail this…water out…hurry!"

"Do what he says!" Bruce yelled. "Bail the damn water out, or we're going under!"

While Marvin did his best to recover from his near-drowning, the other two men grabbed a pair of plastic pails and did their best to bail the water flooding the flimsy life raft—a seemingly impossible task, seeing as every time another wave crashed over the deck, it filled up the raft with more water than the measly amount the men had managed to bail out.

Coughing and spluttering, his throat burning from the seawater he'd swallowed, his muscles both freezing and burning at once, Marvin grabbed a pail and joined the others in bailing water out of the raft. All three men worked with a desperate fervor, scooping and tossing out water over and over, often falling when the lurching of the vessel on the stormy sea became too violent.

They had all clipped themselves back in to avoid being swept away, so each could only bail out water in his particular area of the raft. The struggle initially seemed like a completely futile one, but as the men valiantly and tirelessly fought against the ocean, which was doing its utmost to fill their little raft with water and swallow it, they slowly began to get the water level to subside.

The process was painstaking, though, and it required tremendous and ceaseless effort.

"Bail!" Marvin roared hoarsely with each sweep of his pail. "Bail! Bail!"

The wind lashed the raft, and the rain continued to come down in bucketing torrents, with the sea heaving. Being on the raft felt like being stuck on a rollercoaster ride that had no end; the men had no control over where they were being thrown by the cruel waves, which battered them with sheer and utter relentlessness, hammering the raft and washing icy water across their bodies.

Despite all being clad in waterproofs, the sheer volume and ferocity of the waves and the knee-deep water that filled the deck of the raft meant that everyone was soaked to the skin. Not even the best waterproof clothing could resist the relentless water.

Marvin wasn't sure how long he had been bailing by the time the vicious storm finally began showing signs of subsiding, but it felt like hours. Finally, though—and without any easing of pace by the men in their desperate labor—the wind slowed, the driving sheets of rain became a steady fall, and the surging waves, which had turned the ocean into a churning landscape of tall hills and deep troughs, began to calm, flattening the sea out somewhat.

"Keep...bailing," Marvin gasped, his throat raw from yelling "bail" over and over for what felt like hours on end, his limbs feeling like jelly, every muscle in his body burning with excruciating pain. Every cell of which he was composed was howling at him, begging him to stop, to rest, to crumple into a deep and well-deserved sleep, but he resisted these urges, as intense as they were, and continued to bail water out of the raft with his burning, exhaustion-weak limbs.

So did Hank and Bruce. Each of them—especially Bruce, who wasn't nearly as fit as the other two—was utterly spent, driven beyond the point of exhaustion, utterly burned out. But still, lurching through the waves of the stormy ocean, they kept bailing.

"I...can't...do...this...anymore," Bruce rasped after a while. He wasn't exaggerating. His limbs had stopped working, and his muscles seemed to have rebelled against the authority of his brain, refusing to obey the commands that the organ issued.

"Rest then," Marvin gasped hoarsely.

Bruce collapsed, flopping down into his seat on the side of the raft, his entire body completely limp, like that of a deboned fish. Hank and Marvin, meanwhile, kept on bailing, but their pace began to slow. As fit as they were, and even with their strength boosted by adrenalin, both of them had pushed themselves far beyond their limits.

Finally, Marvin decided it was okay to stop for a while. They had managed to get the water down to ankle-deep. And although the ocean was still choppy, the waves were no longer monstrous in size and strength, and most of them were no longer breaking over the raft.

"Let's...rest," Marvin gasped, dropping into his seat and slumping over limply as if a heavyweight boxer had just delivered a perfect uppercut to his chin.

Hank said nothing; instead, he simply tossed his pail aside and slumped in his seat, his head lolling on his neck as his burned-out body crumpled like a damp rag.

All three of them sat like this for a while, hunched over and limp like geriatric drunks on a street corner. The rain continued to fall, the thunder and lightning subsided, and the choppy ocean grew calmer.

Despite the ceaseless motion of the raft, which made even experienced seafarers like the three of them feel hopelessly seasick, and despite how cold each of them was, being soaked to the bone by the cold Atlantic seawater, all three men were driven so far beyond the point of exhaustion that they all quickly drifted into a deep slumber.

Marvin woke up in pain. He wasn't sure how long he'd been out, but it was still dark when he opened his eyes. He could hardly see anything—the formerly garish green effulgence of the chem light had faded to a soft glow, barely brighter than starlight—so he dug through the bag strapped to his waist (which was soaked and full of water, like his freezing-cold clothes) and got out another chemical light. He struggled to his feet, and on aching legs that felt too weak to take even a dozen steps, he staggered over to the roof of the covered section of the raft and replaced the chem light, providing a fresh source of illumination.

Every muscle and tendon in his body felt as if they had been doused in gasoline and set on fire. He couldn't remember ever having felt this exhausted in his life, not even when he'd been an enthusiastic runner and had run a few ultramarathons a few years earlier. His body felt almost as if it would have welcomed death at this point, simply for the relief it would bring. Throwing himself overboard to be swallowed by the waves almost seemed like an attractive proposition, and only the thought of being reunited with his beloved Caitlin gave him the strength to carry on.

He flopped down onto the floor under the covered section, and the instant he closed his eyes, he was back in the void of deep sleep. When he opened his eyes again, it was still dark, but the storm clouds overhead had largely given way to a clear and starry sky. His entire body was aching terribly as if he'd been in multiple car wrecks, and he barely had the strength to lift his head, let alone get up, but he was feeling slightly better than before.

At first, Marvin thought it was dawn because he could see a red glow on the horizon. But when he took out his watch, he saw that it was too early for sunrise, and when he checked his compass, he saw that the glow was in the west, not the east.

"Oh shit," he murmured, a deep sense of shock rocketing through his system when he realized what he was looking at. "The city's on fire…the whole damn thing is burning down."

12

Declan crept through the night forest as stealthily as any panther stalking its prey. Using both the tricks taught to him in the US Armed Forces and the ancient techniques taught to him by his father—who had learned these methods from his father, who in turn had learned them from his father before him, going back many generations—Declan was able to move undetected by Austin Randall's goons, who patrolled his land day and night.

Declan knew the dogs would pose far more of a challenge than the thugs. The animals' senses were way more intense than even the most alert human's, but he had tricks to get around dogs and could fool them if necessary.

He was deep into Randall's land now, and the journey had been much easier thanks to the EMP's permanent disabling of Randall's many security measures, like electric fences, infrared cameras, and motion detectors.

The sharp crack of a twig and the murmuring of voices made Declan freeze. He scanned the shadowy woods with his dark-accustomed eyes—even at his age, he had sharp 20/20 vision—and soon saw a blaze of artificial light: a pair of camping lanterns.

Holding the two lanterns were two burly men. Each was armed with an AK-47 rifle, and one had a doberman on a leash. They were walking through the forest, swinging their lanterns around and peering through the gloom, while the dog was straining against its leash, sniffing at the cold night air with a voracious eagerness.

A gentle night breeze was blowing, and Declan quickly checked the direction of the wind. He was downwind of the dog, so as long as he remained in roughly his current position and didn't give himself away with any visible movements, he was sure he would remain undetected. He quietly slipped into a hollow next to a large tree, crouched in his ghillie suit, and waited in silence. Just to be safe, though, he quietly took out his .45 pistol and released the safety.

Soon, the men got close enough that Declan could make out what they were saying.

"It's a real shame that Pablo was arrested when he was, is what I told Austin," one thug muttered.

"I know. The timing couldn't have been fucking worse," the other said.

"If Pablo wasn't stuck in a holding cell, he'd already be on his way to get his army, and then we'd be able to walk straight onto Wagner's land tomorrow, slaughter every motherfucker there, and take that shit for ourselves."

"I know…it'd be so damn easy. Don't get me wrong, I don't think we *need* Pablo's cartel army to do the job—it'd just make it way easier for us."

"I don't know, man, I don't know. I heard that old Wagner asshole used to be a US Marine or something like that. He's probably tougher than he looks. And that Indian who's always on the ranch, I heard he's also ex-military or something. And even some of those pricks who take rich tourists on their stupid fucking horse rides, I heard they ain't bad shots with a rifle."

"So, what you're telling me is that you're scared of some old people and horse-riding hippies, is that it?" the first man joked. "I thought you were a stone-cold killer, man, not some pussy scared of a stupid old grandpa and his weak-ass buddies."

"Shut the fuck up, man, before I break your fucking jaw. I ain't scared of shit, especially not some old-ass bitches. I'm just saying that having Pablo's men would make things way easier for us—those Mexicans can go in first and get shot at by the old fuckers. Then when they've softened the old bitches up, we go in and clean up the mess—no danger of taking a stray bullet. I'm cautious, not scared—there's a big difference, asshole."

The other man chuckled. "Whatever, you fuckin'

pussy. Anyway, Austin's plan is to bust Pablo out of that cell tomorrow, and then that fat Mexican fucker can take one of the dirt bikes and ride to where his men are camped out. So, you'll get your wish, you lil' bitch, and have the Mexicans go in first to do all the heavy fighting. Once Pablo brings his boys here, that fucking ranch is ours."

After this point in the conversation, the men passed out of earshot. Neither they nor the dog had had any idea they had passed within a mere fifty feet of an intruder on the land. Declan waited until he could no longer see their lantern's light before getting up.

There was no need to go any deeper into Austin Randall's land. Just in this snippet of overheard conversation, he had learned everything he needed to know about Randall's plans and his sinister goals. He holstered his pistol and hurried back to the ranch, a journey that took several hours.

Although the trip was difficult and tiring, Declan pushed himself onward, refusing to pause for a rest. The information he needed to get to Stanley and the others was of dire importance, and he knew he could only rest after he had delivered it.

When he was finally back on the ranch, an hour before dawn after a long and exhausting night, he spotted his best friend—who had also been up the entire night—patrolling through the woods on the ranch's border with one of his dogs.

"Stan!" Declan called out.

"Declan! You're back already?" Stanley replied, hurrying over to where Declan was waiting in a clearing in the woods.

"I found out what I needed to know, then I came straight back here," Declan said wearily. "No pause, no rest. I had to get back here and tell you what I discovered."

"Judging by your urgency to get here, I'm guessing the news isn't good," Stanley said grimly.

"Not at all, I'm afraid," Declan answered. He went on to tell Stanley everything he'd heard the two thugs on Randall's land saying.

"My God," Stanley murmured grimly, his eyes locked on a pile of dry leaves on the ground, the color draining from his face, "so I was right. I can't say I'm surprised... but it's still a bit of a shock to hear that scumbag is planning a full-scale invasion of our land."

"At least we have some time to prepare for it, now that we know for certain that it's coming," Declan said.

"Indeed," Stanley said, still gazing at the dark ground as he ran a number of ideas through his head. "Hmm... you know what they say about prevention, though, don't you?"

"That it's way better than having to cure an illness, yeah," Declan answered. He narrowed his eyes and stared intently at Stanley. "Are you saying there's a way to stop this invasion before it happens?"

"I think there might be," Stanley said, "but only if we act quickly and decisively."

"I'm all ears," Declan said. "But you heard what I told you, right? These guys aren't wasting any time; they said they were going to break this Pablo guy out of his cell tomorrow—well, technically, today."

"I heard you. I certainly did," Stanley said. "And I'm thinking if we can stop them from freeing this Pablo guy, we can stop them from invading. Or, at least, make it so they don't have some Mexican cartel army backing up their invasion, which will give us a better chance of fighting them off and defeating them."

"I hear you," Declan said, nodding sagely. "And I think that's exactly what we need to do. We've gotta stop them from freeing Pablo. The only thing is, I didn't hear exactly where they're keeping him."

"There's only one town for miles and miles around here," Stanley said, "and I'll bet that son of a bitch is in a holding cell there. I'm pretty damn sure Pablo is the cartel guy who's been hanging around Randall's land."

"I thought all of Randall's cronies were pretty much protected from being arrested because of all the bribes he pays, all the cops he's got on his payroll, though."

"That's true, but if Pablo committed some egregious crime in public, something that a bunch of people saw, the cops would have no choice but to arrest him and lock him up; otherwise, the entire town would realize just how corrupt they are. I'm guessing this guy got into some sort of public altercation, maybe a bar fight or something, and the cops pretty much had to arrest him to save face in public. I'm sure the plan was to quietly release the man during the night so as not to piss off either Randall or the guy's cartel bosses, but then the EMP happened."

"And because of that, the guy is now stuck in a cell, with the cops either having forgotten about him or, more likely, not caring because they have a mountain of their own shit to deal with now that society has pretty much collapsed entirely," Declan said grimly.

"Exactly," Stanley said.

"So, we go to town…then what?" Declan asked. "Shit, are we going to kill this Pablo guy?"

"That's what would make the most sense in terms of the cold, hard reality of the situation," Stanley said grimly. "And I know you find that idea as abhorrent as I do. We've both killed men before, but that was in battle, in a kill-or-be-killed situation, and we both sure as hell know about the scars it leaves on your mind and soul, even though it had to be done. This would be taking things a step further—hell, a few steps further."

"Technically, it'd make us murderers," Declan murmured softly, his eyes locked on the dark, damp soil.

"I know," Stanley said. "And I also know neither you nor I are murderers. Yes, we've both had to kill before… but we're not murderers. Look, you're right that it'd technically be murder to kill this guy, but we have to look at this as if it's a military operation."

"Well, I mean, it *is* pretty much a military operation," Declan said.

"Exactly. And that means we're making a preemptive

strike, the same way any general or colonel would in order to save his men's lives. By stopping this guy from bringing his cartel people here, we'd be preventing a bloodbath. We'd be stopping an invasion that, from the sounds of it, we wouldn't be able to fend off, an invasion that'd likely leave all of us dead and my family's land—and yours, too—in the hands of evil men."

Declan inhaled a long, deep breath, filling his lungs with air, then he exhaled in a slow sigh, shaking his head as he did. Stanley, meanwhile, continued to stare at the safe spot of earth his gaze had been locked on for most of this conversation. Both men understood this was not a decision to be taken lightly. The man, Pablo, was a complete stranger to them, and the only thing they knew about him was that he was a cartel man. This fact alone indicated he was almost certainly a vicious and evil criminal, someone who had almost certainly murdered people, on top of all the drug smuggling and selling he was no doubt involved in. However, that didn't make it much easier for Stanley and Declan to contemplate killing him, especially seeing as he would be unarmed and locked up in a cell. It was one thing to kill an enemy soldier in battle when the bullets were flying, but it was another thing entirely to execute an unarmed and helpless man in cold blood.

Finally, Stanley broke the tense and heavy silence. "Hypothetically speaking, if you could go back in time and kill Adolf Hitler when he was a kid, knowing that you'd spare the world the horror of the second world war, would you do it?"

Declan let out a long, soft whistle. "The answer seems obvious when you think about it as a means to an end—by killing one kid, you save literally millions of lives in the future, you prevent genocide and war and all that terrible stuff...but you still have to murder a kid. I'd like to say I'd be able to do it, but the reality is, even knowing it's technically the right thing to do, the moral thing to do...I don't know if I could do it."

"I don't know if I could do it, either," Stanley murmured. "Even knowing the benefits the world and millions of people would reap from that child's death. But here, we don't have to shoot a little boy. We have to shoot a Mexican cartel man, someone who's definitely a drug dealer and who's probably a murderer, too. We have to do it to save our own lives, the lives of the people we love, and this land. I don't like the idea of it any more than you do, my friend, but I feel like we have no other choice unless we want to have a lot more bloodshed and death down the road."

"You're right," Declan said softly. "I hate to even try to imagine what we're going to have to do, but you're right. It *is* what we're going to have to do."

"We've both been up all night, but we can't afford to get much sleep, not with this urgent mission we have to undertake," Stanley said. "But what we can do is get some sleep in the car. I'll get Nathan to drive us to town in the

Land Rover; we'll have a few hours in which we can catch a few *Z*s in the back. And after that…"

"We'll have a mission to complete," Declan said coolly, slowly patting the pistol holstered on his hip, this minor gesture saying more than anything else he could have uttered.

13

When Caitlin woke, she felt groggy and dazed. The headache that had been pounding in her skull since she had been knocked out by a falling shelf in her office had gotten worse, and now it felt like someone was operating a jackhammer and other tools inside her cranium. She quickly discovered that her hands were bound together behind her back with what felt like zip ties. The hard, sharp plastic was cutting painfully into her wrists.

She was on the sidewalk, in the dark, and she was not alone. Her entire upper body ached with a persistent and ceaseless pain. Instead of focusing on the pain in her skull or the agony radiating throughout her entire upper body, her attention was immediately drawn to the two men standing over her. Fear gushed through her veins, and the memory of what had happened came rushing back to her.

"P-please," she stammered, her voice shaky with dread. "D-don't hurt me…t-t-take whatever you w-want, just d-don't hurt me."

One of them chuckled, but there was no mirth in his laughter. "You think we wanna rob you, you dumb bitch? Oh, sure, we'll take your shit; it's ours now, but that ain't why we pulled you down off that sign. You think we went to all that trouble to steal your damn purse? No… no, girl, it was *you* we were after."

"I…I don't know what you want, or wh-who you think I am—" Caitlin stammered.

"It don't matter who you are, see," the young man said coldly. "What matters is *what* you are. We don't know what's happening here, but we know it's a war. And you might think we're just a bunch of dumb inner-city thugs, but me, I paid at least some attention in school, believe it or not. History was my favorite subject…I especially liked war history. Maybe I should have tried to get into the marines or something. I think I would have been good at that shit, real good at it. Only problem is, I don't like all of that 'yes sir, no sir' bullshit, taking orders, and all that. I like doing whatever the fuck I wanna do without having some jarhead asshole breathing down my neck."

"I…I don't understand," Caitlin murmured, feeling the fear flooding through her system grow even icier, paralyzing her completely with its intensity.

"The point I was trying to make, bitch, is that I ain't no uneducated, dumb fool," the man muttered harshly. "I don't know what's up with the loss of all power, all the cars and electronics being dead, but I do know this is war. And you know what I remember from history lessons at school? Women...young, beautiful women, they're like fucking solid gold bars in wartime. *You*, bitch...*you're* our investment, our currency."

"I'm...I'm your *what?*" Caitlin managed to splutter. Although terror was still gushing with unabated fury through her system, it was now paired with disbelief, which had completely displaced her earlier confusion.

"What the fuck are you, ho?" the other young man grunted, the gaze in his eyes as sharp and as pitiless as flint. "Let me guess, some rich-ass lawyer or accountant or company director or some shit, right? Grew up spoiled, daddy's little girl, went to all the best schools and an ivy league college, right? You think you know everything, right? Well, you don't know shit, as it turns out.

"My boy here," he continued, nodding in his friend's direction, "he's right when he says he's smart. He sure did love history back in school. I couldn't understand my boy's fascination with the subject; it always seemed a little boring to me. Who cares about the dusty old past and a bunch of people who've been dead for hundreds of years, right? Well, I was wrong; I was ignorant.

"Knowledge of history is power, bitch...and the knowledge you had, of how things used to be, up until this power outage, this war shit, all that bullshit that made you so much money, knowledge about finance and laws and how to fuck people over in court...it don't mean shit now. We've gone back to medieval times, at least for now. I haven't seen a cop anywhere since this whole thing started, and you know what that means, don't you?"

"It means that the law is as dead as our phones, as these abandoned cars lining the streets," the other young man said with an evil smirk. "*This* is where power lies now," he said, pulling out and cocking a 9mm pistol. Power lies with whoever is bold enough to take it. Money, it ain't gonna mean *shit* in this new system we're living in. We're going back to medieval times like my friend here says. And do you know what one of the biggest commodities traded throughout human history has been? *Slaves*, bitch, *slaves*. And young, beautiful female slaves have always been the most valuable of all."

Caitlin couldn't believe what she was hearing. Of course, everything that had happened on this fateful night, everything she had experienced, had been utterly surreal, but this was beyond belief. She had dreaded many things about this terrifying new reality in which she'd found herself, but becoming a literal slave had not been at all in the realm of what she'd considered possible. She was so dumbfounded with shock and disbelief that she couldn't say anything; she couldn't even utter a single syllable.

"What, nothing to say, ho?" the second young man growled. "Yeah, I didn't think so. Get up."

"You-you can't do this," Caitlin finally managed to utter. The words felt almost as if someone else was speaking them. She felt as if she were watching herself from some position outside her own body; she simply couldn't accept this was actually happening.

The second young man reached into his jeans pockets and pulled out a switchblade. He flipped the switch on the handle, and the blade darted out like a striking cobra. Even though both young men were shrouded in the gloom of the shadows, the sharp blade gleamed evilly in the darkness, the steel reflecting the oranges and reds of a building in the distance burning down.

"I ain't gonna say it again," he growled. "Get the fuck up and come with us, or I'll hurt you. I won't kill you because I need my merchandise alive and breathing, but I swear to God, I'll make you feel *pain*, bitch."

The tone of his voice and the aggressive confidence of his pose told Caitlin that not only was he perfectly willing to hurt her if she didn't comply, but that he had done it before, to other women. This was a man who was frighteningly comfortable with violence. She had no choice but to obey him.

Still feeling groggy, with a terrible headache thumping in her skull and her entire upper body throbbing with a burning ache, she struggled to her feet.

"Follow me," the young man with the pistol said. "And don't try anything dumb because my boy is gonna be right behind you, and he'll make you pay if you even *think* of fucking around."

Caitlin followed meekly behind the first young man, keeping quiet and staying obedient and non-confrontational, but a thousand thoughts were careening through her mind as they walked. There had to be a way to escape from this predicament. She hadn't gone through everything she had just survived only to be made a slave by these evil people.

She wasn't surprised when they led her into the same building they'd come out of, which turned out to be a rundown apartment complex. One of the men had left a camping lantern inside the entrance hallway, and he picked it up on the way in. They took Caitlin up the stairwell to a door that turned out to lead to an empty apartment.

When they got into the living room of the deserted apartment, she was shocked to see she wasn't the only woman these predators had captured. There were three other young women, all sitting on the floor of the empty, dusty room, which was illuminated by a camping lantern placed on the floor.

The young women's hands and feet were bound with zip ties, and they had duct tape over their mouths. They stared at Caitlin and the young men with terror-bulging eyes as they entered the room.

"Sit there," the young man with the pistol grunted, indicating an empty spot on the floor.

Caitlin had no choice but to obey. When she sat on the floor, the man got some zip ties out of his pocket and bound her ankles together. She didn't bother to try to plead or bargain with him. The men had made their intentions clear, and she understood how futile that would be. After he had bound her ankles, he picked up a roll of duct tape, tore off a piece, and placed it over her mouth, gagging her.

"Don't try anything stupid while we're gone, ladies," the man with the pistol sneered. "And don't worry, you won't be too lonely in here...we'll be back with more merchandise soon." After saying that, he and his companion left, shutting and locking the door behind them.

The room was eerily silent once the men departed. Of course, the sounds from outside could be heard: the gunfire, the occasional boom of an explosion, and the scream of a missile here and there, followed by the thunderclap bang of its impact. And through the windows, which were barred with burglar bars, they could see the lights of flames dancing on burning buildings while the horizon glowed orange from all the fires all over the city. Enormous plumes of black smoke rose into the air like a new temporary set of skyscrapers transplanted onto the dying buildings.

Caitlin looked at each of the women, making eye contact with each one individually, trying to convey some sense of comfort and reassurance through her gaze, even though she was feeling just as terrified as all the rest of them.

All three were younger than her, with the youngest looking like a mere teenager. This girl was utterly terrified, and the trauma and raw fear in her eyes were heart-breaking. She was a young, slim blond, and Caitlin was sure she couldn't have been older than sixteen.

The next oldest looked to be a college student, perhaps nineteen or twenty in age. Like the blond teenager, she was very pretty. She had short brown hair, cropped into a pixie cut, and her bare arms were covered in colorful tattoos, while she sported a multitude of facial piercings. The third girl was a little older, in her early twenties, also a brunette, but with long, silky hair that tumbled around her slim shoulders. The way she was dressed, wearing a cocktail dress that revealed much of her gorgeous hourglass figure, suggested she had been out on a date or a girls' night out when the EMP had hit.

They all seemed paralyzed with fear, and Caitlin couldn't blame them. However, she realized that none of them would be much help when it came to a plan for escape. She would have to come up with and enact the plan on her own, mostly.

She scanned the room, carefully scrutinizing every corner. Aside from the camping lantern burning in the center of the room and the roll of duct tape, there were no other items in this place and certainly nothing that could be used as a weapon. As for the pistol Caitlin had found and taken from the conspiracy theorist's desk, that object, along with everything else she'd had in her bag, had been taken by the young men. She thought it was presumably being stored somewhere else in this apartment, but the fact that she was trapped in this locked room made that point moot.

There was another door on the other side of the room, presumably leading to a bathroom or a kitchen. Caitlin guessed that, like the door they had entered through, this one was locked, too. She figured she would at least try it, though. After all, the men had said they were going out to pick up more "merchandise," and capturing more young women was something they surely wouldn't be able to accomplish in a short timeframe, so she figured she had at least an hour or two to work with.

She tried to stand up but found this was quite impossible due to her sitting position and the fact that her ankles were bound tightly together. However, she knew with some support, she would be able to get to her feet. Right now, she wasn't able to communicate this notion to the other captives, so she knew she would have to do it on her own.

She scooted backward on her butt until she reached the wall. When she was able to press her back into the wall and use it to support her weight at least partially, she was able—with a lot of effort and a bit of pain—to get to her feet. Now, even though her ankles were bound tightly together, she could get around by taking little hops.

The other women had been watching her intently the whole time she'd been going through this struggle, and now, when Caitlin looked at them, she saw something in their eyes that shot a boost of courage through her core: hope. It was there, shining only weakly, like a single candle flame in a black expanse, but its presence was undeniable.

The woman with the short hair and tattoos began scooting backward toward the wall, too, copying what Caitlin had done. Meanwhile, Caitlin was trying to figure out a way to get the duct tape off her mouth; if she could at least talk to the others, their chances of getting some sort of escape plan together would be a lot better.

She made eye contact with the short-haired girl, hoping almost to communicate telepathically with her since their ability to speak had been impaired. She and the short-haired girl locked eyes, and they held their gaze for a few intense seconds. No words were spoken, but both women communicated their desire and willingness to help the other through their eyes.

Caitlin realized that she would need to use a form of sign language and gestures for now. She thrust her chin and jaw forward repeatedly, hoping to convey the idea that she was thinking about the duct tape over her mouth. Then she turned around so her back was facing the short-haired woman, and she wiggled her fingers exaggeratedly.

She hoped that the woman would get the meaning of these primitive-looking gestures: that Caitlin wanted her to come over to her, then she would turn around and help her to get the duct tape off her mouth.

She turned and stared at the young woman with a questioning look in her eyes. She was slightly surprised but very pleased when the young woman, who had now used the same method to get up into a standing position, gave a confident nod.

The young woman hopped across the room to Caitlin. When she reached her, Caitlin turned around, wiggling her fingers behind her back. The short-haired woman squatted down until her face was level with Caitlin's hands, then she pressed her mouth into Caitlin's wiggling fingers.

Caitlin fumbled around until she felt a corner of the strip of duct tape. Slowly but surely, she managed to peel the corner off the young woman's face. When she had peeled enough of the tape off to get a decent grip, she yanked while the young woman jerked her head back.

"You did it, sister!"

This triumphant voice came from behind Caitlin. Hope surged through her at the sound of it and the feel of the loose strip of duct tape in her fingers.

"Turn around, and I'll do the same for you," the short-haired woman said. "And then we can start making a plan to fucking *kill* those evil motherfuckers who did this to us."

14

Frustration and a worry so intense they were almost nauseating seized Marvin, gripping his entire being with the ferocity of a deadly fever. He had known from the moment he had seen the first missiles in the sky that the city would face terrible destruction, but until he had actually witnessed that destruction with his own eyes, he simply hadn't been able to grasp the full, terrible extent of it.

And now, all he could do—even though he knew Caitlin was caught somewhere in the middle of that hellish conflagration—was watch the city burn on the horizon while he sat on the raft, tossed around by the choppy waves, helpless and out of control.

He felt like he needed to wake the others, to force them to get up and start rowing so they could get back to land as quickly as possible, but he knew that would be impossible. His body was aching all over with debilitating pain, partially numbed by the cold from being sprayed and soaked with icy Atlantic water for hours. He was so far beyond exhausted that he felt barely capable of even keeping his head lifted to stare at the red horizon. He knew the others had to be feeling the same after the herculean task of surviving the storm at sea, and it would be about as easy to wake them from their deep slumber as if they'd each drunk a bottle of whiskey.

"Whiskey," Marvin murmured, remembering the bottle he'd taken from Jason.

A sudden pang of sadness stabbed through him when he thought of Jason. In some ways, he felt responsible for his shipmate's death. He had to remind himself that Jason knew full well the risk he had taken when he had chosen to accompany them on the raft, and he had put himself directly in harm's way by failing to clip himself to the raft when the storm had hit.

Even so, the man's death had been tragic, all the more so because it was a tragedy that could have been avoided.

"I should have checked that that stupid idiot had clipped himself in," Marvin muttered, his teeth chattering from the cold, which felt as if it had seeped into the very marrow of his bones and the deepest part of his core. "I should have checked."

He opened his bag—the only dry thing on the raft, seeing as it was certified waterproof even when submerged—and took out the bottle of whiskey. With hands shivering violently from the cold, he popped the cap off the bottle and took a long swig of the liquor.

Its burning passage down his throat brought some welcome warmth to his body. He understood that it wasn't actual heat, but nonetheless, it felt good and comforting.

"And one more for you, Jason," he whispered, the words quickly broken up and carried away by the whipping, icy wind. "Rest in peace, man...rest in peace."

He took another swig of whiskey, then he poured a little out over the side of the raft into the water for his lost comrade.

After putting the bottle back, he dug around in the bag for something to eat. Now that the storm had passed and the pumping adrenalin had worn off, he was seized by a ravenous hunger. He had taken a bunch of ready-to-eat meals from the kitchen—sandwiches, burritos, and such. He wolfed a few down, eating them with the voraciousness of a starving wild beast.

The combination of crushing weariness and food and alcohol swimming around his belly quickly sent Marvin back into a deep, blackout slumber.

When he opened his eyes again, it was light; dawn had gone, and the sun was up. The sky behind the raft was blue, but the entirety of the horizon ahead—on which the outlines of tall buildings and the general city skyline were clearly visible—was an ominous shade of dark, dirty gray.

"I don't think I've ever seen so much smoke in my life."

Marvin glanced to his side and saw that Hank was

awake, too. Bruce, however, was still passed out, snoring loudly.

"I know," Marvin murmured, turning back to face the horrifying sight of the smoke-blackened sky ahead. "It doesn't seem real, does it?"

"This whole thing has felt like some crazy nightmare right from the start, a nightmare that I just can't wake up from," Hank said, his eyes also locked on the gray-black sky over the burning city. "And this nightmare just keeps getting worse."

"Prepare yourself because it's going to be a lot worse when we eventually get to shore," Marvin said. "You ain't seen nothing yet."

"I'm trying to prepare myself, believe me," Hank said. "But how do you actually do that? How do you prepare yourself for, well, the end of the world?"

"I don't think there's anything you can do to truly prepare yourself for something like this," Marvin answered. "But I guess it'd make it slightly easier if you didn't think of it as the end of the world, as such, but rather, the end of *a* world. The planet is fine. It's not like a huge meteor like the one that wiped out the dinosaurs is hurtling toward us. Life will go on for thousands, hell, millions of years—unless Earth is unlucky enough to get hit by another world-destroying meteor—it's just our modern civilization that's been destroyed. And yeah, obviously that's pretty damn catastrophic for ninety-nine percent of people in this country, but if you're adaptable, if you're willing to learn to live in an entirely new way in a completely new system, life will go on."

"How...how the hell *do* you adapt to this, though, sir?" Hank asked despondently. "I know you're into hiking and hunting and stuff when you're on land, but I've never eaten anything that didn't come from a store. Shit, I've been working on ships for the last two years, but I've never even been fishing! I've never even caught a fish or picked a wild berry. I wouldn't even know where to begin when it comes to feeding myself."

"You're not alone there, kid," Marvin said, smiling sympathetically at Hank. "Most people are in the same boat. But I know you're resourceful, you're adaptable, and you're a hard worker. Those are the qualities you'll need in order to survive in this new world we're in."

"But...where do I even begin? Where do I go? My parents are in Minnesota. I don't know how I can even begin to plan to get there without a car, without any form of modern transportation. And the apartment I'm renting is right there," he continued, pointing at the burning city. "In the middle of that. Shit, everything I own has probably already burned to ashes. I'm freezing cold in these wet clothes, but they're all I've got now, sir...I literally have nothing but these clothes and the few items I brought from the ship. I can't even begin to imagine how I'm going to survive, what I'm going to do."

"First up, Hank, you don't need to call me 'sir,'" Marvin said. "We're not on the ship anymore, and that world is dead and gone. "Second, if you're willing to work hard and maybe even fight, if that's what's needed—"

"I'm willing to do whatever it takes to survive," Hank said hastily. "Obviously, within reason. I wouldn't do anything that goes against my moral code, and I wouldn't screw other people over, no, definitely not, sir—I mean, Marvin. But yeah, I'll work my butt off to survive, to get by."

"All right," Marvin said. "Well, my parents have a ranch inland, a few hundred miles from the city. My ma, she's been really into permaculture and off-grid living for a long time now. The land has been in my family for many generations, and we know it well. It used to be a horse ranch, mainly for tourists, but on the side, my ma has been growing a ton of crops with permaculture and aquaculture and everything like that. There's enough food there to feed a lot of people, and there will be, well, pretty much indefinitely, as long as there are enough people to work the land. But even though the land is isolated and far away from everything and everyone, it's not exactly safe. We've got this neighbor. He's a real piece of shit…he grows poppies for heroin. Everyone knows about it, but we haven't ever been able to do anything about him because he's got all the local law enforcement on his payroll."

"Oh man, that doesn't sound good," Hank said. "I bet he's gonna have his eyes on your family's land now, especially if he knows about your mom's garden and all that."

"I know he will," Marvin said grimly, "and I also know

now that the rule of law is out the window that nasty son of a bitch is going to do whatever it takes to take my family's land. I know we're going to have to fight him for it sooner or later...if I can make it back there in one piece, of course."

They both turned and stared at the burning city and the smoke-darkened sky for a while.

"I'll help you fight this guy," Hank said, breaking the silence. "I mean, I don't really know how to fight...but if you put a gun in my hands and show me how to use it, I'm willing to do what I can to help you and your family. If it hadn't been for you, I'd still be stuck on that ship, waiting for a rescue that'll never come. I owe you my life, Marvin, and I'll do whatever it takes to repay that debt."

Marvin looked directly into Hank's eyes, and then he nodded somberly. "Thank you, Hank. I certainly appreciate the offer, and you're welcome to accompany me to my family's ranch. You're also welcome to stay as long as you need to—I know you're a good, honest young man who ain't afraid of a little hard work. In the short time I've known you, I've seen that part of your character plain as day."

"There's no need to thank me, sir—I mean, Marvin," Hank said humbly. "Hell, I'd just be another mouth for you guys to feed, no matter how much work I put in. You'd be saving my life all over again."

Marvin smiled. "Well, like I said, you're welcome to come with me. The only thing is, there's something I have to get done before I can even think of beginning the long journey inland to our ranch."

"Oh yeah? What else do you need to do?" Hank asked.

Marvin pointed to the burning city. "I have to go right into the center of that chaos…and I'm not leaving it, no matter how bad or crazy things are there, not until I've found and rescued Caitlin."

15

Tremendous relief washed over Caitlin when the other girl ripped the duct tape off her mouth. There was a brief and sharp sensation of burning pain when the tape came off, but that didn't matter.

"Oh my God, I can open my mouth again...I can talk again. Thank you, thank you so much," Caitlin said as she raised herself to her full height from the squatting position she'd been in. "I'm Caitlin, by the way."

"Anna," the short-haired girl said. "I'd say it's nice to meet you, but considering the circumstances in which we've met…"

"Don't worry, I understand," Caitlin said, smiling with warm gratitude as Anna turned around to face her. "Let's get the others' gags off, then we can figure out what to do about this situation we've found ourselves in."

"Got it," Anna said. Then, however, her jaw tightened, and a cold hardness gleamed in her big gray eyes. "Man, I swear to God I'm gonna fucking *kill* those evil psychos who did this to us. I'm gonna cut their fucking balls off and shove 'em down their fucking throats! Those sick, evil fucks! Did they tell you that they're planning to make us *slaves?* Literal fucking *slaves* in the twenty-first century! I can't believe this shit!"

"They told me that, yeah," Caitlin said. "And it's clear that they're monsters, total monsters, but let's not worry about what we'd like to do to those animals right now. Let's get the others' gags off, and then see what we can do about getting these zip ties off our wrists and ankles."

"You guys saw how we just got the duct tape off, right?" Anna said to the other two women, who were still sitting on the floor.

Both of them nodded, their eyes still wide with shock and terror.

"All right, well, we're gonna do the same for you two," Anna said. "Caitlin and I will come over to you two, and we'll turn around, then you gotta get your mouths in our hands, okay?"

Again, the other two girls nodded.

Caitlin and Anna hopped over to them, and soon enough, they'd managed to get the duct tape off both young women's mouths.

"Oh my God, thank you. Thank you so much," the beautiful, long-haired brunette said. "My name's Kath."

"And I'm Gina," the teenager said meekly. "Thank you, I feel so much better now that I can talk…but I'm still scared, still really scared. What if those guys come back now?"

"They won't be back right away," Caitlin said. "They've gone out looking for more women to kidnap, and considering how deserted the streets outside are, I don't think it's going to be a quick mission."

"How did they capture you?" Kath asked. "They got me—"

"We can talk about that later," Anna said sternly. "Right now, we don't have time to waste because even if those two psychos don't come back in the next few minutes, we have to act like they might. We can't squander this window of opportunity that's opened. We have to make the best use of this time that we can."

"I agree," Caitlin said. "We can't just assume we have time, even though it seems like we do."

"All right," the teenager, Gina, said. "The first thing we need to work on is getting our hands free. How are we gonna do that? Do any of you guys know how to break out of zip ties or anything? I was thinking maybe there's some, like, technique or something?"

Caitlin looked down at the zip ties around her ankles, which were the same size as the ones around her wrists. They were thick, heavy-duty zip ties, and not even a massive powerlifter or football player would be able to break them with sheer force. "There's no way any of us are breaking out of these with brute force," she said, "and I doubt that there's any technique, even taking leverage principles into account, that could snap these things."

"We could try to gnaw through 'em with our teeth," Anna suggested. "It'd take a while, but if we kept chewing, we could probably get through the plastic."

"Oh my God, I just had my teeth professionally whitened," Kath gasped, looking utterly horrified at Anna's suggestion. "Do you have any idea how badly that would damage them? I don't mean to sound vain, but I have a side gig as a model, and—"

"We don't have to try to chew through them," Caitlin said as an idea suddenly popped into her head. "I think I've got a better, faster way for us to get out of these things."

"Oh yeah?" Anna asked. "How?"

"I'm gonna need your help," Caitlin said. "See this copper bracelet on my wrist?" She held her wrists out in front of her and gestured with her chin at one of the many bangles and bracelets she wore. "It's a soft enough metal to bend easily."

"Okay, so what should I do?" Anna asked.

"I'm going to get it off my wrist first, then I'll tell you," Caitlin said.

She held her wrists up to her mouth, then gripped one end of the bracelet—which only partially encircled her wrist—in her teeth. She hated the feeling of metal against her teeth, for she had always been someone who'd been afraid of dentists. Nonetheless, she pushed through the discomfort and used her teeth to bend and leverage the bracelet off her wrist. When it dropped to the floor, she squatted and picked it up.

"Now I need your help, Anna," she said.

"Sure. What do you need me to do?"

"Take the other end of this bracelet and help me bend it straight," Caitlin said.

Anna walked over to Caitlin, gripped the other end of the bracelet with both hands, and working together, the two women managed to bend the bracelet into a long, straight section of copper.

"Are you planning on using that like a knife or something? It's way too blunt to cut through anything, even plastic," Anna said skeptically.

"I am going to use it to cut through the zip ties, but not in the way you're thinking," Caitlin said. "Come with me."

She and Anna went over to the camping lantern burning in the center of the room. The lantern had a few small gaps between the glass panels, and Caitlin was able to insert her bracelet into the lantern, where the flame quickly heated up the metal. She held onto the bracelet until the heat spreading through the metal became almost too hot to touch. Then she hurriedly pulled it out.

"Hold out your wrists and keep 'em real still," Caitlin said to Anna, who did this.

Caitlin then pressed the hot end of the bracelet against the zip ties binding Anna's wrists. The copper was hot enough to melt through the thick plastic in a matter of seconds.

"You're a fucking genius!" Anna gasped, grinning with

delight and relief as she shook out her aching wrists. "Here, I'll heat it up again and do you."

"Careful, it's really hot," Caitlin said as she passed the straightened bracelet to Anna.

Soon enough, all four women were free, having burned through the zip ties that the thugs had wrapped around their wrists and ankles.

"I can't believe it," Kath gasped. "We're free!"

"Not quite," Anna said. "We still have to get out of this room."

"Can't we just, like, kick the door down, like they do in the movies?" Gina asked.

Caitlin shook her head. "The main door opens into this room. That'd only be possible if it opened the other way."

"What about that other door?" Kath asked. "That one looks like it opens outward."

"We may as well try," Caitlin said, "but I think it only goes to a bathroom or a kitchen or something."

"Leave it to me," Anna said, striding confidently over to the second door. "I do Muay Thai."

"Muay Thai?" Gina asked.

"Thai kickboxing," Anna answered, positioning herself in front of the door.

"Do it, kick it open," Kath said.

Anna aimed a vicious, stomping frontal kick at the door. She delivered the blow with power, and the thump it made rattled the windows and shook the walls. The door held firm, though. Anna stepped back and then aimed another potent kick at the door. This time it smashed open, swinging violently inward.

"Shit," Anna muttered after she stepped into the dark room beyond to check it out. "I don't need to bring the light in here to know this ain't nothing but a bathroom."

"Does it have a window?" Kath asked.

Anna walked around the bathroom, examining the space in the gloom. "Yeah, it's got a window, but it's small and secured with burglar bars. We can't get out this way. It's a dead end. The only way out of this room is through that main door."

All this time, Gina had been next to the main door, her ear pressed against the grubby wood, which had long ago been painted white, but which was now a grimy shade of brownish yellow, stained by age and many years of cigarette smoke in this shabby apartment. Her eyes suddenly grew wide with fright, and her jaw dropped open.

"What's wrong, Gina?" Caitlin asked, perceiving the teenager's alarm.

"It's them!" Gina gasped, the color draining from her face. "Our kidnappers! They're coming back!

16

"Come on, guys, keep pushing. We're almost there, almost there," Marvin urged, dipping his oar into the water and giving a strong pull.

"I'm trying, man, but seriously, I think I'm gonna have a heart attack or something," Bruce gasped, looking and sounding completely haggard, breathing hard. "I don't think I've ever felt this exhausted in my life…or been in this much pain. Holy shit, every single part of me hurts, even parts I never even knew existed!"

"I'm hurting, too, and feel like I just ran ten marathons back to back," Hank gasped, dipping his oar in for a powerful stroke, in perfect tandem with Marvin's, "but we have to keep rowing! We're so close. We're only about a mile out now…just think about the feeling you'll have when you finally get to put your feet on solid ground again."

"That's easy for you to say, kid," Bruce gasped,

paddling feebly with his oar, his hands, arms, and shoulders all trembling. "I also felt bulletproof when I was your age! Us old guys, we don't recover nearly as quickly as you kids do! But you're right, man, you're right, just thinking about being on land again is enough to give me a little more strength. And I'll tell you what, kid, once I make it back, I'm never setting foot on another damn ship!"

"Enough talk," Marvin said. "Save your breath and row."

The men got to rowing, using what little strength and energy was in their weary, pain-racked bodies to propel the raft toward the shore, slowly but surely. Marvin had chosen a quiet beach a few miles from the city to land on. Usually, the waters around this beach would be patrolled by the coast guard, but Marvin wasn't surprised to see that any coast guard vessels in the water were deserted, aimlessly adrift.

The beach was empty, too, as Marvin had expected it to be. Nobody in their right mind would be hanging out on the beach while the entire city was burning down and civilization was collapsing.

The approach to the beach felt as if it was taking forever, with each oar stroke barely pushing the raft through the choppy water, but although progress was slow, it was progress nonetheless, and eventually, the men navigated the raft into the breakers.

At that point, there was little need to keep rowing, for the force of the waves now dragged them shoreward.

After a brief and rocky ride through the waves, they finally washed up on the beach. The men, bedraggled and utterly spent, grabbed their bags from the boat and staggered through the final few yards of frigid water, abandoning the life raft to the waves.

Finally, they got onto the beach, and all three of them collapsed onto the cold, wet sand.

For a long time, Marvin just lay there, sprawled out on the beach, staring up at the sky. It was a surreal feeling, being on the stable, immovable firmness of solid ground after their terrible ordeal at sea, being tossed and hurled around like a leaf in a washing machine.

As determined as he was to get into the city and begin the daunting task of locating and rescuing Caitlin, he just couldn't seem to get his limbs to obey the commands his brain was issuing. A crushing weariness, like nothing he had ever experienced in his life before, had come over him.

"I…can't…move," Bruce groaned. "I…just…need…to sleep…for a…long, long…time."

Even the youngest of them, Hank, who was fit and healthy, was utterly drained. "I want to…get up…but I…can't," he murmured hoarsely.

The morning sun was shining on them, unobscured by the pall of dark-gray smoke that covered the entire western half of the sky. Marvin knew if he truly wanted to get Caitlin out of the city as quickly, as safely, and as effectively as possible, he couldn't do it while feeling like a zombie. As much as time was of the essence here—and it truly, urgently was—he had to admit that he and the others badly needed rest.

"Let's just...lie down...and rest...for a while," he managed to gasp.

The others murmured their agreement with this idea, and within seconds all three of them were asleep.

"He ain't dead, man...he's breathing."

"Then shut the fuck up. You're gonna wake him up!"

The voices sounded distant and garbled as if Marvin was hearing them underwater.

"Take the bags, asshole, and let's go before these motherfuckers *do* wake up!"

Marvin opened his eyes, feeling groggy, totally exhausted, and completely drained, as if he'd only been asleep for a minute or two. He blinked, the sunlight searing his eyes, and through the dazzling haze of brightness, he saw the silhouettes of what looked like three teenagers standing over him. One of them had his bag in his hands.

"Hey, get your hands off my bag!" Marvin tried to yell, the words emerging from his throat in a weak, rattly rasp.

"Shit, run!" one of the teenagers yelled.

Marvin tried to grab the boy's leg, but the teenager was too quick for him, and he darted out of the way of Marvin's grasping hands. Fighting through the crushing weariness, which felt as if it had taken possession of every molecule of which he was composed, he struggled to his feet, but by the time he was standing, the teenagers were long gone, sprinting away down the beach…and they had stolen all three of the men's bags.

"Son of a bitch," Marvin growled. "Shit! Dammit!"

"Wh-what's going on?" Hank groaned, only waking up now.

Bruce, meanwhile, was still fast asleep, snoring like a chainsaw.

"We just got robbed," Marvin muttered sourly. "Some damn kids just stole all our stuff."

Fighting through both confusion and exhaustion, Hank rubbed his weary eyes and got up into a sitting position. He followed the direction of Marvin's angry gaze and saw the three young thieves vanishing into the trees at the far end of the beach.

"Shit," Hank muttered. "Those fucking little jerks."

"We're in some deep shit now," Marvin muttered. "All our food was in those bags…our water, first aid kits, dry clothes, my gun and ammo, the chemical lights…everything. Now we've got jack shit, nothing but these cold, damp waterproofs we're wearing."

"Oh man…what are we gonna do?" Hank asked.

Both men knew it would be completely futile to attempt to chase down the teenagers. They were still beset with a deep and debilitating weariness and could barely walk, much less run. Marvin had been hoping to replenish this lost energy with a good meal when they had woken up from their sleep, but now there was no chance of eating anything anytime soon.

"The first thing we need to do is get off this beach,"

Marvin said. "I don't know about you guys, but I'm starting to feel that sun now."

"Let's go to my place," Bruce suggested. "That's where I was planning on going anyway. There'll be food there, and I'd be happy to give you guys some clothes... although, uh, I can't promise they'll fit you two, given our size differences."

"Where do you live?" Marvin asked.

"Not too far from here, actually," Bruce answered. "I've got a basement apartment on Twentieth Avenue. Old building, nineteenth century, I think, but it's well-maintained."

"That's a nice neighborhood," Hank remarked.

"Ain't as nice as it used to be, but yeah, it's still a good place," Bruce said. "Well, uh, it was, until this shitstorm happened. God knows what it's like now, or if I'll be able to even think of staying there with all this madness happening—"

"You won't," Marvin said. His tone was firm, and there could be no denying the truth of these two simple words, but the delivery was gentle and sympathetic. "I'm sorry, Bruce, but your home isn't going to be your home for much longer. The reality of this situation is that you could maybe hold out for a few days, certainly, maybe even a few weeks if you somehow came across a large cache of drinking water, but eventually, you'd have to leave. Leave or die."

Bruce swallowed a dry gulp of nothing, staring blankly off into the distance as the implications of what

Marvin was saying sank in. Finally, he nodded. "Yeah... yeah, I guess you're right. I...I'll have to say goodbye to my place. I loved that apartment, man, it was...it was *my place*, ya know? *Mine*. And that fuckin' mortgage was almost paid off...almost."

Marvin put his hand on Bruce's shoulder and gave it a sympathetic squeeze. "I'm sorry, Bruce. I truly am. If it's any consolation, just know nobody in this city is going to be able to stay here. Everyone's in the same boat; not even the ultrarich in their fancy penthouses will be able to stay here. They've lost everything, too, the same as everyone else."

Bruce nodded slowly, his eyes still wide, his face locked in an expression of disbelief.

"I'm sorry, man," Hank said. "I don't own a house or an apartment or anything, only my truck, which I'm paying off anyway, but I've also lost everything. I know it's not the same as you, but...I'm sorry anyway."

"Thanks, kid," Bruce said wearily. "I...I don't even know what to say at this point."

"Let's go to your place," Marvin said gently. "At the very least, we can eat something and get some dry clothes to wear."

"I still don't know what I'm going to do after we get to my place, though," Bruce said.

Marvin didn't know Bruce as well as he knew Hank, but he knew him well enough to know he was a good man at heart, and although he was sometimes lazy, he would work tirelessly when it was necessary. He told

Bruce about the Wagner family ranch and explained everything to him the way he'd explained things to Hank, telling him that if he wanted to travel there with them and live on their land, he was welcome to, as long as he was prepared to commit himself to the responsibilities involved: that of working hard on the land, and that of very likely having to fight to defend it. Without hesitation and expressing an infallible sincerity, Bruce declared he was ready to make such commitments.

The men trudged along the deserted beach, listening to the eerie and discordant symphony of the crashing waves, the hiss of the surf, and the forlorn cries of seagulls, combined with the distant booms of explosions in the city, peppered with pops and crackles of gunfire and faraway screams and yells. Missing from this soundscape was the expected howl of sirens—both police and ambulance sirens were completely and eerily absent from the mix. Things got even eerier when the men passed through the parking lot at the far end of the beach—which was filled with deserted vehicles, many with doors left wide open, and towels, gym bags, and bathing suits strewn across the seats or abandoned on the ground—and they walked up to the top of the steep road, winding up a hill, which led out of the carpark and overlooked the harbor and part of the city's waterfront.

Usually, the view from up here showed a vibrant part of the city, with cafés and bars along the promenade and plenty of boats in this section of the harbor, which was reserved for smaller vessels and pleasure vehicles rather than the huge merchant ships, which docked in a different section of the harbor, which was a few miles away.

The men now looked out over a very different scene. The waterfront cafés and bars, usually buzzing with activity, were completely deserted. Not a single living soul could be seen, and at least a third of the buildings had been completely destroyed by what looked like a missile strike or a major explosion. Near the huge mounds of rubble and debris were a number of blood-soaked corpses lying out in the open.

"My God," Bruce murmured, his jaw hanging wide open.

"That's only a little taste of what we're going to see," Marvin said grimly. "Trust me, this is mild compared to what's in store for us."

"It's like a zombie movie, but without the zombies," Hank said, his eyes locked on the frightening scene.

"Come on," Marvin said, trudging wearily onward on his aching legs. "We can't afford to waste time. Let's move."

Weary, starving, and despondent, the other two men followed him, all walking along the deserted streets in stunned silence. The road took them through a residential area. This part of the city consisted of old, impressive mansions, many of which dated back to the early nineteenth century. Some had been bulldozed for more modern hotels and apartment buildings, but many still stood, proud and somber. Although most looked deserted, a number were being guarded by their owners and their families, who stood in the driveways or on porches with shotguns and hunting rifles, or makeshift melee weapons like baseball bats, staring with strange expressions on their faces—a mix of terror, confusion, and aggression, warning these three interlopers to keep walking and not even think about approaching any of these grand old buildings.

"It doesn't look like we'll be getting any help from anyone around here," Bruce remarked gruffly.

"I can't say I'm surprised," Marvin said. "These people are frightened and confused—they know the city's under attack, but they don't know what to do about it or where to go. I'm guessing most of them think the power and the water will eventually come back on. So, for now, all they can do is try to protect their property from looters."

"What I wanna know is, what the hell is the government doing about all of this?" Bruce asked angrily. "Where's the damn president? Where are the cops? Where's the army?"

"I doubt the cops have a single clue about what's going on," Marvin said. "As for the government, the president, and the military, well, they sure as hell do know what's going on, but I'm guessing they're concentrating all their efforts on fighting back against whoever is attacking us.

"If the enemy, whoever it is, is trying to land troops on American soil—which I'm sure they must be—our armed forces are going to have to be doing everything in their power to prevent a full-blown invasion. And I'm sure they must be counterattacking with a swift and brutal response. Either way, though, there's no way any enemy could land troops anywhere near here, not for a hundred miles, because the navy would have spotted enemy ships in these waters days, hell, weeks ago. No, the attack is likely to have come from much farther north.

"And I'm guessing it's been aided by traitors in our own armed forces, who, for whatever reason, turned a blind eye to the enemy movements that had to have taken place leading up to this attack.

"Anyway, we could talk about and speculate about this stuff for hours, but like I said earlier, we don't have time to waste. And my main point is this: as terrible as what's happened to this city is, it's probably happened—and is still happening—to every city along the East Coast, probably to plenty of cities inland, too. No help is going to come, not anytime soon, at least. We can only help ourselves."

"I never thought I'd see something like this, not in a million years," Bruce murmured, looking completely shellshocked. "It's just...it's beyond belief. Everything that's happened since the power went down on the ship has felt like some long, fucked-up nightmare."

As the men talked, they walked up another steep road, which led to the top of a hill that overlooked a few main roads leading into and out of the city. As soon as the men reached this hill's top, all three stopped dead in their tracks. They had expected to see a shocking sight when they reached the top of the rise, but nothing could have prepared them for the vista before them.

Down below, the main roads were completely full, packed with hundreds of thousands of people, all moving in the same direction in a slow, weary march out of the city. It was a mass exodus on a scale never before seen in this country.

"My God," Bruce murmured as the three of them stared in shock and disbelief at the scene below. "It really is the end of the world, isn't it?"

17

"Stan, wake up. We're getting close."

Stanley groaned and opened his eyes, squinting and blinking against the morning sun streaming through the tall trees in half-second flashes, alternating with flickers of shadow. Despite the bumpy ride, with the speeding Land Rover lurching and skidding relentlessly around on the dirt road over the last few hours, Stanley and Declan had both slept through most of the ride, having been awake for most of the night.

"Should I get onto the main road or stay on the dirt track?" Nathan asked from the driver's seat, keeping his eye on the bumpy dirt road as it wound its serpentine passage through the dense, hilly woods that bordered the town.

"Stay on the dirt track," Stanley said, yawning and stretching his stiff limbs. "We're much less likely to attract any unwanted attention here. And stop before you get anywhere near any houses. We'll take the bikes from that point on."

"Got it," Nathan said.

They drove on for another half hour or so in silence before Stanley instructed Nathan to pull over and kill the engine.

"Are you sure you don't want me to come with you?" Nathan asked.

"Stay here and guard the Land Rover," Stanley said. "Declan and I will be okay on our own. And if you hear any shooting or yelling or whatever, anything suspicious nearby, start up the motor and get ready to hightail it outta here."

"Got it. And just so we're clear, if you guys aren't back by two o'clock?"

"You drive back to the ranch and tell the others that we didn't make it," Stanley said grimly. "And if that happens, God forbid, you and Eileen will be in charge."

"Let's hope it doesn't come down to that," Nathan said, looking worried.

"I think we'll be okay, won't we, old friend?" Stanley said, giving Declan a quick elbow in the ribs.

Declan, who had been snoring contentedly up to this point, awoke with a start, scrambling for his pistol in a moment of frightened confusion. When he saw that he was safe and sound in the back of the Land Rover, though, he breathed a sigh of relief and slid his hand off the grip of his firearm.

"Uh, yeah, yeah, we'll be okay," Declan murmured hoarsely.

Both men drank their fill of water, checked their firearms and their backpacks, said a quick farewell to Nathan, and then took their mountain bikes off the rack on the back of the Land Rover and set off on a hiking trail that led through the woods and into the town.

They were dressed in camouflage gear, and each was armed with a pistol, with a few clips of extra ammunition just in case. In addition, they carried enough food and water to last them a day, first aid kits, multitools, chemical lights, and a few other essentials. On their backs, along with their backpacks, each man also carried a crossbow. These weapons were deadly but silent, and the men intended to use them as their primary weapons, only using the pistols as a last resort because of the attention loud gunfire would draw.

They rode in silence along the trail, the only sound being the quiet whirr of their bicycles and the crunching of dirt and pebbles beneath their tires. While they were fully alert and acutely aware of their surroundings, each man was also lost in his thoughts, thinking of the dark task that lay ahead of him.

Soon enough, they began to pass houses, all of which were quiet and looked deserted. Everything looked perfectly normal in the bright morning sun, but there was a feeling hanging in the air, an omnipresent but invisible fog that assured both men things were anything but normal. Unlike the faraway city, many miles beyond the eastern horizon, none of the small towns in this area had been attacked, either by missiles or by forces on the ground. Thus, nothing was on fire. There were no destroyed buildings or plumes of smoke, no sounds of gunfire or explosions…only a thick and almost menacing silence. It felt almost as if the creatures and insects of the woods, spooked by what was happening in the world of the humans, had also fallen silent.

After the houses they passed began to be situated closer together, with yards around them rather than large grounds, Stanley signaled Declan to pull over.

"We're getting into town now. We'd better hide the bikes and go on foot from this point on," Stanley said.

"Agreed."

The men found a thick bush a couple yards off the trail and hid their bicycles under it. Now, ready to proceed on foot, they each cocked and loaded their crossbows, keeping them ready to fire.

A few dozen yards down the trail, the dirt path became a concrete sidewalk between two houses into a parking area. Beyond that was a street. The men had discussed their strategy prior to setting off on this mission. They would sneak through people's backyards rather than walk out on the street in the open. At this stage of their mission, stealth was their primary tactic; they wanted to get as deep into town as they could without being seen. This was for a variety of reasons, not least of which was the threat of being spotted by Austin Randall and his men, who were also surely on their way to town, if not here already. These men were also headed to the police station where the cartel man, Pablo, was being held, but they were heading there for a very different reason. Whoever got there first would almost certainly determine the fate of the Wagner family's ranch, and many lives hung in the balance here.

"How close do you think Randall's goons are?" Declan whispered to Stanley when they reached the safety of a patch of shade under a cherry tree after they had darted across someone's backyard, moving in a low crouch.

"I don't know, but so far, I haven't heard the sound of any vehicles moving through town," Stanley whispered back. "That's either good news, though, or very, very bad news."

Declan said nothing in response to this; neither he nor Stanley wanted to think about just how dire the consequences would be for all of them if it turned out that Randall's men had already been here and freed Pablo.

They moved on, climbing over a wooden fence and winding their way through the overgrown mess that was the neighboring backyard. Afterward, they hopped another fence and found themselves on a street. At that point, there was no way to avoid traveling along the streets, for there was no other way to get to the police station.

"I'd have felt a lot better about this section if we'd been able to do it in the dark," Declan said.

"Me too," Stanley said grimly. "But there was no way

that would have been possible; you haven't stopped moving since you first overheard Randall's plans to free this son of a bitch last night, and we got here as quickly as we could."

"I know, I know, but I feel seriously exposed walking around like this," Declan said, his eyes darting from side to side as he shifted uneasily on his feet.

"The only thing we can do now is to move as fast as possible, get in, do what needs to be done, and get out."

Without another word, Stanley took off at a brisk jog, his crossbow in his hands, and Declan followed closely behind him. As they had been trained all those long decades ago, the men moved like parts of a well-oiled machine. When one raced across a section of open pavement, darting from one section of cover to another, the other waited and provided cover, scanning the landscape with an eagle's gaze, his weapon raised, his finger on the trigger. Then, when the first man reached his destination, the roles would be reversed.

They covered a number of blocks like that, getting steadily closer to the center of the small town, where the police station was located. For the most part, the place was deserted, although, on a few occasions, the men had to duck behind cover—a fence, a dumpster, or into a doorway or a side alley—to avoid being seen by other people they saw.

They observed these people closely from their hiding spots, using binoculars they had brought along. All, thankfully, were townsfolk, most of whom they recognized. None seemed to be Randall's men, most of whose faces the two men knew.

As for the townsfolk they saw, most of them appeared more confused and worried than anything else. The power had now been out for well over twelve hours, and with phones, vehicles, and electronic devices completely dead, everyone had figured out that this was no regular power outage. As to what it actually was, though, Stanley was sure none of them really had a clue.

Most of the people were walking around openly armed, mostly carrying hunting rifles or shotguns, with a few also with pistols holstered on their hips. None of the stores had been looted, however, and from what Stanley and Declan could tell from the demeanor and poise of the townsfolk, they weren't out to form a mob or to break into anyone's store and loot it...at least not yet.

Although they hadn't seen a single law enforcement official of any kind, it was clear that these people still had some unspoken respect for the rule of law. Neither Stanley nor Declan was surprised by this; most of these people were good, honest folk. Both wondered just how long this respect for the rules of civilization would last, though, when the food and drinking water ran out.

They were almost at the police station, and the closer they got to their goal, the greater each of them felt a feeling of dread pulsing darkly within each man. In some ways, both of them were almost hoping that Randall's men had gotten to Pablo first—if he had already been broken out of the cell, they wouldn't have to do the thing they were so dreading having to do.

They knew, however, that such hopes were selfish and shortsighted. Pablo had to be stopped at all costs; if he escaped this town and went to fetch his army of cartel warriors, the ranch would be overrun, and everyone in it would be slaughtered. As ugly as the task was, Stanley and Declan both knew it had to be done, and there was no getting around that.

The sun had passed its zenith, and it was beginning its descent toward the western horizon when the men finally reached the police station. The station itself was a freestanding building, with a public parking lot out front and a private, locked parking section around the back. The men made sure the street in front of the station was truly as deserted as it appeared to be and scrutinized the station with their binoculars, making sure it was empty. When they were sure it was safe, they moved out from the shadows of the alley they were hiding in, hurriedly crossed the street, and went straight up to the front door.

"You ready for this?" Stanley asked Declan, pausing outside the front door.

Declan nodded grimly. "I'm ready."

"Let's do this then."

Stanley tried the door but found that it was locked.

"We can go around the back," Declan said. "I've been in those holding cells—they're in the basement, but they have small windows that look out into the cops' parking lot. The windows are real small…but they have enough of a gap for us to...you know, to do what needs to be done."

"All right, let's move."

The men hurried around to the rear of the police station, scaling a tall chain link fence to gain access to the cops' private parking lot. With their hearts in their mouths, they walked past the dead police cruisers toward the three small windows, which were around ankle height, only a foot high, and around three feet wide.

With Declan watching his back, Stanley knelt and peered through the first window. The cell was empty. With his pulse racing, his mouth dry, and a feeling of dread and nausea percolating in his guts, he moved on to the second window. The second cell was also empty.

"Shit," Stanley muttered. "One to go."

"Let's get it over with then," Declan said coolly.

They moved on to the third and final window. This cell wasn't empty.

"Hey, who the hell are you? You gotta get me outta here! I ain't had nothing to drink since last night, not even a single glass of water!"

The man speaking to them from inside the cell was a short but powerfully built Mexican man in his forties. He was dressed in a bloodstained white wifebeater—clearly, he had been in a brawl the previous evening—and grubby jeans. Both Declan and Stanley recognized his face at once. They had seen him on Randall's land. The man in the cell didn't recognize them, though. He got up from his cot and stared up through the window, squinting at them with his scarred face scrunched up in an expression of confusion.

"What's your name, friend?" Stanley asked coolly, keeping his loaded crossbow out of sight of the man in the cell.

"Why do you care, man? Just let me outta here. I know my rights! I got human rights, man. You people can't keep me locked up with no food or water! Hell, there ain't even been no electricity in this dump since last night, and the damn pigs just left and never came back! Who the fuck are you anyway, dressed up like some army motherfucker? Get me the fuck out of this cage!"

"Tell me your name, and I'll get you out of there."

The man rolled his eyes with anger and frustration, balling his tattooed hands into tight fists at his sides. He glared up at Stanley with rage burning in his small, dark eyes. "Pablo, my name's Pablo Moreno, okay?" he growled through clenched teeth. "Now fucking get me some fucking water and get me outta here, gringo!"

Now both Stanley and Declan knew for certain that this was the man they had come here to find…and they knew what had to be done.

However, just as the two men were about to raise their crossbows and take aim at their target, who was a sitting duck with nowhere to hide from the deadly crossbow bolts, a thunderous barrage of gunfire broke out from the other end of the parking lot…and the bullets were aimed at Stanley and Declan.

18

"Oh my God," Kath gasped. "What are we going to do? They'll kill us when they see we're trying to escape! They'll kill us. They're gonna kill us!"

"Not if we kill them first," Anna growled, curling her hands into fists and clenching her jaw.

"Impossible," Caitlin said, shaking her head.

"There's four of us and two of them," Anna said defiantly. "You saw my Muay Thai kicks, girl. You know I can throw down."

"This isn't some Hollywood action movie," Caitlin countered. "Those men are both much bigger and stronger than any of us, and, what's more, they've got weapons on them, guns and knives. I don't mean to sound like a total bitch, Anna, but I don't care how good your martial arts skills are. It'd be suicide to try to fight those guys."

"If we all bum-rush 'em—" Anna began, but already

the aggressive rage was dimming in her eyes and faltering in her heart.

"It won't work," Caitlin said stubbornly. "It'll only get us hurt or killed. If we had weapons, it'd be a different story, then we'd have a chance…but we don't, and physically, we're no match for them. I hate to say it, but it's the cold, hard truth."

"Well, what *are* we going to do?" Kath cried, her voice almost cracking and breaking into a scream. "They're coming up the stairs right now! We have to do *something!*"

"We can't do anything right now," Caitlin said, trying to control her racing mind, which was threatening to careen out of control as cold fear and icy panic began to surge through her.

"Guys, guys, they're almost here," Gina whimpered, tears filling her eyes as she pressed her ear against the door. Not only her hands but indeed her entire body was trembling with fear.

"Put the duct tape back on your mouths," Caitlin said, "and hook the broken zip ties back around your ankles. Hurry! Sit in roughly the same places we were all in before and keep your backs against the wall. If we can fool them into thinking we're still tied up, they'll probably leave again, and hopefully, next time, they'll be gone long enough to actually give us enough time to escape."

There was nothing else the women could do at this point, so they each grabbed a strip of duct tape, stuck it over their mouths, then hurriedly got back into the same places they'd been sitting in previously, hooking the broken zip ties around their ankles to make it look like they were still restrained.

The last of them, Gina, had only barely managed to get into position when they heard the ominous sound of a key turning in the lock. But just as the door handle began to turn, Caitlin noticed something that almost gave her a heart attack and which sent blasts of terror and panic so cold and so dread-inducing through her core that it almost paralyzed her: sitting on the middle of the floor, only a foot or two away from the camping lantern, glaringly bright in its hue of red, was a broken zip tie, one of those that had been used to bind the women's wrists. If the men saw it, they would know what the women had done…and if they found out their prizes weren't actually bound and gagged, as they were pretending to be…

Caitlin almost threw up, for the twin sensations of panic and dread were beyond overwhelming. She shuddered to think of what the two thugs would do to them if —or, rather, *when*, for how could they fail to notice that bright-red piece of damning evidence on the floor?— they discovered their victims' act of deception.

The door was flung open, and the two burly young men strode in, dragging another victim behind them. This one was a young Asian girl, a pretty, slim woman in her early twenties, wearing an expensive business suit. Caitlin guessed that, like herself, the Asian woman had been working late in one of the nearby skyscrapers when the EMP had hit a couple hours earlier.

With her heart thumping with such intense violence in her chest that she thought it might actually break through her ribcage, Caitlin did everything she could to avoid looking at the broken zip tie on the ground, even though its presence to her seemed about as glaring and as impossible to miss as a naked person walking down a crowded city street. She prayed silently and desperately that somehow her captors would not notice it.

"Say hello to your new friend, ladies," the man with the pistol said, grinning evilly. "I think she's gonna bring in some good business," he added, "like the rest of you. My man," he continued, high-fiving his thuggish friend, who was gripping the girl's arm tightly with his free hand, "we've got ourselves a real harem here, don't we? Shit, this whole war thing might just have been the best thing to ever happen to you and me. We're gonna be rich, powerful motherfuckers when it's all over...and you, ladies, are the merchandise that's gonna do that for us."

Caitlin's heart continued to pump wildly in her chest, but outwardly, she retained a façade of calm collectedness. Despite the icy panic gushing through her every vein and artery, a glimmer of hope flickered to life within her; somehow, the men hadn't noticed the broken zip tie on the ground...at least not yet.

"Let's get this one tied up," the man with the knife said, dragging the whimpering young women over to the corner of the room nearest the bathroom door.

Again, a fresh surge of dread raced through Caitlin's system, and she was sure that the same horrible sensation was tearing through the other women, too. They had shut the bathroom door before the men had come in, but it wasn't—and couldn't—close properly because Anna had broken it with her powerful kick. So, right now, the door was sitting slightly ajar, and even a slight breeze would surely blow it open...and that would also blow the women's secret wide open.

The men got busy binding and gagging their newest victim, and as they did, Caitlin noticed that both their backs were facing her. She knew she had to take this opportunity, for there was only a very, very narrow window where the act she was considering would be possible. It was now or never...

Moving as swiftly but as silently as she could, she suddenly darted up from her sitting position, lunging across the floor. The other women saw her doing this, and their eyes nearly popped out of their sockets with shock. But when they saw her grabbing the broken zip tie, they knew why she was taking the immense risk.

Caitlin snatched the zip tie off the floor, then darted back to her place, hastily securing the broken zip tie back around her ankles and then whipping her hands—which were gripping two broken zip ties—behind her back, just as the two young men finished their work on their newest prisoner.

They turned around, and immediately the man with the pistol stared at Caitlin, a glint of suspicion gleaming in his dark eyes. Caitlin stared back at him, keeping on a perfect poker face, even though she felt as if she was about to have a full-blown panic attack.

"If you're thinking of trying something, bitch, I'm gonna say this to you once," the young man growled, brandishing his pistol at Caitlin. *"Don't.* Seriously, *don't.* We don't wanna damage our merchandise, but also, I won't hesitate to make an example of you if you fuck with us."

Caitlin shook her head, indicating that she had no intention of trying anything.

"Come on, man, let's go get some more merch," the man with the knife said.

"Hold on," said the man with the pistol, who was still glaring menacingly at Caitlin. "We've picked up five tasty lil' snacks already. That's a good number. I think we should celebrate our success quickly."

Dread and fear wormed their cold tendrils through Caitlin's body when her captor said this. She didn't want to even begin to imagine what kind of "celebration" this evil monster had in mind.

The young man took a bottle of expensive single malt whiskey—which had clearly been looted, for it was something that someone like him never would have been able to afford to buy—out of his backpack. Grinning almost maniacally, he unscrewed the cap, pressed the bottle to his lips, and sucked down a few hefty gulps of the amber liquid.

"Mm, mm, mm!" he exclaimed heartily. "Now *that, that's* some smooth-ass shit! Come on, man, have some!"

"All right, all right," the other man said, sauntering over to his friend with a swagger in his step, grinning with eager anticipation. "Gimme that." He grabbed the bottle and drank a few slugs of whiskey, letting out a satisfied sigh and wiping his mouth with the back of his hand when he was done. "Damn, that's good; that's real good," he said.

"You know what I'm thinking?" the man with the pistol said.

"What you thinking, man?" his companion asked.

"I'm thinking these hoes should have some of this, too. They all looking all scared and shit; they need to calm the fuck down. A few good swigs of whiskey should help, right?"

"That's a good idea, man. Yeah, I think this shit'll help 'em chill the fuck out."

"What do y'all think, ladies?" the man with the pistol asked. "Have a drink on us. How about that shit? It's party time, y'all, hahaha!"

The man with the knife stepped over to Gina, who was the nearest of the women. He squatted down next to her, ripped the duct tape off her mouth, and then, without waiting for her to say or do anything, he gripped a fistful of her hair with one hand, pulling her head back, then he shoved the bottle into her mouth, and tilted it up, forcing her to drink.

He chuckled as the teenager, who had never had an alcoholic beverage, coughed and spluttered violently, almost to the point of retching, when he finally pulled the bottle away from her lips after she'd had the equivalent of at least six or seven shots' worth of whiskey.

"How do you like that, lil' girl?" the man with the pistol asked mockingly. "Drink up, bitch. It'll put some hair on those ripe young titties of yours, hahaha!"

The other man slapped the duct tape back over Gina's mouth, even as she continued coughing and retching, and then he moved on to Anna. One by one, they forced each of the women to drink five or six shots' worth of neat whiskey. Caitlin was the last one they got to, and she glared defiantly at the man as he painfully yanked her head back by her hair and then crammed the bottle into her mouth. Unlike the other women, she was something of a whiskey connoisseur, and she was perfectly fine with drinking neat whiskey—although perhaps not quite so much in a single go.

She swallowed the liquid without coughing and retching like the others had.

The young man grinned savagely as he slapped the strip of duct tape back over her mouth. "Hey, man, did you see how this one just sucked that shit down like it was water?" he asked his companion.

"I sure fuckin' did," the man with the pistol said, leering at Caitlin. "Makes me wonder what else she swallows so well…we'll find out tonight, I promise you. We have to try out our merch to make sure it's good enough for buyers, my man."

"We sure as fuck do, brother," the other man said. "And I can't wait to do that."

"Later, man, later," the one with the pistol said. "First, we have a lot more work to do. Let's get on with it."

The man with the knife set the bottle of whiskey—now only half-full—onto the floor, and then he and his companion left the room, locking the door behind them. The women waited for at least a minute, giving the men ample time to get down the stairs and leave the building before they moved, slipping their arms out from behind their backs and removing the broken zip ties from their ankles.

"You said we couldn't take on these scumbags without a weapon," Anna said to Caitlin as soon as she ripped the strip of duct tape off her mouth. Then she pointed at the bottle of whiskey the men had left on the floor. "Well, now we've got a weapon."

19

"It's the end of a world, the world we all knew up to this point," Marvin said, staring at the throng of refugees as they trudged along the road, carrying whatever they could in backpacks, gym bags, or other receptacles, with many pushing shopping carts filled with their possessions along. "But it's not the end of the world. In another way, it's the birth of a new world…a world that's going to be much harder to survive in, but not impossible, not if you can adapt."

"I'll do whatever it takes to adapt," Hank said determinedly. "Just tell me what to do, sir, show me how to do it, and I'll do it. I'm not ready to die just yet, and I don't want to join the rest of those sheep, wandering aimlessly around, not knowing what they're doing or why just going along with what everyone else is doing because they don't know any better."

"I don't have all the answers, Hank," Marvin said

gently, "but I think I know at least a little more about this new world we've been thrown into than most of them. And one of the things I do know is that time is of the essence. Every second that passes is a second that things get worse in what's left of this city. Half of it's already on fire…the rest is going to follow before too long."

"Come on, guys, we'd better get to my place before it burns down if that hasn't already happened, knowing my luck," Bruce muttered. "We've still got around two miles to go."

"Yeah, let's get moving," Marvin said. "And although I don't think anyone is going to try to rob us, considering that right now we look like a couple of bums who got washed up after half-drowning in the harbor, and we have literally nothing for anyone to take except these damp waterproofs we're wearing, we need to remain vigilant. These are crazy times we're in, and anything could happen. People are going to act in very unpredictable ways. Treat 'em like you you'd treat a herd of bison you somehow found yourself stuck in the middle of—walk with confidence, but avoid eye contact, and definitely don't do anything that would antagonize anyone."

The three of them set off, feeling utterly exhausted, with the acute pains of hunger stabbing through their bellies with every step and the terrible dryness of an intense thirst parching their mouths.

They went down the hill, passing a few newer apartment buildings, one of which had been completely destroyed by a missile, two of which had suffered partial damage and were on fire. Most of the buildings, even the undamaged ones, seemed to be deserted, and the streets around the neighborhood, which would usually be bustling with activity, were eerily quiet.

The air was getting increasingly difficult to breathe. The smoke was thick here, hanging like a toxic fog. It filtered out the sunlight, giving the atmosphere an eerie, gloomy twilight feel despite it being late morning.

"Man, this air is burning my throat," Bruce rasped, coughing.

"And my eyes," Hank added, coughing and rubbing his watering eyes.

"Another reason we need to get in and out as quickly as possible," Marvin said, his own throat feeling as if someone were dragging a section of barbed wire through it, his eyes stinging as if from the aftermath of being pepper sprayed. "We don't know how many toxic chemicals are in this smoke. Breathing this crap in is probably taking a year off our expected lifespans every hour."

The men walked on in grim silence, all coughing, spluttering, and rubbing their burning eyes. The going was getting increasingly difficult, made all the more so by the painfully gnawing hunger and thirst that continued to plague them.

They passed a few stores, but a cursory examination of these buildings, whose doors and windows had all been smashed in, quickly revealed that all had already been looted of anything edible.

"Son of a bitch," Bruce growled after the three emerged from a small convenience store that had been cleaned out of absolutely everything, even the pet food. "These people are fucking animals! Not even twenty-four hours have passed, and they've stripped every store bare, like a bunch of, of fucking piranhas stripping a skeleton clean in a river."

"If only those little assholes hadn't stolen our stuff," Hank grumbled. "We had plenty of food and water in those bags, and we wouldn't have needed to be scrounging like a couple of rats here."

"Yeah, those little scumbags," Bruce growled, clenching his fists and shaking them at the empty streets. "Man, if I could get my hands on those fucking punks, I'd wring their scrawny little necks!"

"Guys," Marvin said, "forget about that. There's no point in wasting energy on bullshit we can't change. What happened, happened, and all we can do is try to get over it and move on. It was the first time someone tried to rob us—and yeah, they succeeded in doing that—but it won't be the last."

After they had traveled another block or two, they came across a store that hadn't been looted—a dry cleaning store. The front door was locked, but a quick glance down the alley next to the dry cleaners quickly revealed that the side door had been left open.

"You guys could maybe get some dry clothes from in there," Bruce suggested. "I mean, like I said, I'm happy to give you some of my clothes, but I'm short and fat, and you guys are tall and lean—I'm pretty sure nothing I own is gonna fit you."

"I think you're right," Marvin said. "It would be a good idea to get some fresh clothes from this place."

"Isn't that, like, stealing, though?" Hank asked.

Marvin shrugged. "I guess it is, technically. And believe me, I'm no thief. I've never stolen anything in my life. I didn't even think of shoplifting candy when I was a kid. But realistically, nobody's ever going to collect the clothes in that shop—the owners of those clothes are probably either dead or in that throng of hundreds of thousands of refugees currently on the long trek out of the city. The clothes will rot in there over the next few years, or, more likely, they'll be destroyed when the fires reach this part of the city…and judging from how much smoke there is around here, I'd be placing my bet on that last possibility. So yeah, we would technically be 'stealing' those clothes, but I'm pretty damn sure they'd be going to waste otherwise. This is a survival situation we're in. I'd say it's justified."

"He's right, kid," Bruce said. "You're going to have to get comfortable with a whole bunch of stuff that you never would have considered to be okay in the old world of yesterday. And I suspect that stealing a bunch of abandoned clothes is going to be pretty mild compared to a lot of the other stuff we're probably going to have to do to survive."

"All right," Hank said, sighing and shaking his head, "I guess we'd better go in and get some clothes then."

While Bruce kept watch, Marvin and Hank entered the dry-cleaning store through the side door. It was gloomy inside, but there was enough daylight streaming in from the large windows of the storefront to illuminate the space. After rummaging through the piles of clothes that were ready to collect, both Marvin and Hank found stuff in their sizes. Both men were only able to find business suits, which weren't exactly ideal for their current circumstances, but these were nonetheless far better than their sweaty waterproofs, which were making the already-challenging trek through the burning city a lot more difficult and strenuous.

"What's this, a bunch of lawyers going to court?" Bruce chuckled when the two of them emerged from the store wearing their freshly pressed suits.

"It's all we could find," Hank said.

"We'll get something more suitable when we can, but right now, these suits feel way better than those damn waterproofs," Marvin said.

"I bet they do. I'm sweating my ass off in these damn waterproofs," Bruce grumbled. "Let's get moving so I can get myself some clean clothes, too."

They left the dry-cleaning store and walked quietly along for a while, doing their best to ignore the persistent pangs of hunger and thirst. Finally, Hank broke the silence…by talking about the silence.

"This silence is so…freaky," he murmured, peering around him at the deserted streets and buildings. "I've never, ever seen the city like this. I never imagined I'd see it like this. I guess you get so used to hearing the sound of traffic filling in the background that when it's gone, you really, *really* notice its absence."

"You should try going into the mountains sometime, kid," Marvin said, smiling weakly with his cracked, dry lips. "It sounds like this all the time there…minus the occasional yells, gunshots, and explosions that—"

Just as he said that, a massive explosion blasted its bowel-rumbling boom through the empty streets like a thunderclap out of the blue. It sounded like it had come from only a few blocks away. All three men instinctively dropped to the ground, covering their heads. They waited warily in this position until they were sure they were safe.

"As I was saying, explosions that occasionally shatter this eerie silence," Marvin continued dryly.

"Man, what the hell was that?" Bruce gasped. "My ears are ringing!"

"It could have been anything," Marvin answered with a shrug as he dusted himself off and continued onward. "In fact, it may not have even been deliberately set off. A lot of things in this city are going to spontaneously explode at a certain point because of the breakdown of maintenance systems. Chemical factories, gas stations, and possibly even some power stations. This whole place is a powder keg, waiting for a spark…and I do mean that almost literally."

"Shit…all the more reason to get the hell out of here,"

Bruce said. "We're almost at my place, by the way. Just around that corner up ahead on the right."

They trudged wearily onward, thankful their trek through the ruined city was almost at an end. When they got to Bruce's building, the others saw that it was a relatively modest apartment block, around ten floors in total, which looked like it had been built in the 1950s or 60s. While a large and much more modern apartment building a little ways down the street had been almost completely demolished by a missile, reduced by the potent weapon to a pile of rubble around a twisted steel skeleton, Bruce's building was completely intact.

"This is it, home sweet home," Bruce said with a sigh as they walked up to the entrance of the building. "Thankfully, I kept my keys in my pocket, not my bag," he added, unlocking the front door. "Otherwise, we'd have really been screwed when those punks stole our stuff."

They walked up the stairwell, which was as dark and as eerily quiet as the rest of the building, to Bruce's apartment. He unlocked the front door and took them through the small, neatly kept apartment to the kitchen.

The men were practically drooling by the time they got into Bruce's kitchen. After their marathonic ordeal at sea and the long walk through the city, with barely anything to eat or drink, they were beyond ravenous.

Bruce clapped his hands together and rubbed them eagerly. "Lucky for us, I always keep a full fridge and cupboards," he said. "And since the power hasn't even been off for twenty-four hours, I'm gonna go ahead and say that pretty much everything in the fridge is okay to eat and drink. So, go ahead, boys. Help yourselves. Take as much as you want because it ain't like the fridge is ever gonna come on again, and everything inside it is just gonna go to waste."

The others didn't need to be asked twice. Bruce yanked open the fridge door, grabbed a takeout container of lasagna and a beer, and started going to town on them. Hank snatched a bottle of orange juice from the fridge shelf and started chugging it down, while Marvin, the most sensible of the three, grabbed a bottle of Gatorade to efficiently rehydrate himself.

The three of them pillaged the fridge until they'd had their fill and the relentless feelings of hunger and thirst that had been plaguing them all day had been satiated.

At that point, their weariness was kicking in in an almost irresistible wave of sheer exhaustion. The lack of sleep combined with their overfull bellies hit them like the most potent sleeping pills.

"I think," Bruce said, pausing to let out a long, sustained burp, "that we should take a quick nap before doing anything else. What do you guys think?"

"I agree," Hank said, his eyelids heavy, letting out a yawn.

Marvin was desperate to get going and search for his beloved Caitlin while they still had daylight to work with, but he couldn't deny that he was just as exhausted as the others were. He felt like he had been given an immensely powerful sedative, and it was all he could do to keep his eyes open. He desperately needed sleep—as they all did—and he knew if he didn't get any soon, he would likely collapse in the streets outside.

"All right," Marvin said. "We can nap for a couple minutes, but we can't afford to sleep for hours. We have to make use of the daylight that's left."

"I've got this old wind-up mechanical clock that belonged to my grandmother," Bruce said, walking over to a kitchen shelf and taking an antique clock off it. "It should still work, right?"

"It'll work perfectly," Marvin said. "No electricity or electronics involved. It won't have been affected by the EMP."

"I'll wind it up quick, then set the alarm for, say, an hour's time?" Bruce asked.

"Hmm…maybe make that forty minutes," Marvin said.

"Man, only forty minutes? Sheesh…I could sleep for days, literally days," Bruce said, sighing.

"As could I," Marvin said, "believe me. But the thing is, if you did that when you closed your eyes to sleep, it could end up being the last time you ever closed them. It's not safe to sleep in this city. The missile strikes may have stopped, but we don't know what's coming next. And then there are the fires and the smoke. Thankfully your place is all closed up, but even so, I can smell a hint of that smoke in the air, and it's only going to get worse. When it does, anyone who tries to sleep through it is only going to end up dying from carbon monoxide poisoning."

"Yeah, yeah, I get it, I get it," Bruce muttered. "All right, forty minutes, I'm setting this thing. I'm taking the bed, but it's a double, so one of you can sleep next to me, and the other can take the sofa."

"I'll take the sofa," Marvin said.

He staggered wearily over to it, collapsed onto the soft cushions, and was asleep within seconds.

It felt as if he had only been slumbering for a mere minute or two when he awoke…but it wasn't the alarm clock that roused him. Instead, it was the cold, hard steel of a gun barrel shoved in his face.

20

"Don't fucking move, don't even blink, motherfucker," a voice snarled at Marvin.

It was a man's voice. The guy in question was a large, heavily built man in his thirties, dressed all in black, with a black balaclava covering his head and face. He was holding a pump-action shotgun and had the muzzle pressed right up into Marvin's face. His finger was on the trigger, and his small, ice-blue eyes were wild in their shallow sockets.

He wasn't alone. There was another man behind him, this one taller and skinnier in build but also dressed in all black, wearing a black balaclava. He, too, was armed and pointing a nine-millimeter pistol at Marvin. Both men had long knives on sheaths on their hips and canisters of pepper spray clipped to their belts. Each of them was also carrying a large, empty duffel bag. Their aim here seemed quite clear to Marvin.

"All right, fellas, all right," Marvin said calmly. "Don't worry, I'm not gonna move."

Unlike most people, this was far from the first time he'd had a firearm shoved in his face by angry, belligerent men. Also, a number of subtle cues that Marvin quickly picked up clued him in to the fact that these people were amateurs—their stances, the way they were holding their weapons, and even the tone of voice the man with the shotgun was using. They were nervous and afraid—probably a lot more afraid than he was. That also made them dangerous, though, but dangerous in terms of posing the risk of accidentally blowing off his head with the shotgun rather than doing it deliberately.

"That's right, motherfucker, you keep real still, real fucking still," the larger man growled.

"Okay, that's what I'm doing," Marvin said, remaining perfectly calm and motionless while continuing to assess his assailants, quietly working out a plan to disarm them and keeping his eyes open for an opportunity to do so. "Would you mind telling me exactly what it is you want, though? I'm guessing you're here to rob me."

"We want food and water," the man with the shotgun growled. "Everything you've got in this dump. We're gonna take it all, and you're gonna stay right here, you understand me?"

"Tie him up, man. Make sure he don't try nothin'," the skinny man said, trying but failing to disguise his nervousness.

"I don't have anything to tie him up with, you fuckin'

moron!" the larger man snapped, turning his head to glare at his companion. "I told you we should have brought some zip—"

As soon as the big man turned his head, Marvin knew his opportunity to act had arrived. Moving with lightning speed, he snatched the shotgun out of his assailant's hands. He whipped it around in his hands in a perfectly executed disarming maneuver. In the blink of an eye, the tables were turned, and Marvin had the shotgun aimed up his assailant, the barrel mere inches from the man's mouth, which had dropped wide open with shock and fright.

"Drop it, you son of a bitch, or I'll pump you full of lead!" the thin man yelled, gripping his pistol with both hands and aiming it at Marvin's chest.

"I might have taken your threat seriously if it hadn't been for one very significant detail," Marvin said coolly.

"Drop it now, motherfucker! This is your last chance!" the man screeched.

"Your safety catch is still on—I can see it from here," Marvin said calmly. "And I'll blow a football-sized hole straight through your chest if you even think of trying to flip that switch. Set the pistol on the floor, back away from me, and I'll let you two clowns walk out of this place with your lives."

At that moment, Hank came rushing through from the bedroom, brandishing a baseball bat. "What the hell's going on in here?" he yelled.

"Don't worry, it's all under control…isn't it, boys?" Marvin asked, his tone smooth and utterly calm.

The thin man realized Marvin was right—he had forgotten to take the safety catch off his pistol, and as such, the weapon was useless.

"I've seen active combat, my man," Marvin said to the man. "You won't be the first person I've killed, and you probably won't be the last, either. But this doesn't have to end with you and your stupid friend dying on the floor of this apartment. Set the pistol down nice and slow, and then walk out of here, and you both get to live another day. It's a simple choice…a real simple choice."

"You fucking idiot, Jake," the large man snarled.

"You're the one who let him disarm you!" the thin man snapped.

"I'm running out of patience here," Marvin growled. "I'm going to count to five, and if that pistol isn't on the floor by the time I'm done, I *will* execute both of you, and that's a promise."

"Shit!" the thin man muttered, and he bent down and set his pistol on the floor.

"That's a wise choice you just made," Marvin said. "Now get the hell out of here. And in the future, I suggest raiding places where the owners aren't home."

The two would-be robbers slunk out of the apartment, and as they did, Hank ran over and grabbed the pistol from the floor.

"Are you okay?" he asked, his face pale with fear and shock.

Marvin chuckled and sat up, placing the shotgun across his lap. "Oh, I'm fine, son, just fine. Those amateurs didn't know their heads from their asses, and I was never in any real danger. I'm pretty damn happy they decided to try to rob us, actually. Now we've got some firearms, at least. Hand me that pistol, please."

After checking the firearms, Marvin discovered the shotgun had eight shells while the pistol had nine rounds. He gave Hank a few tips on how to use the pistol, then handed him the weapon while carrying the shotgun.

"Is Bruce still asleep?" Marvin asked.

"He was when that yelling woke me up," Hank answered.

"We'd better get him up and get moving."

Bruce was so deep in slumber that it was almost as if he was in a coma, and it took quite an effort to rouse him.

"Oh man, when are we gonna get to actually sleep?" Bruce groaned, rubbing his weary eyes. It was only after a few moments that he noticed that Marvin and Hank were now armed. "Hey, uh, where did you guys get those?" he asked, scrunching his face with confusion. "I don't have any guns."

"We'll tell you about it while we pack," Marvin said sternly. "But right now, we need to grab as much food and water as we can carry and get moving."

"All right, all right," Bruce groaned.

Bruce gathered every large backpack or gym bag he owned, and he and the others packed as much food and water as they could into them. Bruce, meanwhile, took a few small items of sentimental value, too.

As they walked out of the apartment, Bruce turned and looked back at the place with tears in his eyes. As eager as he was to get going, Marvin stopped and allowed Bruce to have a few moments of grieving.

"You know, I made a lot of good memories in this place," Bruce murmured sadly, his voice cracking. "Especially when Helen was still around before cancer took her away from me…I-I can't believe that this is…that this is probably the last time I'm gonna see this place…ever."

"Take a good picture of it with your mind, Bruce, and keep that picture in the same place you keep all your best memories," Marvin said.

Bruce let out a long sigh, taking in as much of his apartment as he could in these last few moments in it. Finally, he nodded. "All right," he croaked, barely able to speak, being so choked up with emotion. "I'm ready."

Armed and carrying as much food and drink as they could handle, the men set off from Bruce's apartment building. It was early afternoon now, but it looked like the dying moments of dusk. The smoke was so thick that it was blocking most of the sunlight from above, and it was also making it increasingly difficult to breathe. Every few steps the men took, at least one of them would have to stop for a while to cough.

"Man, we need some gas masks or something," Bruce wheezed before breaking into a violent coughing fit. "I feel like we're all gonna have lung cancer by the time we get out of this dump."

"Yeah, or we'll be dead from smoke inhalation long before we even make it out," Hank rasped. "My throat's burning, my nose is burning, my eyes are burning, and I just can't seem to catch my breath."

Marvin was feeling like that, too, but there was no way he could deviate from his mission. No matter how dire things got, he wasn't going to leave this city without finding Caitlin or at least discovering what had happened to her. He realized, though, that this wasn't fair on the other two men.

He turned to them with a grave look on his face. "Guys, you don't have to come with me to do this," he said somberly. "You two can join the throng of refugees and leave the city while you can still breathe before this air gets truly toxic—toxic enough to kill within *hours*, not *years*—and believe me, it's going to get that way sooner rather than later. I'll give you detailed directions on how to get to my family's ranch. As seamen, you guys both know how to use the night sky to navigate. The stars, combined with following the backroads I tell you about and keeping an eye out for the right landmarks—"

"I'm coming with you," Hank said resolutely.

Marvin raised both eyebrows with surprise. "Are you sure, kid? This air is getting worse by the minute, and it'll likely have long-term consequences for your health. You need to think about the implications of what that's going to mean in a world without hospitals and doctors..."

"I'm coming, too, Marvin," Bruce said, folding his arms across his chest. "And nothing you say about lung cancer or throat cancer or whatever is gonna stop me."

"We would both have been condemned to a slow, horrible death on the ship if it weren't for you, sir—I mean, Marvin," Hank said. "We owe you our lives."

"The kid's right," Bruce echoed. "Hell, we may have even been forced to resort to cannibalism...or become the victims of others forced to indulge in 'long pig,' as actual cannibals call it. And man, you not only gave us the chance to escape that horrible fate, but you also gave us a chance of a new life, of continued survival, in this crazy new world, in which, well, let's face it, in which most people are gonna die."

Marvin nodded slowly, and he felt his heart swelling with emotion. He knew this feeling well, for it wasn't the first time he had experienced it. This was the feeling that accompanied the forging of a powerful bond, a bond that often lasted a lifetime. It was a bond beyond friendship—a band of brothers shared between men who had experienced the hardships and horrors of war, who'd had each other's backs at the darkest of moments. After leaving the Navy SEALs, Marvin had thought the days of forging such bonds were behind him, yet here he was, in the midst of one of the greatest cataclysms in history, forging such bonds anew.

"Thank you, guys...from the bottom of my heart, thank you," was all he could say.

"I think we need to find some gas masks," Bruce said,

"and I think I know where we might be able to find some."

"Oh yeah, where?" Hank asked.

"There's a police station two blocks away. With all the recent protests in the city—you know, the big riots that made news headlines all over the world—I know the cops from that station are well stocked up on riot gear."

"Good idea," Marvin said. "And we could also pick up some body armor and possibly some more weapons."

The men headed straight over to the police station, traveling warily through the deserted, smoke-choked streets, which were getting almost as dark as they would be at night due to the ever-increasing denseness of the smoke.

When they got to the police station, which was one of the city's largest police stations, they were dismayed but not surprised to find it locked up.

"Let's not give up on this just yet," Bruce said, pausing to cough and retch. The smoke was becoming truly unbearable now; the men felt as if they were caught in a gigantic and inescapable fog of teargas. "There's an underground parking lot under the station where the cops keep all their vehicles. We can walk right in, and the door to the station down there might be unlocked."

"It's worth a shot," Marvin said, also coughing badly.

They went around to the rear of the station and entered the underground parking lot, which was protected only by a boom gate and thus easily accessible. It was almost pitch-black down below, but they had brought a single camping lantern from Bruce's place—the only camping lantern he possessed. Bruce carried the lantern while Marvin and Hank kept their firearms at the ready.

Along with the usual police cruisers, a number of riot vehicles were parked down there. When the men tried the sturdy steel door that led into the police station and found it locked, a fresh idea popped into Marvin's head.

"Shit, what are we gonna do now?" Bruce groaned. "Never mind getting lung cancer in a couple years from this smoke. I'm starting to worry about making it through the next couple of minutes!"

"Inside the station isn't the only place they keep riot gear," Marvin said, walking over to one of the armored vehicles.

They tried the doors on the first riot vehicle they came to, but these were locked. The back doors of the hulking van were locked from the outside by a sturdy padlock rather than a lock built into the door, and Marvin figured it was worth possibly wasting a shotgun shell on attempting to blow it open.

"Stand back, guys," he said, placing the shotgun's muzzle against the padlock.

With a thunderclap that resounded in a booming echo through the parking lot, he fired the shotgun. A second later, the tinkling clang of metal fragments hitting the concrete sent a surge of triumph through the men's veins.

They hurriedly pulled the remnants of the lock out of

the catch, then they flung open the back of the van. As Marvin had suspected, there were no firearms in the vehicle, nor was there any ammunition, but there were a number of other useful items—and chief among these were gas masks, which the men hurriedly strapped onto their faces.

"Oh God, it feels good to be able to breathe again without every damn breath feeling like you're drowning in corrosive acid," Bruce gasped, his voice muffled by the gas mask.

"Put on some body armor," Marvin instructed. "It may come in handy."

The men put on some items of riot armor, and they each took a nightstick, which they tucked into their belts. Bruce took a riot shield as well.

Marvin looked his companions up and down. For all intents and purposes, they looked like cops ready to take on a rioting mob. He knew, though, that in the hours and days to come, they were going to have to face challenges far more deadly than any angry crowd.

"All right, boys," he said grimly, gripping his shotgun tightly, his determined voice muffled by the gas mask. "We're going in."

21

Neither Stanley nor Declan had any time to aim their crossbows at Pablo, let alone shoot him. All they could do, as the hail of bullets tore up the concrete around them and hammered the police cruisers, was to sprint for cover.

The nearest cover was a large police SUV only a few yards away, and both men managed to dive behind it before any flying bullets found their flesh.

"Son of a bitch!" Declan growled, his heart thumping madly in his chest. "Who's firing? Where's it coming from?"

With his back pressed against the side of the SUV, Stanley set down his crossbow and whipped out his pistol. His heart, like Declan's, was also pounding wildly, but even though it had been many decades since his career in the military, his training kicked in, as did his muscle memory, and a calm collectedness came over him, steadying his nerves and allowing him to focus.

"I don't know," Stanley said, "but I'm gonna give the bastards some lead in a second or two when they have to reload."

"Me too," Declan growled, unholstering and cocking his .45 as the bullets peppered the SUV they were hiding behind, popping the tires with a hiss, slamming into the bodywork in a drumming rhythm, and shattering the windows and windscreen, showering him and Stanley with little chunks of broken glass.

Stanley, meanwhile, used his knife to pry the side mirror out of its housing on the SUV's door. He then used the mirror to scan the parking lot to try to see where the firing was coming from. He didn't have to look for too long. He soon saw three of Austin Randall's thugs standing on the roof of the house behind the police station parking lot. All three were armed with AR-15 rifles and were wearing bulletproof vests.

"Up on the roof, the big house behind us," Stanley said to Declan. "They're wearing bulletproof vests, and they've got AR-15 rifles; it's not going to be easy to take 'em out."

"You fire from the rear of the car; I'll fire from the front," Declan said. "They've gotta reload soon."

Just as he said this, the rate of enemy bullets hammering the car slowed dramatically, and then, after a second or two, it stopped altogether. The men knew this was their opportunity to counterattack and that they had to seize it quickly.

Stanley popped his head out from behind the rear of the SUV and opened fire on the men, while Declan did the same from the front. Although their adversaries had the advantage of higher ground, being up on the roof meant they had no cover whatsoever, and they were sitting ducks for Stanley and Declan, who emptied their magazines on them in a series of rapidly fired but well-placed and accurate shots.

Declan took one man in the chest with his third or fourth shot, and although the man's bulletproof vest saved him from getting a hole blown through his lungs, the shot was indirectly lethal. The .45 bullet gave him a kick as hard as if a heavyweight boxer had punched him in the chest, which caused him to lose his footing and then fall and tumble off the roof, plummeting to his death there on the hard concrete five floors below.

Stanley also put a shot on target, but his bullet ripped through his enemy's upper leg. The man screamed with pain, dropped his rifle—which tumbled down the slanted roof and then dropped five floors down, leaving him unarmed—and then he slipped, lost his balance, and fell to his death.

The third man, though, managed to reload his rifle just as his companions fell, and he returned fire with a furious vengeance, flipping his modified AR-15 to fully automatic mode and spraying hot lead in a vicious storm at Stanley and Declan, who had no choice but to take cover as the bullets riddled the SUV.

"One of 'em left," Stanley growled, hastily reloading his pistol. "We take him out, then we complete our mission."

"Emptying his clip like that, he's gonna need to reload in five, four, three, two—" Declan said, slapping a fresh clip into his pistol.

Just as the two of them were about to counterattack, concentrating their fire on the remaining man on the roof, though, they heard a sound that neither of them had expected to hear at all: the roar of a large vehicle racing through the nearby streets and veering into the police station parking lot.

"We've got company!" Stanley yelled, and as he popped out from behind the SUV to fire at the man on the roof, an old but well-maintained Land Cruiser—an early 80s model—came careening into the parking lot.

Armed men were hanging out of the windows, and as soon as they saw Stanley, they started shooting. There was no doubt in anyone's mind that these men were anyone other than Austin Randall's goons, here to help break Pablo out of the holding cell.

Now, the tables had turned completely, leaving Stanley and Declan outgunned and outnumbered, but the whole situation had changed. The men were now caught in a fight for their lives, and each immediately realized that if they wanted to survive the next few seconds, the only option was to retreat.

"Shit, we've gotta run!" Declan yelled.

"Agreed! We're dead if we stay here and let 'em surround us!" Stanley said.

The nearest exit point was a six-foot-tall brick wall only a few yards away. The challenge, however, would not only be to get over the wall but to simply get to it in the first place, covering dangerously open ground and completely exposing themselves to fire while doing so.

"I'll cover you while you go over the wall!" Stanley said, preparing to pop out from behind his spot of cover and open fire, just as the Land Cruiser came skidding to a stop in the center of the parking lot, its tires screeching and smoking as the driver slammed on the brakes.

There was no time for Declan to do anything but agree. He gave Stanley a grim nod, every muscle in his body taut and ready to explode into a rapid sprint. "I'll cover you as soon as I'm over so that you can do the same," Declan said.

"Got it. Three, two, one, go!"

Stanley popped out, opening fire on the Land Cruiser just as its occupants were piling out of it. The men had no choice but to duck for cover as Stanley's bullets peppered the vehicle. Meanwhile, Declan charged for the wall, clambering over it the instant he reached it, with adrenalin tearing through his veins and bullets from the man on the roof tearing chunks out of the bricks around him.

In a second, he was over the wall, and just as he dropped down into the yard on the other side—the backyard of someone's house—Stanley ran out of ammo and had to duck back behind the vehicle. Now it was Declan's turn to provide cover for Stanley, and he climbed onto a nearby potted plant, a large outdoor specimen that allowed him to get his head and shoulders above the top of the wall. This gave him an unobstructed view of the Land Cruiser and its occupants, and the instant he got these targets in his sights, he opened up with his .45.

Stanley, meanwhile, took this opportunity to race across the perilous open ground between the bullet-riddled SUV and the wall, and he scrambled over the obstacle in record time, with bullets flying around him and tearing chunks out of the wall.

Just as he dropped over the wall and landed on the other side, Declan's ammunition ran out, and he was forced to duck as the enemy returned fire, spraying the wall with hundreds of bullets in the space of only a few seconds.

"Go!" Stanley yelled, pointing at the right side of the house as he popped the empty clip out of his pistol and slammed a fresh one into his firearm.

This was the only escape route, and Declan didn't need to be told twice to take it. He hopped off the large potted plant, and then, reloading as he ran, he sprinted behind Stanley, the thunder of gunfire which came from behind the retreating men a deafening din, a riotous cacophony that had utterly shattered the eerie fog of silence in which the town had been blanketed.

With their hearts pounding, the men ran down the

side of the house, then raced across the front yard, pausing behind the large truck parked in the driveway to scan the street, which they quickly discovered was empty.

"They're gone. Hold your fire!" they heard a distant voice yell—that of the man on the roof, who from his vantage point had seen them run past the side of the house.

The men raced across the street and skidded to a halt behind a van parked outside one of the houses. The gunfire had stopped, but the silence wouldn't last long; a deafening boom thundered through the town.

"I think they just blew the front doors of the police station open with some sort of powerful explosive," Stanley said grimly, his ears ringing with a shrill whine and his pulse racing.

"Then we've failed," Declan muttered, slamming his fist against the concrete. "They've freed Pablo…and now he's going to bring his army to your ranch."

22

"I...I don't know how much chance we stand with a whiskey bottle against a gun and a knife," Kath said nervously, staring at the half-full bottle of single malt whiskey in Anna's hands.

"Much more of a chance than we'd stand empty-handed," Anna said, her eyes shining with determination and simmering aggression as she slowly slapped the bottle onto the palm of her free hand over and over.

The new girl—the beautiful young Asian woman the two thugs had recently captured—started to try to say something.

"Hold on, let me get that off your mouth," Caitlin said. She hurried over to the young woman and removed the duct tape from her mouth.

"Oh my God, thank you, I could barely breathe with that over my mouth," the young woman said.

"We'll get the zip ties off next," Caitlin said. "We'll

have to heat up my bracelet with the lantern, then burn through the plastic."

"Yeah, please hurry. These things are cutting into my flesh and cutting off my circulation," the woman said. "God, those two assholes are absolutely psychotic! I thought they were gonna murder me! I mean, I was terrified when all this insane shit started, with the power failure, the explosions, the—"

"What's your name, and what did you wanna say when we were talking about weapons and taking those two psychos down?" Anna asked, somewhat brusquely, interrupting the young woman, who clearly enjoyed talking. "You got some kinda idea that might help us?"

"Oh, sorry, I should have introduced myself," she said. "My name's Delia. And what I was trying to say is that the bottle isn't the only weapon we have. Those jerks took my handbag, which had my gun in it, but when all this madness started, I took my backup weapon out and put it in one of my coat pockets. I never got the chance to use it because those psychos ambushed me when I was trying to get down into the subway—"

"Why were you trying to get into the subway?" Gina asked. "You know the trains aren't running, right, and it'll be pitch dark in there."

"Sure, I knew," Delia answered, "but I still figured it'd be a safe route out of the city. I take the subway every day to get in and out of the city—my husband and I live in the western suburbs—so I figured I'd walk all the way along the tracks. Most of the network is deep underground, so it'd be safe from the missiles and bombs and stuff, and—"

"Tell us about your backup weapon," Anna said, sensing Delia was getting sidetracked.

At this point, Caitlin had gotten the bracelet hot enough to melt through the zip ties, so she freed Delia from these painful bindings.

"Thanks, oh my God, that feels a lot better," Delia said, shaking her wrists and rotating her ankles.

"No problem," Caitlin said.

"Oh yeah, the extra weapon," Delia said. She reached into one of the pockets of her suit jacket and retrieved what looked like a stick of lipstick. "Pepper spray, disguised as lipstick," she said with a wicked smile. "And this isn't the cheap stuff. This is pure OC spray of the highest grade. The strongest stuff you can get. Also, it's the gel, not the spray, to be technical, so there's no danger of getting blowback in your own face when you use it."

A smile broke across Anna's face. "Good…yeah, that's really good."

"How were you planning to navigate the subway system without a flashlight or something?" Gina asked, still seemingly fixated on the idea of getting through the subway system in conditions of complete darkness.

"I've got this too," Delia said, producing a Zippo from another pocket in her jacket.

"That could also be used as a weapon," Caitlin said. "I saw something in the bathroom. Let me go check it out."

Caitlin hurried into the dusty bathroom. The small room was mostly bare, but a can of air freshener spray was next to the toilet. The can had rust around the edges, and it looked like it'd been sitting there for years, but Caitlin picked it up. She could feel there was at least a little liquid left in it. She gave it a shake and then a test spray, and a burst of air freshener came out.

She checked the small print on the can, and, as she had suspected, there was a section saying, "WARNING: highly flammable. Keep away from open flames."

Caitlin strode back out into the room and went straight over to Delia. "Could I borrow your lighter for a second?"

"Sure."

Caitlin held the lighter in her left hand and the can of air freshener in her right. "Stand back, everyone," she warned.

"What are you gonna do with that?" Kath asked skeptically. "Freshen those two monsters to death?"

"Just watch," Caitlin said, grinning.

She flipped up the Zippo and ignited it, then held the nozzle of the air freshener can a few inches from the flame and gave a quick burst of spray. The extremely flammable vapor became a roaring torrent of fire as it passed through the Zippo's flame, creating a flamethrower-like fire blast that shot out over at least three or four feet.

"Whoa!" Gina gasped.

Kath's skepticism quickly transformed into awed wonder, and both Anna and Delia were just as impressed.

"How the hell did you know how to do that?" Kath gasped. "That's like a freakin' improvised flamethrower!"

Caitlin chuckled. "Growing up with two older brothers who loved messing around with anything to do with fire and explosions," she answered. "I never thought the old 'deodorant flamethrower' trick would come in handy, but it might just end up helping us to save ourselves from those monsters."

"All right, this is good, this is good," Anna said slowly. "We've got a whiskey bottle, we've got some OC spray, and we've got an improvised flamethrower. Those evil motherfuckers might be a lot bigger and stronger than us, but there's only two of them and five of us, and we've got weapons now."

"Even so, we can't be gung-ho about this," Caitlin cautioned. "One of them has a pistol—maybe the other, too, if they've searched through my bag and Delia's, both of which contain firearms. And the other has a knife, which is less immediately lethal than a pistol, but seriously, it's not a weapon you can afford to underestimate. It's very easy to deal out some horrendous and lethal wounds very quickly with a knife, especially if the wielder knows what they're doing."

"We have to fight these guys, though," Anna said. "I'd rather die fighting for my freedom than be a coward and let them rape me and turn me into a literal slave."

"I agree," Caitlin said, "but I'm saying that we need a

plan of attack. We're the underdogs here, even though we outnumber them. Without a solid plan, we're going to fail, and some of us will almost certainly get killed."

"We've got another weapon we can use," Gina suddenly said. "In conjunction with the flamethrower."

Everyone turned to look at the shy teenager.

"What's this other weapon, kid?" Anna asked.

Gina pointed at the bottle in Anna's hands. "The whiskey. It's flammable, right? So, if we dumped some whiskey over these guys, then used the flamethrower on them, they'd go up in flames, right?"

Anna chuckled darkly and nodded. "You're more of a badass than I thought, Gina. Yeah, whiskey will burn, all right. Sure, it ain't gasoline, but it'll burn."

"Wait, if we're talking about flammable liquids and gases, I think we've ignored the most obvious one, one that just so happens to be sitting right in front of us," Caitlin said, pointing at the camping lantern.

"Sure, the gas canister in it is full of some very flammable shit," Anna said, "but as far as I remember when you take the canister out of the lantern, it's impossible to get the gas out unless you puncture the canister. You know, safety mechanisms and all that. And we don't have a blade or anything to puncture the canister with, so as potent a weapon as it could be, I don't think we'll be able to use it."

"Hmm, yeah, I guess you're right," Caitlin said. "We're going to have to work with what we've got: some whiskey, the bottle that whiskey is in, some OC spray, and an improvised flamethrower. Oh, and wait, there might be one more weapon we could use."

She hurried back into the bathroom and checked the toilet cistern. A small burst of triumph and hope flared to life within her when she discovered that the cistern top was an older type, made of thick, heavy porcelain. She removed it from the toilet. She also noted that the toilet cistern was full of water. It wasn't ideal, but they could drink it in an emergency, depending on how long they ended up being trapped in this place. She was already feeling thirsty, and she knew this feeling would only get worse. She suspected the others were feeling the same. Tucking the heavy cistern cover under her right arm, she carried it into the room.

"You could easily crack a motherfucker's skull wide open with that," Anna said, nodding approvingly.

"That's exactly what I'm planning on doing with it," Caitlin said, gripping the cistern cover in both hands and giving it a few test swings. "Okay, everyone, we don't know how soon these psychos will be coming back; it could be in a few minutes or in a few hours. Either way, we can't afford to waste any time. We need to get a solid plan of attack together."

It took the women around fifteen minutes to devise a good plan. The ambush wasn't guaranteed to be successful, and indeed it was fraught with risk and peril, but at this point, it was all they had.

Once everything was in place, all they could do was wait in tense suspense, with each of them rotating watch shifts, which involved sitting with one's ear pressed against the door, listening intently for the dreaded sound of their two captors coming up the stairs.

Slow minutes dragged by, eventually becoming hours. As frightened and traumatized as the women were, they all managed to get a little sleep on the hard, cold floor, for a deep exhaustion, exacerbated by the state of fear and stress they were in, soon overcame them.

Caitlin took her turn, watching the door sometime in the early hours of the morning. Since none of them had a working watch, there were no set time periods for the sessions at the door; each woman simply did it for as long as she was able to.

Caitlin wasn't certain just how long she sat at the door with her ear pressed up against the wood, shifting sides when the dull pain in one ear got too much to handle, but looking out through the window, she watched the dark sky becoming lighter before she finally couldn't take it anymore and decided to ask someone else to take over.

The dawn was the darkest one she'd ever seen; the thick smoke that blanketed the entire city blocked out the light of the rising sun almost completely, and only a subtle change in the level of gloom indicated that daybreak was approaching.

The air in the apartment was stuffy, humid, and stale, but Caitlin resisted the urge to open the window; she knew as bad as the air in here felt at the moment, opening the window would make things a hundred times worse. They could survive the stuffy, humid air with some discomfort, but they surely wouldn't be able to survive the toxic smoke for very long.

Caitlin lay down on the floor with the cistern cover next to her, ready to snatch it up in a moment's notice if necessary. With her throat parched with an almost painful dryness and a persistent hunger gnawing painfully at the inside of her belly, she closed her eyes and drifted into a fitful sleep.

While her body may have attempted to shut down during this period of slumber, her mind did not. Nightmares of falling plagued her sleep; she kept dreaming that when she jumped out of the burning skyscraper, her parachute disintegrated on her back, crumbling into ashes, and she plunged in a terrifying free-fall plummet to her death below. She would wake up with a violent start every time this happened, shaking with fear and then slip back into a restless slumber.

She wasn't sure how much time passed in this cycle of nightmares and fitful sleep, but finally, she was awoken for good by a frantic hand shaking her shoulder.

"Wake up, Caitlin, wake up!" Gina said, the pretty teenager's face contorted into an expression of worry and dread. "They're coming! The psychos are coming!"

23

"We haven't failed just yet," Stanley said, steeling his resolve with fierce determination. "We can still ambush them when they try to drive out of here. I doubt that Land Cruiser is bulletproof, and we can take Pablo out with a few well-placed shots."

"We can try, old friend, we can try," Declan said.

Stanley took out his stainless-steel liquor flask, which he kept in one of the chest pockets of his jacket. He took a swig of the whiskey within, wiped his mouth off with the back of his hand, then offered the flask to Declan. "Something to calm your nerves after that battle?" he asked. "It's the first firefight I've been in for decades, and I have to say, it's left me a little shaken up."

"Thanks, and yeah, I'll admit that it got my heart pounding and my adrenalin racing, too," Declan said, taking the hipflask from Stanley, glugging down a hefty swig of whiskey, then passing it back. "Good thinking bringing that along, by the way."

"This thing got my dad through the second world war and storming the beach at Normandy," Stanley said as he tucked the steel flask back into his pocket. "It's been my good luck charm ever since my dad gave it to me on my eighteenth birthday. I wouldn't have left home without. Forget about that, though. Let's talk about what we need to do to take out Pablo."

"You still think we've got a chance?"

"I sure as hell do. There's only one main road out of town back to our land, and they're going to have to use it to get Pablo out," Stanley said. "And I'm thinking they have to go through the old tunnel under the railway line. That's a perfect spot for us to ambush them. If we hurry, we can get there before they do."

"We can't be sure that's the way they'll go, though," Declan countered. "I mean, yes, it *is* the only road outta town toward home, but there are other ways they could get there if they drive through fields and cut across farms and stuff. I doubt Randall's goons are too worried about trespassing."

"I know," Stanley said, "but since they're aware that we're after Pablo and that we know what their plans are in terms of trying to take my ranch, they're going to want to move as fast as they can. Going the long way around and cutting across fields and farms is going to add at least an hour, more likely two, to their journey. There's a chance they'll take the long way, sure, but if they do, there's no way we can stop them anyway. At least this way, we have a shot at it."

"You're right," Declan said. "If there's a chance we can stop them, we have to take it. And even if our odds aren't too great, being armed only with pistols instead of something a lot more suitable for a mission like this, like AR-15s modded to fully automatic, we have to try."

Stanley flashed Declan a boyish grin. "Hey, it could be worse. We could be trying to take these guys down with a couple of slingshots or something, right?"

Declan had to chuckle, grateful for this moment of levity. "You're damn right, Stan, you're damn right. And hey, it might not be a rifle round, but a well-placed shot from a .45 sure as hell can ruin someone's day."

"It definitely can. Come on, let's go."

The men raced off through the streets. Their passage through town did not go unnoticed, though. The sound of the gunbattle had drawn the attention of the town's residents. Some of them were merely peeking out of their windows with frightened, worried stares, but others came out with their own firearms, ready to fend off whatever enemies they thought were invading the town.

The quickest way to the old railway tunnel was directly down the main strip of the town, and although Stanley and Declan would have preferred not to go that route, they were racing against time and had they had no real choice.

They hoped they would be able to get through the

town without running into any major obstacles, but these hopes were quickly dashed. As they turned a corner, running almost a full-tilt sprint, they were confronted by a group of armed townsfolk. There were almost a dozen men, all armed with either hunting rifles or shotguns, and these men leveled their firearms at Stanley and Declan as soon as the two of them came running around the corner.

"Stop right there!" yelled the leader of this mob, a large, portly man in his sixties—the principal of the local elementary school, Philip Pratt. Over the course of a long career in education, he had learned to infuse his sonorous voice with a commanding air of authority, and his booming yell was almost more of a factor that got Stanley and Declan to halt in their tracks than the firearms aimed at their chests.

"That's Stanley Wagner!" a voice from the back of the crowd yelled. "I know these guys. They're good men."

Stanley and Declan lowered their pistols, not wanting to give any of the men—who were clearly on edge and racked with nerves and fear—an excuse to accidentally squeeze their triggers.

"Easy now, fellas, we aren't looking for any trouble," Stanley said. "You heard Jim there. He knows us. And looking at you boys, I know most of your faces, too."

"That may be so," Pratt said, eyeing Stanley and Declan with undisguised suspicion in his gaze, keeping his shotgun aimed at Stanley's chest, "but what the hell was all that shooting a couple minutes ago? And that car we heard racing through town, what was that about? All of our trucks are as dead as doornails, our wives' cars, too. Hell, everything with a motor seems to have just spontaneously caught some sort of deadly mechanical fever and perished. Yet now we hear someone tearing through town, and then there's some sort of gunbattle going on near the police station. You two know what's going on. You're mixed up in this business, I can tell that much…and we're not letting you pass until you tell us exactly what you're doing here and what you know about all of this insanity."

There was a murmur of general agreement from the group, even from Jim, who had vouched for Stanley and Declan. A few of them had lowered their firearms, but more than half still kept their guns aimed at the two men.

A sense of frustration was rising rapidly within Stanley. He wasn't worried about being shot or detained by these men; he just didn't want to waste precious time explaining everything to them.

"There it is again!" someone yelled as they all heard the sound of the Land Cruiser racing through the streets.

As he heard this sound, Stanley's frustration reached boiling point. He knew now, without any shadow of a doubt, that Randall's thugs had succeeded in freeing Pablo from his cell, and now they were on their way out of town. The window in which a successful ambush was possible was shrinking by the minute.

"Yeah, I hear it, I hear it!" another yelled.

"Boys, you'd better open those mouths of yours and tell us exactly what's going on," Pratt growled.

"We don't have time, dammit!" Stanley snapped. "We're not here to steal anything or raid any stores or anything like that—we have to stop the men in that Land Cruiser. My family's survival, hell, our very *lives* depend on it! Let us pass, and I'll explain everything after we take those guys out!"

"No," Pratt said coolly. "No, I'm sorry, Mr. Wagner, but you and your friend aren't going anywhere until you tell us what's going on and what you're doing here."

Declan spoke up before Stanley could answer. Always one to get straight to the point and never one to beat around the bush, Declan didn't pull any punches here. "You want to know what this is, man?" he growled. "It's the end of the world, and I *do* mean that *literally*. Nothing will ever be the same, so you all better figure out how you're going to survive in a world with no running water, no electricity, no internet, no phones, no cars, none of that bullshit.

"And what Stanley and I are doing is trying to save our land and a lot of lives from a drug lord and his thugs who are planning on stealing that from us and killing everyone we love. He's driving that car—it works because it's an old model, pre-80s—and if we don't stop him before he gets out of town, it's all over for us. Do you want our families' blood on your hands, man? Because if those sons of bitches get away because of you and they destroy our lives, I'll come for you, and I'll make you pay, I swear to God. Do you understand what I'm saying?"

"Let 'em pass, Phil," someone said.

"Yeah, let 'em go," Jim echoed.

Philip Pratt continued to glare at the two men. For a few seconds, he kept his firearm leveled at them, but as murmurs of agreement with Jim began to swell in the group, he reluctantly lowered his shotgun and indicated to the others that they should do the same.

"Go then," he said, "go on, do what you need to do. But if you've got any decency, you'll come to find us when you're done, and you'll give us some detailed information about what's happened and what's going on—this whole 'end of the world' thing you're talking about."

"Thank you," Stanley said, infusing his words with genuine gratitude and respect. "I appreciate that. And yes, we'll come to find you when we've completed our mission. But what my friend here just told you ain't no exaggeration; this thing we're living through really *is* the end of the world we've known all our lives up to this point."

Without another word, he and Declan raced off, their hearts pumping, their muscles burning, a sense of urgency driving them on and allowing them to push through the pain and weariness. They wound their way through the streets of the small town and encountered a few more people, some of whom yelled at them or brandished firearms at them, but most of whom simply watched them with frightened, confused eyes from behind locked and barred doors and windows.

All the while, the two men could hear the sound of the Land Cruiser tearing through town, getting ever closer to the railway tunnel, the final barrier they would need to cross before getting out onto the open road.

"Shit, do you think we're gonna make it?" Declan gasped, breathing hard from the exertion of sustained running at a speed close to a sprint.

"We *have to*…we *have to* make it," Stanley gasped back.

"Two more…blocks, right?" Declan wheezed, finding it increasingly difficult to catch his breath.

"Yeah, two more," Stanley answered as he veered around a corner, his pistol aimed out in front of him.

As Stanley raced around the corner, though, he was met with a storm of gunfire and a hail of bullets…and one of them slammed into his chest. Everything went black as he dropped limply to the ground.

24

"Oh God, shit, all right, all right, everyone, get ready," Caitlin urged, her heart in her mouth and her pulse racing as she scrambled to her feet.

Everyone had their own roles to play in the unfolding plan of ambush. Delia had her OC spray, which was the first thing the thugs would be hit with the moment they opened the door. Waiting behind her were Gina and Kath, who had filled their mouths with whiskey. Gina would spray her mouthful of whiskey all over the first man, and Kath—who also had the lighter and the can of air freshener spray—would first spray her mouthful of whiskey over the second man, and then she would blast fire all over both of them, setting them aflame for a few moments.

And in those crucial few moments in which the flammable whiskey, which would be all over the men's heads and upper bodies, went up in flames, the heavy hitters would charge in: Anna with the whiskey bottle and her Muay Thai kicks and Caitlin with the heavy cistern cover.

If the men had another captured woman with them—which they most likely would—it was Gina's job to yank the newest captive out of harm's way so she didn't get caught in all the flames, the OC spray, and the swinging weapons.

Caitlin's heart was pumping in great, booming thumps in her chest, and her entire body was tingling, racked with nervousness and an almost crippling feeling of fear. Aside from some roughhousing with her older brothers when she'd been a little girl, she had never been in a physical fight in her life...and now she was going to be doing her utmost to severely incapacitate or even kill two large, armed men in a hand-to-hand fight.

The women waited in tense silence as the men came up the stairs. The two goons had no idea that anything was out of the ordinary; they stomped up the stairs, talking and joking loudly and brashly, full of confidence and swagger.

As they got closer to the door, a debilitating feeling of nausea suddenly surged from Caitlin's guts all the way up the back of her throat, and she tasted the bitter burn of vomit in her mouth, which she had to use all her willpower to force down. Everything felt completely surreal and dreamlike—but then again, this was how things had felt ever since that fateful moment the night before when all the lights had gone out and the whole world had changed irreversibly in the blink of an eye.

"Courage, girls, courage...this is the fight for our lives," Caitlin whispered to the others as they heard the dreaded sound of the key turning in the lock.

The men flung open the door and stomped in, freezing in their tracks when they saw that their captives were no longer bound and gagged on the floor but instead standing in a semicircle all around them in the doorway...and at that moment, all hell broke loose.

The two young thugs had no time to react before the women's plan of attack kicked into action. Moving like a well-oiled machine, the women all attacked in sequence. Moving with astonishing rapidity and accuracy, Delia gave them both a heavy blast of OC spray, the gel coating the men's eyes and noses. Before she was even finished with this, Kath and Gina spit their mouthfuls of whiskey all over the men's heads, and then Gina yanked the thugs' newest captive—a beautiful black teenager—out of the way as Kath used the "flamethrower" on the pair of them.

The men howled with both rage and pain as their whiskey-soaked heads and shoulders went up in flame with a sudden whoosh, but both of them were already fighting through the shock and agony of this unexpected attack and were scrambling for their weapons.

At this point, Anna and Caitlin charged in. Caitlin took on the man with the pistol. Although her first primal instinct was to smash the heavy cistern cover over his head, she knew she had to get the pistol away from him before she could even think of incapacitating him. Hence, she took a vicious swipe at his right wrist just as he curled his hand around the grip of his pistol.

The heavy porcelain cistern lid smashed into the thug's wrist, and there was a sickening crack as the impact shattered his wrist bones. He dropped the pistol and staggered back, howling with agony and rage as his head and shoulders burned with furious flames and a sharp, fierce pain shot up his arm.

Next to him, Anna attacked his friend just as ruthlessly. She came in with the heavy whiskey bottle, bringing it down on the thug's flaming head as hard as she could. The impact shattered the bottle and caused the young man's knees to buckle beneath him. It wasn't a strong enough blow to knock him out cold, though, and roaring with a vengeful fury while fighting through the agony of the OC spray and the hungry flames dancing around his skull, he whipped his knife out and lunged blindly at Anna.

Her Muay Thai training came into play here, and she swiveled her hips and dodged the vicious lunge as if it were a kick, and then she stabbed the sharp, jagged end of the broken bottle into the side of his neck and, as he staggered backward, with blood spraying in a sickening arc from the wound the razor-sharp glass had opened up in his neck, Anna charged forward and planted the most powerful kick she could throw between his legs.

As the man went down, his arterial blood spurting with such violence from his neck that it sprayed a streak of red across the ceiling, Caitlin prepared to smash the cistern lid over the other man's head, but just as she was about to bring it down on his skull, two deafening thunderclaps blasted through the room.

The man's body jerked twice as the bullets tore through his chest, and then he fell flat on his back, sprawled out in a spreadeagled position as he breathed his final ragged breaths, a few flames still burning on his head, shoulders, and chest. Next to him, his friend was feebly trying to cover the gaping cut in his neck, which was no longer spurting blood, but was still bleeding copiously...and fatally.

Caitlin slowly lowered the cistern cover and turned around. She saw Delia standing there, both hands gripping the pistol the thug had dropped, a thin wisp of smoke rising from the barrel.

"Help me," the dying thug rasped weakly, frothy blood gurgling from his lips. "Please...help me...I don't wanna die...I don't wanna die."

Delia calmly aimed the pistol at his face, then she fired one more shot. After the deafening clap of the shot faded away, the second man's body became as limp and as lifeless as his friend's.

25

The women all stood in stunned silence for a while. The vile smell of burned hair and scorched skin hung in the air, and drops of crimson blood dripped slowly from the ceiling and dribbled down the walls. Outside, the morning was almost as dark as night as the clouds of smoke grew thicker.

"Holy shit," Kath eventually murmured, the first to break the silence, her eyes wide and her jaw hanging open. "Did we just...did we just *murder* two men?"

"We didn't murder anyone," Anna muttered. "We killed two criminals in self-defense. No court of law in this country would convict us of any crime. Ain't that right, Caitlin? Delia? You two are lawyers, ain't you?"

"Well, there was an element to the attack that was premeditated," Caitlin said, "but that doesn't matter; it's irrelevant. If we hadn't done what we just did, these men would have raped us and sold us to other people who would also have raped us."

"I don't feel a single iota of guilt about shooting those two monsters," Delia said calmly. "As far as I'm concerned, they signed their own death warrants when they proudly declared themselves to be slavers, violently kidnapped us, held us here against our will as captives, and threatened to rape and enslave us."

"It had to be done," Kath said. "Those two were pure evil, absolute psychopaths. I don't even want to begin to imagine what they would have done to us if we hadn't defended ourselves like this."

"They deserved to die…and I wish they'd died a much slower, more agonizing death."

Everyone turned to look at the new girl; this was the first time she had spoken. She was staring at the two men with a look of ferocious loathing in her dark, beautiful eyes, which were bloodshot and puffy from weeping and rimmed with tears.

"These two animals murdered my little brother when he tried to protect me from them," she continued, her voice cracking. "They just…they just shot him, like it was nothing. My kid brother…Michael, he was only…he was only seventeen, and these disgusting pieces of shit shot him."

"I'm so sorry," Caitlin said, walking over to the young woman. She put her arms around her and hugged her tightly. "What's your name, sweetie?" she asked softly.

"Jemma," the young woman whimpered. Then she

burst into tears, weeping bitterly and hugging Caitlin tightly.

"I'm so sorry about your brother, Jemma," Caitlin said, doing what she could to comfort the young woman. "I wish I could say that justice has been served, somehow...but I don't know how much justice any of us have seen or will see in the days to come."

"I'm sorry about your brother too, Jemma," Anna said, although her almost cool tone did not convey quite as much sympathy as Caitlin's had. "But we can't stand around this dump, feeling sorry for ourselves all day. We're free now, and I don't know about the rest of you ladies, but I wanna get the hell out of here."

Caitlin got the sense that everyone, aside from Anna, who was headstrong and more than a little domineering, was looking to her for leadership, simply by virtue of her being the eldest among them but also because she had been the one who had initially freed them from their bonds and come up with the plan of attack that had defeated their captors.

After slowly disengaging from her embrace with Jemma, Caitlin drew in a deep breath and then addressed the others. "I'm not going to tell anyone else what to do, and I'm not going to claim to know exactly what's going on here, but I can tell you that wherever you intend to go later, we have to get out of this city and get as far away from it as we possibly can. There's no time to waste. The longer we're here, the more danger we're putting ourselves in. That smoke out there isn't just darkening the sky. It's poisoning the air we need to breathe to stay alive."

"I intend to stick with my original plan of getting out of here via the subway," Delia said.

"Would you mind if some of us came with you?" Caitlin asked. "The experience we've just been through is a stark reminder of just how much danger we're putting ourselves in by trying to navigate this city as lone individuals. Society has been plunged into chaos, anarchy rules the streets, and each of us is now going to be seen as a target—these monsters were the first to attempt to take advantage of us, and I guarantee they won't be the last. We're stronger and safer in a group."

"Anyone who wants to come with me can come with me," Delia said. "Caitlin's right—as women, we need strength in numbers. I'm not sure what my husband is going to want to do, but I have to get to him. You all are welcome to stay at our house for the next day or two until we all figure out what to do next. All I know for sure is that we have to get out of this city, and we have to do it soon."

"You said you live in the western suburbs, right?" Gina asked meekly.

"Yeah, that's right."

"I'll come with you then if that's okay," Gina said.

"Of course. Who else is coming?" Caitlin asked.

"I'm not even from this place," Kath said. "I was just visiting town with my friends, having a mini vacation. I don't know what happened to the rest of them…I was out on a Tinder date, and I was supposed to meet them at a club after the date. Well, the power went out at the restaurant halfway through dinner, then my jerk of a date just bailed on me, running away like a coward and leaving me on my own. Anyway, my point is, I don't have anywhere to go, so if it's okay, I'll go with the rest of you through the subway and figure something out when we're safely away from the city."

"Anna?" Caitlin asked.

Anna shrugged. "Look, I'll be honest, I'm probably much more of a lone wolf than the rest of you ladies, and if you haven't already figured it out by now, yeah, I'm a lesbian. I was trying to raid some stores for supplies when those two motherfuckers caught me, and my aim was to get out of this city on my own, get into the hills and the woods, and live off the land for a while. My apartment building was destroyed by one of those fucking missiles. I'm really glad I wasn't in it when it got taken out, but literally, everything I own was in that apartment, and now I'm officially homeless and penniless, and I have nothing but these clothes I'm wearing. Still, I figure I could make it in the wilderness. I grew up in a mountain town, and my dad raised me on his own, teaching me to hunt and fish and forage, all of that. I'm pretty independent and tough. But, uh, I guess you guys are right. We have to stick together, strength in numbers, at least until we get out of this hellscape of a city."

"We're happy to have you with us," Caitlin said. "The more of us there are, the safer we are." Finally, she turned to Jemma. "What about you, Jemma? Do you want to come with us?"

Still weeping, all Jemma could do while she tried to compose herself was to shrug, sniff, and wipe her teary eyes. Eventually, she spoke. "I don't have anything anymore," she said, her lower lip quivering, tears rolling down her cheeks. "My brother and I went out to get takeout for dinner for our family…then, the world ended. We were walking back home with our food when the power went out and those missiles started coming down. One of the missiles hit our apartment building…it was totally destroyed. Our parents are dead, all our things are destroyed, and now my brother's dead, too, thanks to those…those disgusting monsters," she cried, pointing with a trembling hand at the corpses on the floor. "I've got nothing…nothing. And nobody, and nowhere to go."

Caitlin took Jemma's hand and squeezed it gently. "Come with us then. We'll look after you. We'll protect you, won't we, girls?"

Everyone murmured their agreement with this sentiment, and Jemma beamed a tearful smile of gratitude at them.

"All right, it's settled then," Caitlin said. "We're all journeying through the subway together. What happens when we're out of the city? Well, we'll cross that bridge when we get there. We'd better gather whatever supplies we can because it's going to be a long walk, a difficult and dangerous one."

The women's handbags and other items the thugs had stolen from them were all stacked together in a pile in the apartment hallway. Caitlin found her pistol and the other items she'd had in her bag were all still there; the goons had clearly been waiting for a better time to go through their loot.

"God, I'm parched. I'm so damn thirsty I'd gladly drink dirty water from a puddle in the street," Anna muttered as she slung her backpack over her shoulders.

"There's fresh water in the toilet cistern," Caitlin said.

"I feel just as thirsty as Anna," Kath said, her face scrunching up with disgust, "but there's no way in hell I'm going to be drinking from the *toilet*, like a dog...ewww!"

"She's not talking about the toilet bowl, Barbie," Anna said sarcastically. "The cistern is the tank above the toilet, you know, where the water that flushes the toilet comes from. Sure, it ain't spring water from the fjords of fuckin' Norway or some shit, but it's clean enough. The only thing is, how long has it been sitting there?"

"There was no sign of stagnation," Caitlin said, "and there's a new roll of toilet paper in there. I think our two psychos were using that toilet, so I'm sure it's been flushed very recently. I'm pretty sure it's fresh. I'm going to drink some myself."

The others followed her and watched as she headed through to the bathroom, bent over the toilet cistern, and cupped her hands, dipping them into the water. As much as she logically knew the water was clean and fresh, there was a psychological barrier in her mind—like Kath had said, it did feel like drinking from a toilet, like a dog.

Caitlin pushed through this psychological barrier, though, and drank the water. "It tastes fine," she declared.

Everyone else drank their fill, and by the end of it, the cistern was almost empty.

"If anyone wants to go to the bathroom, now's the time," Caitlin said. "This is probably the last safe bathroom we're going to come across—next time you pee will probably be squatting over the subway tracks in the dark. Sorry to be so blunt, but that's how it's going to be. Obviously, we can't flush the toilet, but even so, it'll be way nicer than having to do it on the subway tracks."

One by one, each of the women emptied their bladders. Then, finally, they departed the apartment that had been their prison for well over twelve hours.

There was a subway stop a mere block from the entrance to the apartment building, and the women hurried down into the darkness, coughing and retching from the acrid smoke that filled the air. The smoke was so thick in the eerily silent streets that it was difficult to see even twenty or thirty yards.

The camping lantern from the apartment was the women's only light source. Caitlin had found two spare gas canisters for it in the kitchen of the apartment, though, so she wasn't worried about running out of light in the middle of the subway system.

She was, however, worried about Marvin. She knew if he was somehow able to make it back to land from the open sea, he would come straight back to the city to look for her, no matter how much danger that would put him in. And now, with no phones, no email, no means of communication at all, there was no way of sending him any sort of message to let him know where she was going.

Suddenly, however, she realized that there *was* a way. She unraveled the scarf around her neck—that colorful, unique scarf from their trip to Africa—and went over to Anna.

"Help me get to the subway station sign, please," she asked.

Anna and Kath helped Caitlin to get up to the sign that hung over the subway station entrance, and she wrapped her scarf around this sign. If Marvin came this way, which she hoped he somehow would, he would recognize the unique scarf right away, and he would hopefully understand that its presence here was a message, telling him that she had gone through the subway.

Caitlin whispered a prayer that, against all odds, Marvin would find her. Then, she and the others began their descent into the inky darkness of the underground tunnels.

26

Declan heard the gunfire in the nick of time, skidding to an abrupt halt before he rounded the corner and got caught in the middle. He saw Stanley fall, though, and he knew his friend had been hit.

Most other people would have frozen in shock in this situation and would have been unable to act or think. Declan's training and battle experience kicked in right away, though, and he hastily scanned his surroundings, searching for a position from which he could return fire. His primary concern was getting to his wounded friend, to get him out of the way of taking any more bullets—if he was still alive—but to do that, Declan needed to return fire at their attackers, to get them to take cover long enough for him to get to Stanley and drag him out of harm's way.

At that moment, Declan was taking cover behind the corner of a store. It was a printing supplies store—not exactly the sort of place someone would think of breaking into and not somewhere that would be raided in a situation like this one. Declan figured that if he could get into the building, he would be able to get a few good shots at their attackers from the door around the corner and hopefully drag Stanley inside.

The firing stopped, but Declan knew this was only because his attackers were waiting for him to pop his head out so they could resume shooting, hoping to take him out with a few well-placed shots.

The door on this side of the building was glass, so a single shot from his .45 shattered it, allowing him to gain access to the building. Keeping his head below the windows, in case his enemies were watching them, he rushed through the store to the back room, which had a much smaller, higher window. From there, he was able to get a look out at the street and the surroundings beyond it.

"Man, I hope you're okay, Stanley. I really hope you're okay," he murmured under his breath, dread coursing through him as he tried to come to terms with the horrible fact that his oldest and closest friend, a man as close to him as any blood brother, might be lying dead in the street at this very moment.

He peeked out of the little window in the back room and saw that their attackers were positioned on top of the railway bridge—there were four of them on the train tracks, hiding behind makeshift items of cover, with old oil drums and sacks they'd dragged into place. Their rifles were aimed at the corner, clearly waiting for Declan to step around it.

"An ambush for our intended ambush," Declan muttered.

Randall had to have anticipated that Stanley and Declan would try to ambush his vehicle at this crucial thoroughfare, and therefore he had set his own trap for them.

He ducked down, worried that if he stayed in the window too long, his enemies would spot him. He waited there, his mind racing, trying to figure out how he was going to rescue his friend. Bright sunlight was streaming through the window, its warm luminescence at odds with the dark mood.

Suddenly, an idea popped into Declan's mind. The sunlight…it could be just what he needed. He had noticed a large mirror on the wall when he first charged into the store, and now he was sure he could use this item against his enemies.

He raced back through the store, yanked the mirror off the wall, and then ran back to the side of the store facing the men. What he was about to do involved great risk, but if it worked, it would hopefully buy him just enough time to rescue his friend.

Declan gripped the large mirror, drew in a deep breath, and steeled his nerves. Then he jogged out right in front of one of the largest windows, in full view of the men on the bridge…and as they caught sight of him and swung around to aim their rifles at him, he angled the mirror to reflect the dazzling sunlight right into their eyes.

"Can't shoot me if you can't see me, you sons of bitches!" Declan yelled as a beam of blazing light from the large mirror burned into the men's eyes, temporarily blinding them.

They opened fire anyway, and Declan dropped the mirror as the bullets started flying. The windows all shattered under the hail of lead, but as they did, Declan charged out of them, running through the rain of flying glass shards, firing his pistol wildly at the men on the bridge.

They ducked behind their makeshift cover, and Declan saw Stanley lying flat on his back a few feet away, his arms sprawled out, his pistol lying on the street. There was no time to think, no time to check Stanley's vital signs. The men would surely open fire again in a mere second or two, so, with his strength boosted by the adrenalin surging through his system, Declan grabbed his limp friend's collar and dragged him along the sidewalk at a run, only barely managing to get safely around the corner by the time the bullets started flying again.

"Stanley, dammit, man, can you hear me? Are you there?" Declan asked, staring at Stanley's closed eyes.

He looked down over his friend's chest, expecting to see his jacket stained dark with blood...but although there was a bullet hole in the fabric in his chest area, there was no blood.

"What the hell?" Declan murmured.

Suddenly, Stanley let out a gasp, and his eyes fluttered open.

"You're alive!" Declan gasped. "Holy shit, man, you're alive!"

"My pistol, where is it?" Stanley asked.

"I couldn't get it. It's out in the street there," Declan answered. "Those sons of bitches have the bridge totally covered. I've only got one more clip left for my .45, and… shit, there it is."

The two men heard the sound of the Land Cruiser roaring closer. It was racing along the streets parallel to them, and from the sound of where it was, they both knew the window of opportunity was closed. The Land Cruiser, with Pablo inside it, would make it through the tunnel and be out on the open road in under a minute.

"No," Stanley gasped, his face falling. "No."

They heard the Land Cruiser racing through the tunnel, a sound followed by cheers and jeering from the men on top of the bridge. At that moment, they both knew even though they had tried their hardest, their mission had failed. A hostile, brutal, and merciless army would be coming to take over the Wagner family ranch… and neither of them knew if there was any way to stop it.

27

It didn't take long for Marvin, Bruce, and Hank to understand why they had seen refugees streaming out of the cities in such great numbers. After trekking deeper into the burning city—a journey made much easier by the gas masks they were now wearing—they saw a sight that was at once reassuring and worrying. Barricades were set up across the major streets that led to the heart of the city and what was—or, rather, what had once been, since it seemed to have been the primary target of the missile attack—the financial district, which was also where many of the city's government buildings had once been.

There were no improvised barricades set up by worried citizens trying to do what they could to defend their homes. Instead, they were well-constructed barricades made of coils of razor wire and sandbags, and they were manned by US Army and US National Guard servicemen.

Behind the barricades were large numbers of tanks and military transport vehicles, all of which were working perfectly and which appeared to have been stored somewhere that had been shielded from the effects of the EMP.

"What's this now?" Bruce asked as he and the others stopped in their tracks right after turning the corner onto the main street, staring at the barricade located around a hundred yards down the road.

A group of soldiers was patrolling the streets beyond the barricades, and as soon as they saw Marvin and his companions, two of them fired warning shots into the air.

"You three!" the sergeant in charge of the group roared, his voice muffled by the gas mask that he—like all the other soldiers—was wearing. "Get the hell out of here! The entire city is under martial law, and this is now a restricted zone!"

"My wife's in there somewhere!" Marvin yelled back, pointing beyond the barricades. "I'm not going anywhere until I have her with me!"

Of course, he and Caitlin weren't officially married, but he figured the statement would carry a lot more gravitas if he said they were.

"If your wife is still behind those barricades, that can only mean one thing, that she's one of the tens of thousands of charred corpses in there!" the sergeant yelled back. "If she was still alive when we set up our zones, then she'll be long gone. She will have joined the other refugees by now! Either way, civilian, your wife isn't there! Now move on! This is your last warning!"

"We'd better not mess with these guys," Bruce murmured nervously. "He did say the city's under martial law now, and that means he can shoot us if we piss him off."

"I know what it means," Marvin muttered angrily. "But I also know my wife is still in there somewhere."

"Are you deaf or just fucking suicidal, civilian?" the sergeant yelled. "You have five seconds to comply, or I *will* order my men to open fire on you! Now you have four seconds! Three seconds."

"All right, all right. We're going, we're going!" Bruce yelled. "Come on, guys, I don't want to have gone through all the insane shit we survived just to get killed by our own army. Marvin, we can figure out what to do about your girl when we're out of sight of that trigger-happy asshole."

"Please, Marvin, let's just go somewhere where they can't see us," Hank pleaded.

It made Marvin's blood boil to be bossed around and threatened by the sergeant, but he knew his companions were right. Without a word, he turned around and stalked off, with Bruce and Hank following hastily behind him.

"Don't even think of trying to come back here!" the sergeant yelled behind them. "If we see you three clowns anywhere near the restricted zone again, you *will* be shot on sight! You've been warned, you crazy sons of bitches. You've been warned!"

The three men hurried back around the corner, and then, just to be safe, they continued a few blocks farther, knowing that the soldiers would be expanding their patrols through these streets. When they finally found a safe place to shelter in—an empty convenience store, which had been thoroughly looted—they stopped for some food and drink and to figure out what to do next. They went down into the basement, which wasn't as badly affected by the smoke, and they took off their gas masks, relieved to be able to breathe without restriction for a while, even if the air was acrid and burned their airways.

"Man, I almost shit my pants when it seemed like those soldiers were gonna shoot us," Bruce muttered, shoveling a sandwich into his mouth.

"We'd better make sure we stay well away from them," Hank said. "I guess one good thing about seeing them there, though, is at least the government is doing something about this whole insane situation."

"Who knows," Bruce remarked with a shrug. "And they probably don't know much about all this bullshit, not if they let this whole thing happen in the first place. They should have known something was up way before this. It's like Pearl Harbor or 9/11 all over again, except the damage this time is way, way worse."

"Where do you think all those refugees have been told to go to?" Hank asked, biting into an apple. "I mean, I thought they were just kind of aimlessly fleeing the city, trying to get away from this place before it all goes up in flames. But it seems like there's some sort of plan in place for the refugees."

"I doubt there's any sort of serious plan," Marvin said, speaking for the first time in a while. "They've probably cooked up some half-baked idea just to get as many people as they can out of this place before it gets totally destroyed or before the smoke becomes toxic enough to start killing people within *hours* and *minutes* rather than years. Maybe they've put up a few tents in a field or something out in the city, but beyond that, I really don't think they have any idea what they're doing or the true scope of what they're dealing with."

"What are we going to do about your girlfriend, Marvin?" Hank asked. "I mean, if they say she isn't there, or if, God forbid, she's dead—"

"She's not dead," Marvin insisted stubbornly. "I know it sounds crazy, but I feel like I'd *know* if she was dead."

"All right, I get that, and, uh, I'm sure she's alive and well," Hank said, feeling a little nervous about challenging Marvin, who he still saw as an authority figure, "but even so, what are we gonna do? You heard that jerk of a soldier—they're gonna shoot us next time they catch us in the restricted zone."

"Yeah, man," Bruce added, "don't get me wrong, Hank and I, we both want to help you find Caitlin, but we also…we don't want to get killed. We've all risked our lives—I don't know how many times—since last night. If

I were a cat, I figure I'd be on my ninth life right now, you know what I'm saying?"

Marvin wanted to argue with them, and anger was undoubtedly rising within him, but he knew Bruce and Hank were right. It wasn't fair to ask them to risk their lives yet again after already having been through such danger.

"You guys are right," he said. "And I'm not going to ask you to risk your lives any longer. I'm going to give you detailed directions to my family's ranch and this signet ring of mine so you can prove to my parents that I sent you if I don't make it out of this city alive. But I can't give up searching for Caitlin, not until I either find her or find out what happened to her. I'm going to sneak into the restricted zone—I have to."

Bruce and Hank looked at each other. Neither knew what to say.

"It's okay, guys," Marvin said after a few moments, his words breaking the heavy silence. "I don't feel like you're letting me down or abandoning me. Not at all. I wouldn't dream of asking you to put your lives on the line any longer. This is where we part ways, my friends. I hope I'll see you both again at the ranch."

"How are you planning on getting into the restricted zone?" Hank asked, a guilty look on his face. "I mean, there were a lot of soldiers, and I'm guessing they've barricaded every street and alley, right down to the smallest access point."

"There is one form of access they may not have barricaded, at least not yet," Marvin said. "The subway."

"Yeah, that's true. It might be a way to get in," Hank said.

"Hey, uh, we could use the subway to get out of the city, too," Bruce said. "We could come with you for some of the way, Marvin. We've got enough camping lanterns between us for you to take some and for us to take some."

"Sure, I'd appreciate the company," Marvin said, smiling. Despite the grin on his lips, though, there was a weariness and a deep sadness in his eyes. Neither Bruce nor Hank could help but feel at least a little guilty about not going with him into the restricted zone.

They finished the rest of their meal in silence. When they were done, they slipped their masks on and headed back into the ruined city and the billowing clouds of toxic black smoke. The smoke was a double-edged sword for the three of them. At the same time, it provided cover from the patrolling bands of soldiers, but it also meant the soldiers were concealed from their eyes. There was a distinct possibility of having an unexpectedly close encounter with a bunch of nervous, trigger-happy troopers, a prospect none of them relished.

"There's a subway station two blocks that way," Bruce said, pointing up the street, "but there's another one four blocks that way," he continued, turning around. "That one is a little farther away, but it's much closer to the restricted zone. In fact, judging by where those soldiers have set up their barricades, I think it's right on the edge of the restricted zone. We should go to that one to get down into the subway, I think."

"That would definitely be a help for me," Marvin said.

"All right, let's head there then," Bruce said.

The three of them set off on their journey to the subway station, and the landscape they passed through on the way there was in utter ruin. This section of the city had been hit hard by the missiles, and many buildings, formerly proud skyscrapers, mighty towers of gleaming glass and steel, had been reduced to smoking piles of rubble. More ominous and disturbing than the sight of the destroyed buildings, though, were the occasional glimpses the men caught of stiff, bloodied arms and legs sticking out of the piles of broken debris. They all saw these corpses, and all of them were quietly wondering just how many thousands—tens of thousands, even—of people had been killed when the skyscrapers and apartment blocks had come crashing down, but none of them vocalized these things.

They walked cautiously along the streets strewn with rubble, abandoned vehicles, and more than a few twisted, torn-up corpses out in the open, their senses on full alert, always scanning the landscape for any sign of soldiers.

Finally, they turned a corner and found themselves on the street where the entrance to the subway station was.

"We're almost there," Bruce said. "You'd be able to see the entrance if it weren't for these thick clouds of smoke."

As soon as they got close enough to see the entrance, Marvin caught sight of something that stopped him dead in his tracks and rendered him speechless for a few moments.

"What is it, man?" Bruce asked, looking worried. "Have you spotted some soldiers or something?"

"No...what I'm looking at is something good, something great!" Marvin replied. If his face hadn't been encased in a gas mask, the others would have been able to see the enormous ear-to-ear grin he was beaming out. Hope was now flowing freely through his heart.

"Uh, I'm not following you, buddy," Bruce said, glancing over at Hank, who shook his head and shrugged with confusion.

Marvin pointed to the sign above the entrance to the subway station. Wrapped around part of the sign was an item of clothing he would have recognized anywhere. "You guys see that scarf?" he asked.

"Oh yeah, uh, that colorful African-looking thing?" Bruce asked. "What's that doing there, and why's it got you so excited?"

"It's Caitlin's!" Marvin said. "It's hers. I'm one hundred percent certain of it! I bought it for her when we visited Uganda a couple years ago."

"Holy shit!" Bruce gasped. "Are you sure it's the same one?"

"I'd recognize it anywhere. I could pick it out of a million other scarves," Marvin answered confidently. "Trust me, it's hers...and it's gotta be a sign she left there for me, a message telling me that she's alive and well and escaping the city through the subway system. See? It didn't just get blown there by the wind or something. It's been deliberately tied around the sign. Hank, I'll give you a boost. Get it off the sign, please."

Marvin helped Hank up, and the young man untied the scarf from the sign.

"There's no need for me to try to get into the restricted zone now," Marvin said, overflowing with hope and joy. "Caitlin will be heading out of the city, making her way to the ranch by whatever means she can. All we have to do now is catch up with her. Then we can get out of this hellhole and leave it behind us forever."

Somewhere in the distance, there was a deep, booming explosion that shook the ground beneath their feet with its violence. After that thunderous sound came bursts of automatic gunfire.

"You don't have to tell me twice," Bruce muttered, shook up by the ominous sound of the distant explosion and gunfire. "Let's get the hell out of here."

They lit a camping lantern and headed down into the darkness of the subway. Bruce went up ahead, lighting the way, carrying the lantern in his right hand and the riot shield in his left, while Marvin and Hank followed close behind him, their firearms at the ready. The silence was so intense down here that it felt like a thick, sinister fog, and the darkness was so dense it almost felt like a physical presence. For a long while, the men journeyed through that eerie zone, following the train tracks. The only sounds were their footsteps and the soft, insistent hissing of the flame in the lantern.

After what felt like many hours of trekking through the deep subterranean tunnels and seeing nothing but ink-black darkness, the men finally caught sight of something that both broke the monotony of the blackness and which sent rushes of both hope and worry surging through them: a single light up ahead, perhaps a mile down the tracks.

"Do you...do you think it's them?" Bruce asked.

"I hope it is...I pray it is," Marvin answered. "There's only one way to find out. Speed up the pace, boys, speed up the pace!"

As weary as the men were, the sight of the light injected fresh energy and vigor into their veins. They sped up, almost breaking into a jog, and the distance between their light and the light ahead grew steadily shorter.

When they got a little closer, they saw silhouettes of a number of figures around the light, and they knew those figures had to have seen their light, too.

This was confirmed when a voice from up ahead yelled out at them. "Stop right there! Don't come any closer! We've got three guns with us, we know how to use them, and I promise you, we will use them if you don't stop following us!"

Marvin smiled, for he recognized the voice at once. "Oh really? Well, I bet you're really grateful right now that I taught you how to shoot back at the Wagner ranch all those years ago, sweet thing!" he yelled back.

"Marvin? Oh my God, it can't be, it can't be," Caitlin gasped.

"Come here, sweet thing!" Marvin yelled. "It's me, all right! I've found you, praise the Lord, I've found you!"

They ran to each other through the darkness, with both the men and the women cheering them on, everyone overcome with a new sense of joy and elation, and in the middle of the inky shadows of the underground tunnels, Marvin and Caitlin leaped into each other's arms, finally reunited.

28

Stanley held up the stainless-steel hipflask, marveling at the deep dent the bullet had left in it.

"If you needed any proof that that thing really was a lucky charm, I think you've got it," Declan remarked.

"I still can't believe this thing stopped a bullet," Stanley said. "I mean, I knew it was tough but stop-a-bullet tough? I had no idea."

Declan chuckled. "They don't make 'em like they used to, right?" Then, however, the smile faded from his face, replaced by a far more severe and somber look. "What do we do now, old friend? We failed in our mission to take out Pablo, and now he's going to bring an army of cartel thugs to invade our land. We don't have the numbers or the firepower to stop them, not if as many of them as I think will come end up invading."

"You're right. We don't stand much of a chance if we

try to fight them with conventional tactics," Stanley said, slipping the dented hipflask back into his pocket. "But that doesn't mean there isn't any hope."

Before he could say anything else, Philip Pratt and his group of armed citizens came marching around the corner. "So, you two were involved in yet another gunfight, huh?" Pratt said sourly. "We heard that car racing out of town after all the shooting and figured your targets escaped."

"That they did, unfortunately," Stanley said, rubbing his chest. Although the hipflask had stopped the bullet, the impact had left a painful bruise.

"I'm sorry to hear that," Pratt said, "considering the consequences you said their escape would have for you and your family. But we let you pass, we let you go take care of what you needed to take care of, and now that that's over, you two owe us an explanation. It's time you started talking; we need you to tell us exactly what's going on here."

There was a murmur of general agreement from the group. Stanley sighed, realizing he needed to keep his end of the promise and tell them what was going on. "All right, listen up, y'all," he said. "Who's ever heard of an EMP?"

Stanley explained everything as clearly and as succinctly as he could. When he was finished talking, everyone simply stood there in stunned silence, devastated by the impact of his words, which were soaking into their minds like tissue paper absorbing ink.

"I'm sorry to be the bearer of bad news," Stanley continued, "probably the worst news you've ever heard, short of news of a loved one's death, but it is what it is. This is what's happened, this is the situation, and this is how things are going to be from now on. Whatever future y'all thought you had or hoped you would have is gone. It's gone forever, and like the world we knew, the world that's been destroyed, it probably won't be coming back, not in your lifetime, at least."

Again, there was no response but stunned silence.

Eventually, though, someone croaked out a question. "What are we gonna do?"

"I wish I could give you some good, solid advice," Stanley said. "But all you really can do is try your best to survive in a very challenging new world. If ever there was a time to come together as a community, it's now. There's no way anyone is getting through this on their own, no matter how tough they are, no matter what sort of survivalist skills they have...or think they have. Only the kindness and friendship of your fellow man will ensure your long-term survival in his strange and uncertain new world.

"But if you think about it, that's how it's been for thousands of years for people all over the world. It might seem impossible now, but countless generations have done it before you. Community, y'all, community...it's more important now than ever. And on that note, we need to leave this place and get back to our own community, to help them do whatever they can—

whatever *we* can—to prepare ourselves for what's coming."

Without another word, Stanley and Declan turned and strode away from the stunned group of men.

They left the town the same way they'd entered it—via the hiking trail—and they soon found their mountain bikes where they had left them. They rode back to the Land Rover in silence, and when they got to the vehicle, they found it still parked in the same place.

"What happened, guys?" Nathan asked, the look on his face both eager and anxious. "I heard a whole bunch of gunfire in town…was that you guys?"

"It was," Stanley answered. "And by some miracle, we're both okay. That's the good news. The bad news, however, is that our target escaped."

"Oh no," Nathan murmured. "So, that means…"

"That means that in a few weeks, or maybe even a week, or days if we're seriously unlucky," Declan said grimly, "a bunch of ruthless cartel thugs is going to be coming to our land to take it from us…and if that means killing every last person on the ranch, then that's exactly what they'll do."

"Let's get out of here," Stanley said glumly as he climbed into the passenger seat. "We need to get back to the ranch to start doing what we can to prepare for the inevitable invasion."

They drove back to the ranch in somber silence. Each of them was thinking about the upcoming battle against Austin Randall's forces, but in addition, both Stanley and

Declan were running on empty; both men had been up all night, had barely had any sleep or real rest, and had been through two short but intense firefights. Even though they were both preoccupied with thoughts about Randall's inevitable invasion, they both drifted off into a fitful slumber during the course of the long drive.

"Stanley, wake up, wake up!"

Stanley groaned and opened his eyes, blinking against the low, intense sunlight of the late afternoon sun as Nathan frantically shook him awake. He felt as if he had only just closed his eyes, but when he saw the familiar sight of his ranch gates ahead of him, he knew he'd been dozing for a few hours.

A range of emotions surged through him the moment he opened his eyes and realized why Nathan was trying so urgently to wake him. It wasn't his ranch gates that drew his immediate attention; instead, it was the person standing in front of those gates.

Austin Randall's was a face Stanley knew well—and it was probably the face he hated most in the world. He was a little younger than Stanley but not nearly as fit and healthy. A large man, his flabby jowls were covered by a dense, close-cropped beard of gray. Above this sat a crimson-lipped mouth with a cruel twist to it, and above his bulbous red nose were two close-set green eyes nestled beneath a pair of thick, caterpillar-like eyebrows. He kept his long, greasy gray hair slicked back from his face and tied behind his head in a ponytail.

In his youth, Randall had been a tall, strapping man,

but most of his muscle had faded into flab in his latter decades. Now he sported a barrel-like paunch that strained against the fabric of the black silk shirt he wore, tucked into the designer jeans that he was at least twenty years too old to be wearing.

He was flanked on each side by two of his thugs—all young, powerfully built men armed with AR-15 rifles. As for Randall, he carried his favorite weapon—a gold-plated Magnum .44 revolver—holstered on his hip.

As Nathan stopped the Land Rover in front of Randall and his men, who were blocking the way into the ranch, Randall flashed a crocodile's toothy smile at the vehicle's occupants. His goons, however, glared with naked menace and aggression at the three men.

"What are we going to do?" Nathan hissed.

"Wake Declan up and tell him to get ready to fight if necessary. In the meantime, let me handle this," Stanley answered. He quickly checked to see that his ammunition clip was full, and then he stepped out of the vehicle, locking eyes with his nemesis and gripping his pistol with quiet confidence.

"What the hell are you doing here, Randall?" Stanley asked, walking over to Randall, taking slow, deliberate steps.

"I think we both know why I'm here, Mr. Wagner," Randall said, smiling evilly.

"The answer is still 'not in a million years,' no matter what you're planning on offering me now," Stanley said.

"Now, get the hell out of here before you *really* piss me off."

One of the men whipped up his AR-15 and aimed it at Stanley's chest. "Take one more step, old man, and I'll air you out," he growled.

Randall reached over to his thug, placed his hand on the firearm's muzzle, and slowly lowered it, the crocodile smile on his face unwavering. "There's no need for that, Jose," he said to his henchman. "Is there, Mr. Wagner? We're going to talk like two civilized humans, aren't we?"

"I don't have a single thing to say to you, Randall," Stanley snarled.

"Oh, I think you're going to want to hear my latest offer," Randall said smugly. "Trust me, you're really going to want to hear it. And I promise you, it's going to be the last offer I ever make…cross my heart," he added with a mocking chuckle.

Stanley realized Randall wasn't going anywhere until he'd given him his offer, and he had no real choice but to hear him out. "Fine, go ahead, put your cards on the table," he muttered.

"I thought perhaps you might come around and see a little reason," Randall said. "My offer is this: in light of the new situation we find ourselves in, which is a very *unique* set of circumstances, I've decided to retract the last offer I gave you. I've come up with an entirely new offer, and this is it. You give me your land, all of it and everything that's on it…*for free*. In return, I let you and your family and whoever else is currently on the land walk away with their lives. I'm a reasonable man, so before you give me your usual stubborn bullshit, I'm going to give you forty-eight hours to consider my offer. Even if you tell me to go fuck myself right now—which I'm sure you will, with pride stinging at you like a swarm of wasps—I won't take that as your final answer."

Randall paused to let out a smug, self-satisfied chuckle before continuing, "I'll be back in forty-eight hours after that famous temper of yours has had time to cool off and you've had a good bit of time to think about this situation logically and rationally. At that time, you can give me your answer. You know what's coming, Wagner; I've outmaneuvered you this time.

"As we speak, my friend Pablo is off to gather an army of the most violent and brutal killers you can imagine. I'm sure you wouldn't want your beloved friends and family members to fall into the hands of such men, now, would you? Think about it, Wagner, think about it hard. If you know what's good for you, you'll walk away from this situation alive…with your fucking head still attached to your neck. Pablo's friends, you see, have a penchant for separating those two body parts from each other."

"You son of a bitch," Stanley growled through tightly clenched teeth, white-hot wrath blazing through him. "You evil, conniving—"

"That's not all, Wagner," Randall said coldly. "I want to clarify the terms of this deal for you, just to make sure you understand it perfectly. I don't want to leave out the small print, you know. I'm just getting it all out in the open, putting everything on the table for you so that you have all the details you need while you're mulling over the decision you have to make."

Randall waited for Stanley to respond, but he said nothing. Instead, he simply transfixed Randall with an icy glare.

Randall smiled his mirthless, mocking smile at Stanley, and then he continued, "I want you to know, Wagner, that if you choose the foolish option, if you choose to reject my very generous and compassionate offer...then *you will die*. Everyone you love will die. Every living thing on your land will be slaughtered, humans and animals, including your precious horses.

"Even if you change your mind later and surrender, it won't matter. If you put up a fight and then realize you have no hope of winning—which is, *absolutely and without a doubt*, the case—and then you try to run, to flee into the wilderness, we will hunt you down, every last one of you, and kill you. And we won't stop until every last one of you is dead, no matter how long it takes us to track you all down.

"When that EMP went off—and yeah, I know exactly what an EMP is and what it can do—it changed *everything*. I think you and I both understand that. There are no more cops or laws to save you anymore. The only law that matters now is the law of the jungle: kill or be killed.

"Do you understand what I'm telling you, Wagner? Do you? Is my message getting into that thick skull of yours? If you don't choose to take my offer in forty-eight hours, you're choosing *death* for you and everyone and everything else on your land. And that is a *guarantee*, Wagner, a personal *guarantee*. Think about that. And I mean, *really* think about it."

"Burn in hell, Randall," Stanley snarled.

Randall just chuckled and shook his head. "Forty-eight hours, Mr. Wagner…I'll be back here in forty-eight hours. I suggest you think long and hard about what you're going to say to me when you see me next." He turned to his goons. "Let's go, boys."

"Stick that pistol back in its holster and get back into the car, old man," one of the thugs growled at Stanley, "otherwise, we might just start our hostile takeover right now. And after we're done blowing you three away, we're gonna show all the women on your ranch a real good time…before we cut their throats."

Stanley fired a steely glare into the young man's cruel eyes, completely unintimidated by his brash bravado and his threats of future brutality. He kept his pistol in his hand, ignoring the goon's orders, and got back into the Land Rover.

"Drive in," he muttered to Nathan. "Ignore those pricks."

By this time, Declan had woken up, and he was ready to fight. "What did that evil piece of garbage say to you?" he asked.

"He gave me an ultimatum," Stanley said grimly. "Either we hand over the ranch and everything on it in forty-eight hours…or they kill us all."

29

As tired and hungry as Stanley and Declan were after their long mission, they knew they could neither rest nor eat, not after the ultimatum they had just been given. They called everyone on the ranch together for an urgent meeting. Once everyone was assembled in front of the porch of the main house, without sugar-coating anything, Stanley cut straight to the point. He gave everyone the bad news, telling them exactly what Randall had said to him and the chilling ultimatum he had issued.

"That's how it is," he said after explaining that their mission had failed and after delivering the grim news. "Now, I know I explained to everyone that there was a good chance you'd have to fight for this land and for your lives. Now I'm telling you that this is a certainty… and not only that but also the fact that it's going to be a fight that well…if I'm being completely honest, isn't a fight I'm entirely sure we can win. And it ain't only Randall's regular thugs we're going to be up against; it's a bunch of drug cartel killers. I'm sure I don't need to tell you anything about the reputation of these evil men that you don't already know; they kill for pleasure, for fun, and they have no qualms about torturing people in the most horrific ways."

"Randall has promised us that these monsters will hunt us down, as long and as far as it takes," Declan added. "They will hunt each and every one of us to the ends of the Earth if that's what it takes to exterminate every last one of us. This is what we're dealing with, people…this is the level of evil and hatred we're up against."

"Declan is telling you this not to frighten you," Stanley said, "but just to ensure that you understand exactly who it is you're up against. This isn't a conventional army you could consider surrendering to, who would hold you as captives under the code of the Geneva Convention if things go south. These are psychotic monsters who, in all likelihood, are frothing at the mouth at the prospect of torturing you to death. This is a fight in which no quarter will be asked and none given. I need you all to understand just how serious this is."

"These guys mean business," Declan said. "And that means that if we're gonna fight 'em, we have to be prepared to fight with everything we've got."

"*Are* you going to fight them, though?" someone asked. "I'm sorry, Stanley, I love this ranch as much as everyone, but to me, it sounds like suicide, pure suicide. From what you've told us, it doesn't sound like we have a snowball's hope in hell of winning this fight, and the consequences for us for losing the fight would be…well, I don't even want to imagine how terrible they'd be."

"You're right," Stanley said, sighing. "So, even though all of you have already promised me that you'd stay here and fight for this place, in light of this new development, I'm going to give each and every one of you the chance to reconsider that promise. I won't hold anything against anyone who changes their minds and decides to leave before the forty-eight-hour deadline is up."

"We're not going to put any pressure on anyone right now," Declan said. "You don't have to give us answers right away. We understand that it's difficult to make such a weighty decision on the spur of the moment or even after a night of thinking it over. We also get that it's tough to make that sort of decision in front of everyone. Nobody wants everyone to think of them as a coward or selfish—but I promise you, none of us will think those things about anyone who chooses to leave. Not after the change in the situation we've just told you all about. That evil son of a bitch has given us forty-eight hours to make our decision, and we're going to give all of you the same length of time to make yours."

"That's all we have to say to you, for now, my friends," Stanley said. "All you can do now is go and think long and hard about what you're going to be doing."

The crowd dispersed in silence, and Declan, Stanley,

and Eileen quietly watched them go. Each of them felt as if they had a million thoughts racing through their minds all at once. They stood on the porch for what felt like an eternity before Declan finally broke the silence.

"So, old friend, what are we going to do?"

"To tell you the truth, I don't actually know," Stanley said. "My heart has never once doubted that my choice should be to stand my ground and fight, to give my blood for this land, this land that's been in my family for all these generations. This land that's the only real hope of sustaining ourselves through the catastrophe that's befallen this country."

"I can sense a 'but' coming," Declan remarked.

"Yes," Stanley said, letting out a long sigh and shaking his head slowly. His eyes narrowed as his gaze shifted off to the forested hills in the distance. "Yes, there's definitely a 'but,' my friend. While my heart wants to stay, my head is telling me something else. We can't win a fight against Randall and his men, not with the army they're bringing in. Logically, that's the truth. That's the cold, hard truth.

"Maybe if my boy was here, and he had some good people who could shoot straight with him, it'd be a different story...but we don't know when or even if Marvin is going to make it back onto dry land from the ocean he's on, let alone whether he'll make it back here in the next forty-eight hours...or even if he'll make it back here at all."

When Stanley said this, Eileen let out a soft gasp. She

wrung her hands together, and tears filled her eyes, with a lone tear trickling its way down her cheek. Intense emotion balled in a tight knot in her throat, and all she could do was let out a plaintive gasp. "My boy...my Marvin."

Stanley reached over to her and took her hands in his. Eileen looked up at him with a quivering lower lip, her beautiful, dignified features twisted by a gut-wrenching worry and grief. They both understood that the odds of seeing their only child again were slim at best.

"I'm sorry, guys...I truly am," Declan said. Tears were burning at the corners of his eyes, too. While he had never had children of his own, Marvin had always been like a son to him.

"What I was trying to say," Stanley continued, "is that my head is telling me that to be brashly courageous and defiant now is to not only be suicidal, but it's also even worse...it's murderous, in a sense.

"I'm the unofficial leader of this group of people, this community we've got here on this ranch. And if I stay and fight, it'll certainly inspire at least a few of them to do the same, even if they may not really want to do that. But what is certain, what seems certain beyond a doubt, is that anyone who chooses to stay and fight is going to die. I'd be leading people to their deaths with no hope of achieving victory against the odds we're facing.

"I feel shame and disgust at myself at even considering handing everything over to that monster and slinking away with my tail between my legs...but it may be the rational thing to do, the responsible thing to do. Otherwise, I'm going to have the blood of good, innocent people on my hands…a lot of blood on my hands."

"I know what you mean," Declan said softly. "I was thinking exactly the same thing. If we had a few more people, a few more guns here, it'd be a different story. But the reality of the situation is…we don't. We're hopelessly outgunned and outnumbered here. This land doesn't have very many good defensible spots—even if we were to spend the next forty-eight hours putting up barricades and setting booby traps all over the place—and like you said, logically, we don't stand a chance against Randall's men. It'd end in death for all of us."

"So, is this it?" Stanley asked, his shoulders slumping, suddenly looking as if he had aged ten years in the space of ten minutes. "Is this the end for us? Has the decision already been made? Is there even any point in waiting forty-eight hours?"

"Yes, there is." This time it was Eileen who spoke, and despite tears rolling down her cheeks and her entire body shaking with emotion, fierce courage blazed brightly in her eyes. "What we need is a miracle of some sort, I understand that, and it's not likely to happen…but it just might. So don't tell that snake Randall anything just yet, Stan. Wait as long as you can—the whole forty-eight hours—and maybe, just maybe, God will send some sort of miracle to save us before the deadline is up."

30

"Thank you, guys, *so* much for the food," Kath said, shoveling another handful of peanuts into her mouth. "You don't know how insanely hungry we've all been feeling."

"And like I said, you're all welcome to stock up when we get to my place," Delia said after wolfing down a sandwich. "My husband is a bit of a prepper, I guess you could say. He's got enough food stashed in the basement to last years, literally. He told me not to tell anyone about it, but screw it. I wouldn't even be alive without you guys, and we're a team now. We need to look out for each other."

"Does your husband have weapons?" Marvin asked.

"Guns? Hell yeah," Delia answered with a grin. "He's got a whole room full of guns and ammo. He taught me how to shoot every type of gun he's got, too, from handguns to shotguns to machine guns."

"You mean semi-automatic rifles, modded to fire fully automatic, like someone might do with an AR-15?" Marvin asked.

"Oh, he's got a few modded AR-15s," Delia said, her grin broadening. "But despite how I must look to you—you know, some Asian-American big city lawyer with painted nails and makeup and high heels—I know way more about guns than most people, thanks to my husband. When I say machine gun, I mean *machine gun*. He's got an M60 general purpose machine gun, a Browning M2 Aircraft heavy machine gun, and plenty of ammo for both."

"Holy shit," Marvin murmured, letting out a low whistle. "Your husband isn't messing around when it comes to firepower. We've got a few AR-15s on our ranch, and I've got two pistols modded for high-capacity magazines in our apartment—"

"What used to be our apartment," Caitlin said sadly. "I'm pretty sure it's been totally destroyed by now."

"Yeah, but anyway, what I was saying is that I have—I had—a good few guns myself," Marvin continued, "but nothing like the arsenal your husband has, Delia. Do you think he'd be willing to part with one or two of them? Not the machine guns, of course, but maybe even just one of those AR-15s? It would make a huge difference to us, to our chances of getting back to my family's ranch. I mean, right now, all we've got is a shotgun with a few shells and a pistol with a single clip of ammo. I don't like how our odds are looking with these as our only weapons."

"Billy can be a little, um, possessive when it comes to his weapons," Delia said, "but I'll have a word with him. I'm sure when he finds out that Caitlin and the rest of my new friends saved my life, he'll become a lot more generous than he usually is. Even though he can be a bit of a jerk sometimes, he truly and deeply loves me."

"All right, well, please, if you could, have a word with him when you get to your place," Marvin said.

"Speaking of that, how far are we?" Anna asked. "It feels like we've been traveling through these damn subway tunnels for literal *days*, never mind hours. It's just pitch-black permanently down here. There's no way of telling how much time has passed, whether it's day or night."

"Judging by the last station, we walked past," Delia said, "we've got another two or three miles to go before we get out of the subway, then another four miles of walking aboveground after that, so we're not exactly close, but we're not super far, either."

"God, I hope we get there soon," Kath muttered. "My legs and feet are killing me."

"As for how long we've been down here, and whether it's day or night, I can tell you the time," Bruce said. "I've got my dad's old wind-up watch, see? That's some old-school technology that's about as EMP-proof as you can get," he added with a chuckle. "Let me look in the light quick."

He checked his vintage wristwatch in the light of the camping lantern. "Looks like it's almost eight o'clock in the evening. We've been walking a long, long time, and we've still got a few hours to go."

"How long will it take us to get back to the ranch, Marvin?" Caitlin asked. "I know it's a long drive, but I have no idea how to translate the driving time to the time it'd take on foot."

"Oh boy," Marvin said. "I don't even want to begin to think of how long it'd take to walk there. At least a week, if we walked for around twelve hours a day. Probably more, something like ten days. I'm hoping it's not going to come down to walking it, though. If we're super lucky, we can find a vehicle that's still working, but of course, the odds of that are like winning the lottery. No, instead, I'm hoping we can get our hands on some good bicycles. I think that's a more realistic hope. That'd cut the trip down to maybe five days. It'd also be easier for us in the sense that we could strap a lot of our provisions and equipment to the bikes instead of having to carry it all in backpacks."

"Man, that sounds like a real marathon," Bruce grumbled, sighing. "And I thought what we'd already done up to this point was insane. Sheesh, I knew I needed to lose some weight, but at this rate, I will have lost half my damn bodyweight by the time we get to that ranch of yours, Marv! And I'll probably have the knees of a ninety-year-old by then."

"Hey, Marvin," Hank said, dusting his hands off after

finishing the last few cookies from a bag they had all shared, "remember you told me about your neighbor? The guy who's like, a major heroin producer. Do you think he's gonna make a move on your family's ranch anytime soon?"

"I have no doubt that Randall will try something," Marvin said, "but I'm not too worried about him making any moves just yet. My parents and the people who work on the ranch will be able to hold off Randall's men for a long time—easily for long enough to us to get there and provide them with the extra manpower and firepower they'll need in order to get him to permanently back off. Randall is cunning, I'll give him that, but I very much doubt he ever had any idea that anything like this EMP could ever happen. He doesn't grow any crops on his land, only poppies for heroin, and I doubt he's got more than a couple weeks' food and supplies on his ranch. His goons are nothing more than hired thugs; there's no real loyalty among them, and when they see the food is running out, they'll bail on him."

"Are you sure your parents and their workers will be able to hold him off?" Hank asked. "No offense, but your parents have gotta be pretty old."

Marvin chuckled. "No offense taken, kid. They are pretty old, but you know the saying, 'tough as nails'? That's my dad. He's also a former Navy SEAL, and so is his best buddy, Uncle Declan, who lives on the plot of land next to ours. He was an Army scout. Between the two of them, I'm pretty sure they could handle whatever Randall's dumb goons throw at them."

"We should still try to get there as soon as we can, of course," Caitlin added. "I know your parents are tough, Marvin, but the thought of them having to defend themselves against that sick drug dealer and his henchmen makes me very nervous."

"Of course, sweet thing, of course," Marvin said. "I'm not going to hang around; as soon as we're able to get going toward the ranch, I intend to do just that. Let's hope we can find some bicycles so the journey will be around five days instead of ten."

By that point, everyone had finished eating, so they picked up their bags, put on their backpacks, and resumed their journey through the subway tunnels. The rest of the trek through the dark tunnels was long and tiring but mercifully uneventful, except for the occasional aboveground explosion, which would rattle and shake the walls and ceiling of the subway with alarming violence.

Finally, when everyone's legs were feeling leaden, their feet and joints were aching, and they were so beset with exhaustion and fatigue that they didn't feel as if they could take another step, they reached the end of the subway line.

"This is it, people," Delia announced, navigating her way past an abandoned train and then climbing off the train tracks onto the subway platform. "This is as far west as the line goes. We're into the suburbs now."

"How much farther is your place?" Kath asked, grimacing. "My feet feel like they've been fed through a meatgrinder."

Everyone murmured their agreement with this sentiment.

"There are still around four miles to go, I'm afraid to say," Delia said. "Believe me, I wish it were closer, but that's the truth of the matter. There's still a lot of walking ahead of us. I think we should all take a rest here, though. There are plenty of benches in the subway station."

Nobody was about to argue with this idea, so they spread out through the subway station—staying close enough that they could see each other's lamps, of course, and found benches to sit or lie down on and rest their aching legs and feet.

A lot of people dozed off, quickly falling asleep, but Marvin made sure he stayed awake; someone had to keep watch, for even down here, there was always the possibility of some sort of threat surfacing. He borrowed Bruce's watch to keep track of time, and when it got close to midnight, he began to wake the others. He figured it would be safer to complete the final four miles of the trek under cover of darkness rather than out in the light of day. One never knew who was watching or what sort of opportunistic scumbags were out there searching for victims to prey on.

Everyone grumbled and complained at having to get up and continue walking, but their complaints were short-lived. They all knew the reasoning behind the need to get moving was sound.

"Stay alert," Marvin cautioned as they emerged from the subway station onto the streets. "If you catch a hint of anything even vaguely suspicious, tell me right away. Delia, lead the way. Let's go. Also, don't talk, walk as quietly as you can, and don't do anything that might draw anyone's attention. Eyes and ears open, mouths closed, everyone, firearms at the ready."

They trudged wearily through the dark, deserted streets for the next couple of hours. The entire eastern sky was a canvas of dirty reds and grubby oranges, light from the countless fires of the burning city. Even though the air out here was cleaner than the smoke-thick air inside the city, the smell of burning was heavy on the night breeze.

Abandoned cars littered the streets. The houses were mostly dark, and some had very clearly been hastily vacated, with the doors left wide open, but in a few of them, the walkers could see lamps, lanterns, candles, and fires burning, with silhouettes of frightened figures crouched over these modest light sources. While most people had fled, a few seemed to have chosen to stay.

The group trekked on through the night, each weary step feeling more leaden and painful than the last, with all of them feeling as if they'd just run several marathons back to back. By the time they reached the final stretch of the journey—the long cul-de-sac at the end of which was Delia's house, which bordered some woods—they were all so dead on their feet that not even a live hand grenade being tossed into their midst could have spurred any strength into their weary, aching limbs. Every last one of them felt like a zombie.

"Almost...there," Delia groaned. "The house...at the end."

The final hundred yards felt like a mile up a steep mountain, but finally, they reached Delia's house. Her husband was on the porch, sitting there with a bullet-proof vest strapped on and an AR-15 laying across his lap. He was wide awake, kept alert by strong coffee, which he'd been brewing every hour on a gas stove on his porch.

A muscular, rugged-looking man in his late twenties with long red hair and a bushy red beard, Billy set down his rifle and raced over to Delia the moment he saw her, sweeping her up in his tattooed arms and embracing her tightly.

Delia briefly introduced him to the others and told him about what had happened, and he was grateful to them for what they had done for his beloved wife. In addition, he was happy for everyone to sleep in their large and spacious house.

The next morning, after a long, restful night of sleep, Marvin was up before almost anyone else. His feet, legs, and joints still ached from the long trek the previous night, but overall, he was feeling a lot better.

Billy was also up early and offered Marvin some coffee, which he gratefully accepted. The two of them soon got to talking, and the conversation inevitably turned to the EMP. As it turned out, Billy knew a thing or two about such things, being a prepper, although an EMP attack was never something he had considered a likely possibility. Instead, he had mostly been prepping for a deadly pandemic, a total economic collapse, or a weather-related catastrophe.

"At least you have some preparation done," Marvin said. "And I'm betting that much of what you've done will get you through what's coming, even if your preps haven't been EMP-specific. Delia mentioned that you had a whole lotta food…and a lot of guns."

Billy chuckled and grinned. "I do love my guns, always have," he said. "It was only logical for me to start stockpiling guns and ammo a few years back when I first got into prepping. A man can never have too many guns, right? Haha. I'd say the only thing I like more than guns are my bikes."

This piqued Marvin's interest. "Bikes, huh?" he asked. "What kind of bikes are we talking about?"

"Harleys, mostly," Billy answered. "A few Indians, too. American cruisers; that's my thing. Are you into bikes, too?"

"I've been riding dirt bikes since I was a kid," Marvin answered, "but I never rode anything on the street. I do like Harleys, though. I always thought I'd get one when I finally settled down."

"I've got a whole collection in my garage if you'd like to take a look," Billy said. "I've got at least a dozen bikes in there. All of them vintage, too—classic cruisers from the fifties all the way through to the late seventies."

"Damn," Marvin murmured, his interest now totally focused on every syllable Billy was uttering. "Are all your bikes from those decades?"

"Yep!" Billy answered. "And I restored every one of 'em to perfect showroom condition. A labor of love, man, a real labor of love. Come on, follow me. I'll show you my bikes."

Now Marvin was extremely eager to check out Billy's collection of motorcycles. It sounded as if every one of the bikes would have been completely unaffected by the EMP if they were indeed all of the vintage Billy said they were. Perhaps, Marvin thought, they wouldn't have to undertake a grueling multi-day bicycle trek to his family ranch. Perhaps, if Billy were generous enough, they could get there a lot faster.

When Marvin stepped into Billy's large, almost barn-like garage, it was like stepping into a motorcycle museum. There were over a dozen cruisers, each gleaming in the morning light, shining with a dazzling glow from being lovingly waxed and polished.

"Tell me, Billy," Marvin said, his eyes locked on the spellbinding sight of the spotless vintage motorcycles, "do you have gasoline stockpiled here?"

"I've got barrels and barrels of it for my truck," Billy said, shaking his head sadly and sighing, "which is now as dead and as useless as every other abandoned vehicle strewn across these streets. And now, looking at my bikes and thinking about the fact that I'll never hear the beautiful rumbling thunder of their motors again, it breaks my heart, man, it breaks my heart. All I can do with these things now is look at 'em."

Marvin smiled to himself; clearly, Billy didn't know quite as much about EMPs and vintage vehicles as he did. "Do you mind if I take a closer look at some of your machines?" he asked.

"Sure, knock yourself out."

Marvin walked over to the closest bike, a gorgeous 1976 Harley Davidson Sportster. Like most of the bikes in the garage, the keys were in the ignition. Marvin turned the key, then thumbed the starter. The motor roared to life, filling the garage with its booming rumble.

Billy's eyes almost popped out of their sockets. "How the hell did you do that?" he gasped. "It's...it's *working!* The motor's running!"

"All of these bikes will still work despite the EMP," Marvin said. "Now, speaking of these bikes...I have a proposal for you."

31

The past two days had been two of the most agonizing and depressing days of Stanley's life. He and Declan had spent hours debating over what to do and had trekked back and forth across the ranch, trying to devise a plan to set up effective defenses with their small numbers. But no matter what plan they came up with, the result was the same. There was simply no way the defenders would be able to hold out against the overwhelming numbers and superior firepower of Randall's thugs and their drug cartel allies.

Things were made even more difficult by the fact that at least half of the workers had come to Stanley and told him that they intended to leave rather than stay and fight. He understood completely, of course—with the change in circumstances, the decision to stay and fight was essentially a decision to die.

Even those who courageously had said that they

would stay and fight until the end, though, were showing signs of changing their minds as the hands of the clock moved inexorably toward the hour of Randall's deadline.

Despite the situation looking increasingly hopeless, Stanley had not given in to fear and despair, and he and Declan had spent the final few hours before the deadline setting up defensive barricades, resolving to fight to the bitter end and take down as many of the invaders as they could before inevitably being overwhelmed and killed.

That was, until the final hour. Eileen, who had been a staunch supporter of staying and fighting, changed her mind—not out of a sense of fear but rather of responsibility.

"These people need a leader, Stan," she said to Stanley as he was dragging some sandbags into place for one of his barricades. "If you, me, and Declan all die here—as we surely will when Randall's men invade—we'll be leaving the rest of our people to wander the wilderness aimlessly. I know this isn't what you want to hear, but we'll be inadvertently condemning many of them—these good, honest people who are like family to us—to a slow, horrible death in the wilderness. Especially when winter comes.

"As much as it makes me sick to my stomach to even think about handing over everything we've worked for our whole lives to that monster Randall, I think…and I can't believe I'm actually saying this…but I think we need to do it. Not for our sake, but for the sake of our friends and our son. When—if he eventually gets here, if we've all been killed by Randall's goons, you can bet they'll do the same to Marvin, Caitlin, and whoever else they bring with them. If we walk away and live to fight another day, we can at least wait for them and make sure they don't walk into whatever ambush is inevitably going to be set up for them. We need to lead our people now and help them survive in this new world we've found ourselves in. It pains me to say it, but I think we should save ourselves and give up the ranch."

Stanley let out a long sigh as if his entire being was deflating, and he glanced across at Declan. Declan was also looking utterly defeated, and he nodded grimly. He agreed with what Eileen was saying.

Feeling as if his heart was being ripped from his chest, Stanley nodded. "You're right," he said, and it seemed as if some other entity had taken control of his body and was doing the speaking for him. "I can't believe I'm saying this…doing this…but you're right. For everyone else's sake, we have to give it all up."

"We'd better go pack every item of canned and dehydrated food we've got into saddlebags," Declan said. "And make sure everyone's got two horses and as many firearms and ammo as they can carry. We can get the horses off the land without Randall's goons noticing if we go via the creek. The Land Rover, though…there's no way we can get that out of here without him seeing, and I suspect he's not going to allow us to get away with that."

"Yeah," Stanley said grimly. "I'll get everyone together

and tell them about the new plan. You two, get packing… we don't have much time."

Stanley called everyone together and delegated a specific task to each person. Then he got busy himself, packing with the frenetic and desperate energy of a madman while the final sands of the hourglass trickled from the top chamber to the bottom.

The time passed unbelievably quickly, and it seemed like barely two minutes had gone by when Nathan came running into the main house, breathless and drenched in sweat. His eyes were wide, and his chest was heaving.

"What is it?" Stanley asked gruffly, already knowing the answer to this question.

"Randall's at the gates with his men," Nathan answered breathlessly. "I told him I'd go call you, but I didn't tell him what answer we're gonna give him."

"Does he have the cartel people with him or just his regular thugs?"

"I didn't see any extra men with him," Nathan answered. "Only the same assholes I've seen before."

This gave Stanley a glimmer of hope in this dark hour. Against Randall's regular henchmen, he and his people certainly would be able to defend the ranch. Despite this brief burst of hope, though, Stanley's heart sank again. It was simply a matter of time before the cartel people arrived—it could be hours or days, but they would be coming. And when they arrived, all hope of defending this land would be lost.

"I'll go speak to him now," Stanley said softly. He set

down his bags, and he and Nathan trudged with weary, hopeless steps down the long driveway to the gates.

It was the longest mile Stanley felt he had ever walked, and each leaden step he took was filled with an increasingly crushing sense of despair, getting to the point where he felt almost completely unable to continue and had to force his body to comply.

When they got to the gates, they saw Randall and his thugs waiting for them. Randall had every man who worked for him with him—around a dozen men in total. Each of them was wearing a bulletproof vest and carrying an AR-15 with multiple sidearms. Despite the men's intimidating appearances, Stanley knew he and his people would be able to defend the ranch against them…as long as the cartel army didn't show up to aid them.

"I hope you've come to your senses, Wagner," Randall said coldly as Stanley and Nathan approached. "And before you say anything, I know what you're thinking—where are my cartel men? Don't let the fact that they're not here yet trick you into any false sense of hope. They're on their way; I've got riders on dirt bikes traveling back and forth between here and the advancing force, checking their progress, and they'll be here in two days, three at the most. If you don't believe me, you're welcome to send one of your people with my bike riders so they can see the force with their own eyes. That scrawny lil' piece of shit there can go with one of my boys," he said, pointing at Nathan. "Or, hell, you can go yourself, Wagner. You're not too old to ride a dirt bike, are you?"

Stanley had always been good at reading people—he'd been a great poker player—and he could tell that this was no bluff. Randall was telling the truth, and although the cartel people weren't here right now, they were on their way, and only a miracle could stop them.

"I don't need to go with your people," Stanley said. "I've made my decision."

Randall chuckled coldly and humorlessly. "Well, go on, Wagner, tell me what it is. We're all waiting in suspense here."

Stanley drew in a deep breath, trying to find the strength to utter the words he didn't want to say that he couldn't believe he was about to say. But just as he was about to speak, he paused. There was a strange sound in the distance. It was like the rumble of thunder, but there were no storm clouds in the sky, which was clear and blue overhead. Also, while it was faint, it was growing steadily louder.

Stanley's face-reading skills came into play again when he scrutinized Randall's expression when the big man noticed the sound. An expression of complete surprise, shock almost, came over his face for a split second before he disguised this look with a put-on sense of false confidence. The utter surprise had been fleeting, and it had been displayed almost too rapidly to notice, but Stanley had definitely seen it, and he was sure he knew what it meant. The sound, which they were now all aware was that of a large group of motorcycles approaching, was not the sound of Randall's cartel people coming here.

"Well, it looks like my friends might be arriving a little sooner than expected," Randall said smugly, fingering the grips of his gold-plated Magnum .44 in its holster on his hip. "Hopefully, that drives home the hopelessness of your situation, Wagner. Come on, you know what to do. Tell me the ranch is mine—save the lives of your family and friends and your own worthless life."

For the first time in forty-eight hours, a smile broke across Stanley's face. He chuckled softly and shook his head.

Fury and a naked hatred burned on Randall's face. "You think this is a joke, Wagner? You and everyone you care about are about to be annihilated! Don't tell me you're actually going to make the dumbest, most suicidal choice possible. Surely you're not that much of a pigheaded idiot?"

"Those bikes that are coming this way," Stanley said, "they're not your cartel buddies."

"You fucking moron," Randall growled. "Who the fuck else would they be? Quit stalling for time and give me your answer."

"You've waited forty-eight hours," Stanley said, folding his arms defiantly across his chest. "What's a few more minutes? I want to see your cartel boys in the flesh before I hand over my land, house, horses, and everything I've worked for my whole life to a steaming turd like you. I mean, if you're so sure those bikers are your buddies, you'd be perfectly happy to wait until they get here. Then I'd see your overwhelming force of numbers, and I'd be forced to admit that the only thing I can logically do is to hand everything over to you…right?"

Randall chuckled again, but there was only emptiness in his hollow laughter and doubt in his greedy eyes. He realized he had been outmaneuvered here, and all he could do was wait to see who was approaching. "Fine, Wagner, we'll wait. I can wait a couple more minutes for your land. I mean, I know you're going to make the right decision…the only decision you can logically make."

All of them waited in tense silence as the motorcycles came down the road…and when the first of them rounded the final corner before the gates and Stanley, and the others caught sight of him, hope exploded like a glorious display of fireworks in the night sky within Stanley's chest.

It was Marvin, riding a vintage Harley, and he was not alone. A large group of people was with him, and all of them were armed. One bike was even pulling a trailer with two machine guns on it.

"This is my decision, you piece of shit," Stanley said to Randall, smiling triumphantly. "You can have my land… over my dead body. You want it? Just *try to* take it, you son of a bitch…just *try*."

32

"I really do appreciate you letting us live here, Mr. Wagner," Billy said, enthusiastically shaking hands with Stanley. "And like I said, I've got a whole lot more stuff locked away in my house that we can bring up here if we can take that Land Rover of yours and a horse trailer. Tons and tons more ammo, gasoline, non-perishable food, and medical supplies. They're all locked away in my secret safe next to my basement, so the supplies should be safe from the inevitable raiders and looters."

"Like I said to the people who are already here, son," Stanley said, "anyone who's willing to not only work this land but also defend it with their lives if necessary is welcome here."

"We are willing to fight to the end for this land of yours, sir," Billy said solemnly. "Your son convinced us that this land was the only hope of long-term survival in this crazy new world in which we've found ourselves. My wife, Delia, and I would have lasted a few months in the suburbs, I know much…but beyond that, I wasn't prepared for a truly long-term plan, I have to admit. We would eventually have starved to death or been killed by looters or raiders, like everyone else in the city and the suburbs around it."

"It's a deal that's mutually beneficial," Stanley said, smiling. "Without the extra guns and ammo you brought —and the numbers, too—we wouldn't have been able to defend this land against those ready to take it by force. And let's not forget the motorcycles, which allowed you and my son and the others to get here in the nick of time. We're eternally grateful to you and to everyone else who's come to fight. Now, speaking of that, we need to start setting up our defensive positions. I don't know how soon those cartel scumbags are going to get here, but I suspect it'll be sooner than any of us would like."

In preparation for the battle to come, Stanley, Declan, Marvin, and Billy had sat down and made extensive plans for the defense of the ranch. The arrival of the group on motorcycles had greatly swelled the numbers on the ranch; in addition to Marvin and Caitlin, Billy and Delia, and Bruce and Hank, most of the women from the group had chosen to come along as well. Anna was here, as were Jemma and Gina, who had discovered that her family had abandoned their house and vanished when Billy had driven her through the suburbs on his motorcycle to her home. Only Kath had chosen to go her own way, and she had headed off to join the vast throng of refugees streaming out of the city toward some unknown destination.

Those who knew how to shoot and had shown promise when shown how to shoot were given further training by the former Navy SEALs. Those who couldn't shoot and who wouldn't have been much use as fighters nonetheless had valuable roles to play. Viewing platforms had been erected in the tops of the tallest trees, and the undergrowth in the woods surrounding the ranch had been cleared so the people in these makeshift lookout towers could see an enemy force approaching when they were miles away so that an alarm could be raised.

In addition to being lookouts, other people were in charge of a first-aid station, and others were food, water, and ammo runners. Everyone, no matter whether man or woman, young or old, had been involved in heavy manual labor from sunrise to sunset and beyond. A network of narrow but four-foot-deep trenches had been dug across the ranch, allowing the defenders to move rapidly from place to place without being exposed to enemy fire. Countless grain sacks had been filled with the soil from these trenches, and these sandbags served as valuable barriers that could stop enemy bullets.

Nobody was sure when Austin Randall would launch his attack—only that it was coming, and they used every precious moment to its fullest when it came to preparations. In addition to the lookout towers in the trees,

Declan, Stanley, and Marvin regularly went on scouting missions on horseback through the depths of the woods.

They couldn't get too close to Randall's land because he had his own patrols through the woods there, and on a few occasions, they spotted the men on horseback and opened fire on them. However, they were able to roam freely through the rest of the woods and beyond. It seemed that Randall's men were—for the moment, at least—content to stay within the boundaries of his land until their army arrived.

And sure enough, the army did arrive. Declan was scouting through the woods late one afternoon when he heard a sound that he hadn't heard for a while, a sound that was certainly out of place in comparison to the sounds of the forest: the rumble of car motors.

He spurred his horse and galloped through the forest to a vantage point that looked out from a hilltop over the network of hills and valleys beyond and the long road that snaked a serpentine passage through this landscape. On that road, gleaming in the late afternoon sunlight, he saw a convoy of vehicles. They could only be the cartel members coming to join Austin Randall and his men.

He turned and galloped back to the ranch, pushing the weary horse as hard as it could go until it was half-dead. Leaving the exhausted horse to quench its thirst at one of the troughs, he sprinted to the main house. When Stanley saw the expression on his old friend's face, he knew what Declan was going to say long before he opened his mouth.

"They're coming, aren't they?" Stanley asked.

"They are…a lot of 'em. Way more than I thought there'd be," Declan answered grimly.

"Nobody said this would be easy," Stanley said.

"I never expected it would be," Declan answered, "but I never expected there to be so many of the bastards, either. I counted at least fifteen cars, all of them full."

"We have to estimate high and guess that there are five men per car. That's seventy-five men added to Randall's dozen. We're getting close to a hundred enemy fighters here," Stanley said.

"Good thing Billy brought those machine guns," Declan said. "We're gonna need 'em and all the ammo we can get our hands on."

"That's right," Stanley said. "All the ammo we can get and more."

Both men fell silent for a while as they thought deeply about the situation. Up to this point, both men had been fairly confident about their chances against the invaders since their own numbers and firepower had been bolstered so well by the arrival of Marvin and the others. Now, however, that confidence was faltering. They had both known that Pablo would bring a large number of guys with him, but neither of them had guessed that there would be quite so many.

"We have to make the first move," Stanley said. "It's our only hope of evening the odds. You said you saw the cars from the old lookout point near Eagle Rock, right?"

"That's right," Declan said.

"That means the cars would still need to drive around fifteen miles to get to Randall's place. If we saddle up some horses right now, we can cut through the woods and ambush the cavalcade before it gets to Randall. Hit and run guerilla tactics; that's what we're going to have to do. Even if we only take out a handful of enemy men right now, it'll still put a dent in their numbers."

"I'll round up Marvin, Hank, and Billy," Declan said. "You, Eileen, and Caitlin get the horses ready."

The five of them conducted two rapid hit-and-run attacks on the cavalcade of 1960s and 70s muscle cars, opening fire on them from concealed positions with their AR-15 rifles and then hopping on horseback and galloping away before the cartel people could mount a counterattack. They managed to kill a few of the cartel thugs, enough to put a small dent in the enemy's numbers. Even so, they knew they were still heavily outnumbered.

That night, the mood on the ranch was tense. The horses and other livestock were taken to an underground bunker so they wouldn't be caught in any crossfire. Everyone was issued a bulletproof vest, whether frontline fighters or runners, and watch patrols were tripled in frequency. Stanley suspected that Randall and his cartel allies would not waste any time when it came to attacking and that they would attack under cover of darkness…and he was right.

The two teenage girls, Gina and Jemma, were positioned in the lookout towers in the treetops. Both girls had sharp eyesight, and both were using binoculars. Jemma caught sight of movement in the trees to the north of the ranch, and when she looked closer with her binoculars, she saw that there were men with guns creeping through the darkness...a lot of men.

"Attack!" she yelled, her heart racing, grabbing one of the makeshift bullhorns they had fashioned out of scrap plastic. "They're attacking from the north! We're under attack!"

"Light 'em up!" Stanley yelled.

His command didn't mean open fire—not yet. Instead, he was calling out a command to Billy, Hank, and Marvin, all of whom were carrying crossbows and lighters in addition to their AR-15s. The crossbows weren't for attacking the enemy soldiers. Each crossbow bolt tip was dipped in homemade napalm, fashioned from Styrofoam, gasoline, and a few other substances. The men set the tips on fire with their lighters. Now, with these makeshift fire arrows burning, each of them ran to the northern front and picked his target: one of the many large piles of dry leaves and branches that had been set up along what would be the front lines of the battle.

They shot their fire arrows into these piles, which had been doused with gasoline and oil, and four huge bonfires immediately roared to life, illuminating the entire northern front in orange light.

The attackers, who had thought they would be able to get right up to the buildings under cover of darkness, were caught in the open, with barely any cover. And now Stanley and Declan, who were manning the machine guns, began their deadly work, opening fire on their enemies and strafing them with relentless machine gun fire.

There were over seventy attackers, but the hammering machine guns, from which the cartel men could neither escape nor take cover, cut that number in half in mere seconds. And while the rearmost of the thugs were running into the trees behind them to find cover from the ceaseless, thundering storm of lead scything through them, cutting men down left, right, and center, they found no respite or shelter in the darkness of the trees—for Marvin, Hank, and Billy had already raced out into the darkness with their AR-15s and were spraying the fleeing cartel men with bullets from positions of cover.

The others, Bruce, Delia, Eileen, Anna, Nathan, and many other ranch workers, who were in the network of trenches, armed with hunting rifles, shotguns, and pistols as backup weapons in case the attackers broke through the first line of defense, were now picking out fleeing targets with their rifles and taking them down one by one as the men fled in a blind panic.

Aside from a few stray bullets fired in desperation by the invaders, the defenders came under no real threat. Indeed, they were surprised at how effective their attack was.

"It can't be this easy," Stanley said, finally easing his

finger off the trigger of his machine gun when he saw that nobody in the area lit up by the fires was still moving. "We can't have just defeated them like that in a few minutes...Randall is way too cunning to throw everything into one attack—"

"Another attack! From the south!"

This time it was Gina yelling from her watchtower in the treetops. And this time, the defenders were caught totally off-guard. The cacophony of gunfire from the battle on the northern front had completely covered the sound of vehicles racing through the woods to the south. The cars had been driving with their headlamps off, navigating only by the light of the moon, and now they had crossed the boundary and were speeding toward the buildings...and they weren't only firing guns. They had RPGs too.

"Oh shit!" Stanley yelled as one of the RPGs screamed through the air and smashed into his house, blowing a huge chunk out of the wall and the roof on one side in a mighty explosion.

"Everyone to the rear!" Declan shouted, scrambling to turn his machine gun around.

Believing that the sole attacking force was coming from the north—for that was how things had looked—the defenders had thrown all their numbers, aside from two workers left to guard the south, who were quickly and tragically cut down by the bursts of automatic fire coming from the racing cars.

The machine guns, which were dug into position for

stability, were too heavy and cumbersome to be maneuvered around quickly enough to turn and face the opposite way, so Stanley and Declan quickly gave up on doing this and instead grabbed their AR-15s and scrambled out of the trenches.

Now that there was no need for stealth from the vehicles, the drivers flipped on their headlamps, using their bright beams to blind the defenders while they raced toward them, with men hanging out of the passenger windows, whooping madly as they blasted bursts of automatic fire at the defenders with submachine guns, AK-47s and AR-15s.

Rocket-propelled grenades, fired from the backs of two trucks, streaked through the air and slammed into the various buildings—which were thankfully unoccupied—while the drivers of the vehicles tossed grenades out of their cars as they sped past the trenches, forcing the occupants to scramble out and flee before these deadly explosives detonated.

The tide of the battle had turned completely, and now the defenders were fleeing in terror before the bullet-spewing cars.

"Take out the drivers!" Stanley yelled as he and Declan ran toward the speeding cars.

They each dropped into a kneeling crouch and took careful aim at the lead cars, lining the windshields up in their sights. Then each man fired a burst of bullets. The shots were well-aimed, and they punched through the glass of the cars and riddled the drivers with lead. The two speeding vehicles swerved out of control, with one crashing into a tree, ejecting its occupants at speed, while the other spun and flipped over, tumbling and cartwheeling in a deadly series of jumps and rolls, spitting out broken metal and plastic as well as bodies. These were only two cars out of many more, though, and both men had to dive to the ground and take cover when another car skidded to a halt so that its occupants could take aim at Stanley and Declan, which they did, spitting bullets in their direction with a vehement fury.

Another car sped past the trench Anna and Delia were in, and an occupant tossed a live grenade into the trench as the vehicle roared past. Once a keen and talented softball player, Anna caught the grenade and tossed it straight back into the car, acting purely on reflexes, only realizing what she had done after doing it. There was a brief yelp of surprise from the occupants, cut short by a deafening boom and a blast of light as the grenade when off inside the speeding vehicle, killing all its occupants instantly.

Although the tide of the battle was shifting again, with the defenders now having recovered from their initial surprise and mounting an effective defense, the two trucks at the rear presented the greatest danger with their RPGs, which were laying waste to all the buildings on the ranch.

"We have to take those two out before they destroy everything!" Stanley yelled.

"We can't get to 'em, not with the other cars weaving

around in front of them, spraying hot lead all over the place!" Declan yelled.

Suddenly, an unlikely hero came to the rescue. Behind them, both men heard the chattering thunder of the machine guns breaking out once more, and when they shot surprised glances over their shoulder to see who was operating them, they saw Bruce. He had climbed out of his trench while bullets were flying, cars were racing, and grenades were exploding, and somehow, he had managed to turn each heavy gun around to face the opposite direction. He had dragged the lighter of the machine guns over to the heavier one, and now he was firing them both simultaneously, operating one with each hand, strafing the weaving cars with bullets.

"Take out the trucks!" he roared to Stanley and Declan. "I'll handle the cars! I've got 'em as long as this ammo lasts!"

At that moment, another form of support arrived. Billy came roaring out of the barn on one of his motorcycles, and on the back was Marvin, with two AR-15s—one in his hands and the other strapped to his back. They veered around the edge of the property, aiming to flank the trucks and take them out from the rear, all while spraying the cars with fire from their sides as well.

With Bruce, Billy, and Marvin taking out the speeding cars one by one, Stanley and Declan were able to sprint across the property to get closer to the trucks and their RPGs.

"You take out the left one. I'll take out the right one!" Stanley yelled.

The men in the trucks saw what was happening, and the drivers stomped on the gas, doing their best to turn around and flee. At that point, Stanley saw one of the men on the backfiring RPGs was his nemesis, Austin Randall. On the other truck, the man firing the RPG was Pablo, the head of the cartel men.

Stanley had been planning on taking out the driver first, but now that he had the chance to hack off the figurative head of the snake, he was planning on doing exactly that.

He dropped down into a kneeling crouch fifty yards from the vehicle...and at that moment, Randall saw him and realized what he was trying to do.

"Die, motherfucker, die!" Randall screamed, aiming his RPG in Stanley's direction.

Stanley, however, already had Randall lined up in his sights, and all he had to do was squeeze the trigger, which he did.

The rifle did not kick, nor was there any loud bang or a bright, brief flare from the muzzle. Instead, all that came from the weapon was a soft click. Stanley's entire body went rigid, and his blood turned to ice as he realized that at this crucial moment, he was out of ammo.

Randall grinned, for like Stanley, he had his target lined up in his sights, but unlike Stanley, he wasn't out of ammunition. All he had to do was squeeze his trigger, and his old enemy would be blown into a million shreds of tattered flesh and shattered bones by a rocket-propelled grenade.

"You've had this coming a long time, Wagner," Randall hissed as he began to squeeze the trigger. "Say goodbye, motherfucker...say—"

Randall's head exploded in a grisly shower of blood, brains, and skull fragments, and he dropped the RPG as his limp body toppled over the back of the truck. Fifty yards behind the truck, Marvin—who had fired the killing shot from the back of Billy's motorcycle—took aim at the truck driver as the man tried to speed away. He squeezed his trigger one more time, and the man's brains were blown all over the windshield, and the truck came rolling to a halt.

Declan, meanwhile, managed to take out the man with the RPG on the other truck and then the truck driver. A few cars were still speeding around the ranch, desperately shooting, but now they were fighting for their own survival, not to win, for the invaders realized the battle was lost.

In the end, none escaped. By the time the red sun rose over the eastern horizon, the ranch was almost completely destroyed...but the invaders had been thoroughly defeated, their corpses littering the ground all across the ranch and throughout the woods surrounding it.

It was over...it was finally over.

EPILOGUE

"Who do you think won the war?" Bruce asked, sipping on his whiskey. Although his voice was the same, his face was vastly different from how it had looked three years back, on the day when the old world had died and a new one had been born. He had lost every ounce of fat on his once-podgy body, and now, despite being well into middle age, he was in the best shape of his life, lean and muscular from toiling on the land from sunrise to sunset.

Stanley stared at the bonfire for a while, then he glanced up at the clear, starry sky overhead. He sipped on his tumbler of whiskey before answering. "I don't think anybody won it, to be honest," he answered.

"We still don't even know who started it or fought in it, aside from the United States," Billy said.

"What used to be the United States, you mean? The

entity that used to be the United States of America is now...well, nothing, I guess. It just...ceased to exist, like I'm guessing so many other countries did after what had to be World War III," Marvin said. He, too, took a sip of his whiskey.

This was one substance they had a lifelong supply of—three years back, after they had defeated Austin Randall and his cartel allies, after burying the dead in the trenches, which had since been covered over with grass, and of which there was now barely any evidence—the men had taken over Randall's property.

Although the main purpose of taking Randall's land had been to remove his vast fields of poppies and use the land for food crops instead—an endeavor in which the Wagner clan had seen much success and bounty—they had also checked out their old foe's house. Along with barrels full of hundred-dollar bills, totaling tens of millions of dollars, which in this new world was about as useful as Monopoly money, they had also discovered a cellar full of expensive liquor.

"Oh, we're all pretty sure that was World War III," Caitlin remarked. Unlike the men, she and the other women sipped on wine as they sat around the bonfire. "We saw those fighter jets flying over us a few times in those first few months."

"And there were those crazy bright flashes on the horizon, lighting the night sky up like it was day for a few seconds," Anna said. "We saw those flashes at least, what, a dozen times? More, maybe?"

"Yeah, but for more than two years now, we ain't seen or heard nothin'," Jemma said.

"Nothing at all," Gina echoed.

Like Jemma, she had grown from an awkward teenager into a beautiful, hardworking, and respectful young woman these past few years.

"Yeah, it's been dead quiet for a long, long time," Nathan remarked. "We haven't seen any more raiding bands or refugees for years now."

"Nope," Declan said, swigging heavily on his own tumbler of whiskey. "Not even on our longest-ranging scouting missions, where the boys and I have been out in the wilderness for weeks at a time. It's almost like…like we're the last people left alive in this country. It's downright eerie, is what it is."

"Like I said, there were no winners in that war," Stanley said somberly. "There were only survivors…and far, far too few of us."

"I thank God every day that we did survive, though," Marvin said. "It's a miracle that all of us are still alive and well after everything that happened."

"That's all we can do," Eileen said, smiling. "Keep on surviving. Keep on going. And with all of us working together, we're not only going to keep on living and surviving…but we're also thriving in this strange new world we've found ourselves in."

"To thriving, despite everything," Bruce said, raising his glass in a toast.

"To thriving, despite everything!" they all declared, all

raising their glasses to the starry sky and all wondering what else this strange new world held in store for them in the days, years, and decades to come.

THE END

Made in the USA
Columbia, SC
27 September 2022